I AM SANTA!

KRISTY HAILE

HAPPY BEAN
PUBLISHING

Text copyright © 2010 by HAPPY BEAN PUBLISHING

All rights reserved. Except where permitted under the U.S. Copyright Act of 1976, no part of this publication may be reproduced, distributed, or transmitted in any form or by any means, or stored in a database or retrieval system, without the prior written permission of the publisher.

HAPPY BEAN PUBLISHING

The characters and events portrayed in this book are fictitious. Any similarity to real persons, living or dead, is coincidental and not intended by the author.

Haile, Kristy, 1974-

I AM SANTA : a novel / by Kristy Haile. - 1st Edition

Photography by Armen Asadorian

ISBN 978-0-9827043-0-1 (Hardcover) / 978-0-9827043-1-8 (Paperback)
978-0-9827043-2-5 (eBook)

Imagination is more important than knowledge......
Albert Einstein

Everything you can imagine is real.
Pablo Picasso

CHAPTER 1

Have you ever wondered what it must have felt like to be the mother of an important influential figure? Have you ever even thought about the mother of any important influential figure in history? Have we ever even asked ourselves what the mother of Abraham Lincoln must have felt as she was raising the boy who would eventually become the man that started equality in the United States? Or what about Pauline Einstein, the mother of Albert Einstein, the scientist who grew up to be in many people's view the most influential scientist of all times? And we will probably never truly know nor understand how Alberta King, the mother of Martin Luther King Jr. truly felt as she raised her small child into the man who essentially changed the face of America forever. Even being a mother myself, I have to admit I had never thought about the mothers of any important influential people in our lives let alone the mother's of any important influential figures in my children's lives. That is until I became one.

Looking back, I don't really know nor do I understand why I had never thought about those mothers and how they must have felt when they became the mother of an important figure. I often wonder this and I have realized that I may never truly know but I do know those mothers mentioned before were all strong, influential woman themselves who chose to participate in their child's life and to most importantly believe in their child.

Some believe my son is a real figure who has the potential to make an impact on every child as well as every adult. However, there are those who believe my son does not exist. I often wonder what makes some people disbelieve in his existence. Have they lived their lives in a manner that has put them on the naughty list way too many times or were they simply born without an imagination and the ability to believe in their dreams? No matter the cause of their disbelief, I choose not to listen to them. I choose to believe in my son. I know my son is real and I feel truly blessed that I was chosen to be the mother of Santa Claus.

It all began during a simple shopping trip to the mall. My daughter Holly needed a new dress for her choir concert at school. I was in quite a big hurry so I really wasn't being attentive at all to my surroundings. My son Nicholas however seems to always notice everything!

It seemed as if we had been in the mall for not even a minute when Nicholas began with his incessant amount of questions, "Hey sissy and mommy do you see the old man on the bench? Doesn't he look like Santa Claus? Mommy, can I go see if he really is Santa Claus?"

I looked at my son with a scowl on my face that told him he had just asked the worst questions in the world. Of course I couldn't leave it at the scowl. For some reason I felt the need to stupidly reply, "You know what Nicholas, I told you in the car that we were in a hurry. So please stop asking to do anything! In fact I want you to stop asking questions. All I want you to do is walk right here beside mommy and sissy so we can buy sissy a new dress."

Nicholas dropped his head down and stared at the floor for a moment to gather his happy thoughts before raising his head right back up and asking cheerfully, "So can I go and talk to that man on the bench?"

I found myself simply shaking my head as I sternly replied, "Nicholas I have told you a thousand times, we do NOT talk to strangers! Do you understand?"

For a moment, I started to feel really bad as Nicholas looked up and stared at me with his big green eyes. But I knew I had to stand my ground about the 'no talking to strangers rule.' His daddy and I have seen him numerous times approaching random people out of the blue. Nicholas has never even seen the people before but he goes right up and starts talking to them as if they were best friends!

Since Nicholas didn't reply, I had to sternly ask him again, "Nicholas do you understand?"

His little head fell to his chest as he replied, "Yes mommy, I understand."

We walked through the mall and I guess it wouldn't have hurt if I had taken Nicholas up to the old man on the bench myself so he could say 'hi'. I began to think maybe it would have made the old man on the bench happy that a little boy actually thought he looked like Santa Claus. I thought I would let Nicholas say 'hi' when we were all done shopping if the old man was still sitting on the bench, but right now, I had no time for such a trivial thing.

I watched my disappointed son sadly going through the motions of walking through the mall with his sister and me. I try, well I guess I always have the intention of trying to make Nicholas feel important. But I think he probably feels a bit invisible most of the time in comparison to his sister. I have always been so over the top obsessive about making sure Holly has the perfect everything so sometimes Nicholas does get lost in the shuffle. I began thinking to myself, how excited Nicholas would be to say 'hi' to the old man on the bench if he was still sitting there when we left the mall.

I had been so lost in my own thoughts as we walked through the mall and arrived at the department store. I hadn't even realized my little son Nicholas had wondered away from me. How could I not even notice he wasn't with us anymore?

Holly was actually the one who realized Nicholas was gone. Holly turned to me with a worried look as she asked, "Mom is Nicholas on the other side of you?"

I had no idea what Holly was even talking about so I asked, "What?" As I began looking around me before casually replying, "Oh don't worry about Nicholas he is probably just hiding under one of these racks or something," as I pointed to a clothing rack full of dress pants for sale.

Nicholas always likes to hide under the racks so I really wasn't concerned as to which rack he was hiding under this time, I just continued shopping. Holly on the other hand became increasingly worried about where her little brother possibly could be. She began frantically looking underneath all of the racks. Then ran back to where I was looking at dresses.

Holly was a bit out of breath, her long brown hair looked as if she had been in a tornado and all she could do was say, "Mom....mom! I really can't find Nicholas. We need to look for him now!"

I was quite confident Nicholas was probably under one of the racks hiding or something, watching and laughing at his sister as she looked for him. But because Holly was so upset, I decided to stop dress shopping to help her look for her little brother. We looked every where around us, under all of the racks in the girl's clothing department but neither of us saw Nicholas.

I began to get a little frustrated with my son because he knew we were in a hurry and I didn't have time for his little games today. I have repeatedly told Nicholas he is going to get taken by a stranger if he does not stay with me. But Nicholas unfortunately loves to wonder off and talk to strangers. This time though he was in big trouble with me for wondering off.

It has always seemed as if my little Nicholas lacks any and all type of fear. He has never been afraid of the unknown. For example, he has never asked for a night light to help illuminate his very dark room at night although his sister can't sleep with out one. Of course as a mother, his lack of fear causes me even more fear. I have never been able to sit and talk to the other mom's when Nicholas is playing at the park. No, I have to follow him everywhere at the park. Why? Because my little Nicholas will jump off of the top of any jungle gym. Following him around the park is the only way I feel I can protect him from getting hurt. I have often wondered why and how my son can feel so invincible and untouchable from any and all harm. Does he know I will always be there or does he truly feel no limits in life?

Here I was trying to find my little boy who was missing at the moment and all I was thinking about was his lack of fear. I currently needed to get myself together to find Nicholas and all I needed to think about was how I was going to do that.

Holly and I went to the clerk at the register and I politely asked, "My very active son it seems has wondered off in the store and....well....maybe....well truthfully I think he is just hiding but can you please call out his name on the store loud speaker?"

The clerk looked at me as if I was the worst mom ever as she sarcastically asked me, "What's his name?"

"His name is Nicholas," I quickly replied.

The clerk was an older lady dressed impeccably and I think she would have actually been pretty if she hadn't put her gray hair up in such a tight bun. It made her face look as if it was stretched to the limit. The constant sarcastic frown on her face also made her appear to be a very unhappy person. I was hopeful she would actually call for Nicholas as I had requested and stop staring at me.

Fortunately, after a moment of her judgmental stare, she turned and picked up the loudspeaker and said in a very monotone voice, "Nicholas....Nicholas....Nicholas your mommy is looking for you. Please come to the front of the store where she is waiting for you."

When Nicholas didn't respond to his name over the loud speaker, Holly and I frantically left the store in order to notify mall security that Nicholas was missing and to start searching the mall for our little Nicholas. We looked in all of his favorite stores, even the arcade but we still couldn't find him. I began to wonder if I would ever find my little boy again. A sick feeling began to dig into the walls of my stomach as we continued our search.

I suddenly began to realize how much time I was always giving to Holly and how little time I was giving to little Nicholas. I began to know in my heart Nicholas was reaching out to me for more of my time. Was that the reason why he lacked all fear? Did he know I would always be more near to him if he lacked all fear? Is fear how he thought he could keep his mommy always right by his side?

At this point I had absolutely no idea how I could better divide my time between my two children. Holly had always been the light of my life, ever since the first time I saw her. I remember looking into her beautiful big eyes feeling as if she were looking straight back into my own, knowing exactly how much love I already had for her. That first day, I promised her I would always be there for her, which strangely enough has made her into a more independent and strong person. Sometimes I feel a whisper of a breeze and I always wonder if it's a quick glance from Holly making sure I am still there.

When I looked at baby Nicholas for the first time, I felt as if he were looking straight into my heart feeling an automatic endearment from him. Nicholas has always been so very dependent upon me. Even on his first day of preschool he wanted me to stay with him. Okay, actually he wants me to stay with him at preschool every day and he still cries when I drop him off. I can't deal with the whole crying thing before work so I hand him off to his teacher and I walk away. I remember looking back once seeing his face pressed up against the window. I could see the longing he had for me in his eyes and I saw him mouth the words 'come back'. But I didn't go back, I got into my car and I drove away. I remember asking myself, 'Aren't boys suppose to be automatically strong independent people, or does Nicholas need more of me?'

As I was frantically running through the mall searching for my little Nicholas, I began to realize for the first time I wasn't there for my son enough. I was really trying to find my son but no matter how hard I tried, I couldn't get all of these thoughts out of my head.

I felt so relieved when I finally found my little Nicholas near the entrance of the mall. He was sitting on a bench talking to none other than the old man he was claiming to be Santa Claus. As I was running towards Nicholas, I myself couldn't help but notice the significant resemblance this old man did have to Santa Claus. I didn't want to focus on Santa Claus though. All I wanted to do was hug my little boy.

I felt very relieved and extremely fortunate to have found my Nicholas. But I couldn't avoid thinking of his direct disobedience. I had specifically told him not to talk to the old man on the bench but he did. In fact, he wondered off leaving his sister and me behind so he could talk to the old man. When we reached Nicholas, Holly immediately hugged her little brother. I on the other hand, quickly grabbed Nicholas off the bench and I pinched his little butt.

I found myself lecturing little Nicholas all the way back to the department store we had been shopping in earlier. With a strong lecturing voice I told Nicholas, "Sir, you do not wonder off and you do not talk to strangers. You told me you understood that. But then you go and wonder off and talk to a stranger! I have told you numerous times that I am in a hurry today! You are going to quietly hold my hand the rest of the time we are shopping and you are not going to say a word. And 'yes' I am going to tell daddy about this and 'no' he is NOT, I repeat NOT going to be happy about this one."

Nicholas found himself unable to be quiet though. "Mommy....but mommy the old man isn't a stranger I know him....I really do know him."

Well I know or should I say, I thought I knew everyone my four year old son knows. I was a bit irritated to say the least about Nicholas claiming to know the old man on the bench. I didn't want to have anymore discussions with my son at the mall today. I just wanted to find a dress for Holly so we could all go home.

I finally looked at my little boy and politely stated, "Look Nicholas, mommy has no time to discuss the old man on the bench any further with you. And I have already told you Nicholas that you need to be quiet right now."

Nicholas turned to look at me with a smile on his face that quickly faded as I spoke to him. When I was finished talking to Nicholas he hung his head down in silence.

I truly was very thankful to have found Nicholas and all I really wanted to do was scoop him up, kiss him and hug him, I didn't though. Instead of letting Nicholas know how much I really do love him, I simply continued shopping for the 'perfect' dress for Holly to wear at her concert. A dress seemed so unimportant in comparison to finding my son. Still, I went through the motions of shopping until I found the 'perfect' dress for Holly.

I continued holding on to my baby boys hand very tightly the entire time we were shopping. I could not and did not ever want to imagine a life without my little Nicholas. It wasn't until I was waiting in line to pay for Holly's dress that I decided to make the conscious choice to have two number one children. Somehow both of my children were going to start receiving equal attention and most importantly an equal amount of my time. I also decided a hug can never be too late so I reached down and scooped my little son into my arms and I hugged him very tightly.

As I hugged my Nicholas I whispered in his ear, "I love you sweetheart but you better promise to never walk off by yourself again."

Nicholas gave me a sweet kiss on my cheek and smiled as he answered, "Promise!"

When we got into the car Nicholas refused to stop talking about the old man on the bench. "Mommy you just don't understand….the old man on the bench is now the old Santa Claus….and….well he told me that I am the new real Santa Claus."

I was really not in the mood to discuss the old man on the bench any further. So I sternly said, "Nicholas you are to stop….and I mean stop right now. I do not want you to talk about the old man on the bench anymore. If you don't stop I will pull this car over right now."

Unfortunately, Nicholas knew I wasn't going to stop the car or else Holly would be late for her concert.

So Nicholas continued to excitedly talk about the old man. "But mommy the old man is really, really the old Santa Claus and he is very sick. So that is why he picked me to be the new real Santa Claus."

I don't know why but all of a sudden I found myself in the middle of a Santa discussion with my son. "Nicholas look, Santa lives in the North Pole and not in California."

Still he would not stop about the whole Santa at the mall thing so Holly and I were forced to listen to his story over and over again for the entire twenty minute ride home.

Holly began to get extremely irritated when Nicholas kept saying he was now the new real Santa Claus. I glanced at her in my rear view mirror only to discover her face was so red that I was sure it would explode at any minute.

When she could take it no longer she loudly shouted, "Look Nicholas, you are just a four year old preschooler and not Santa Claus. Just stop saying that you are Santa Claus!"

Nicholas however, refused to give up on his new theory about himself being the new real Santa Claus so he calmly continued, "You know what the old Santa Claus told me? He told me that he had been waiting for me, and the elves will be in touch with me very soon."

The North Pole conversation continued the entire ride home despite mine and Holly's objections. When we finally arrived home we rushed into the house to change and eat dinner as quickly as possible before it was time to go to the concert.

As soon as Nicholas saw his dad he eagerly announced, "Daddy you need to know that I am the new real Santa Claus."

My husband, Garrett looked at me strangely and mouthed the word "what" to me.

I simply stated, "Do not ask."

As my husband and I were getting dressed and ready for Holly's concert, Garrett once again asked me as to why Nicholas was all of a sudden thinking of himself as the new real Santa Claus. I told Garrett the entire mall incident story and about the old man in the mall Nicholas claims told him he would be the new real Santa Claus.

Garrett wasn't shocked at all by the incident at the mall. He knew it was always an adventure no matter where we go with our children.

My husband laughed and told me, "Don't worry, next week Nicholas will tell us he is the *Incredible Hulk* or *Superman* and he will forget all about this Santa Claus thing."

I smiled shaking my head agreeing with my husband even though at the back of my mind I somehow knew the Santa Claus thing wasn't going to go away.

Nicholas is usually very bored at all of the school events we go to, which Holly is a part of. Tonight was different though. Little Nicholas walked in and greeted everyone he saw and he looked as if he was on cloud nine the entire night. Nicholas sat through the entire concert with a huge smile on his face looking truly happy and content. Even after the concert, he told his big sissy she had done a wonderful job. A mother is always happy when her children are getting along so well. So I just chalked up his great behavior as a perfect ending to a not so perfect day.

CHAPTER 2

Seriously, how many Birthday parties do you have to take your children to? When is enough, enough? Couldn't there be like a five birthday party limit per child per year? It's wonderful to take your kids and to let them have fun seeing their little friends but it gets very expensive after awhile! So, here it is the fourth weekend in a row my kids have been invited to birthday parties. This weekend though, they were each invited to their own friend's parties. I will take Holly to her girlfriend's party and Garrett will take Nicholas to his preschool buddy's party.

Therefore, once again we are at the infamous toy store! Nicholas and I were searching the store for the ideal birthday gifts when Nicholas spotted it. He ran over to it, and took it right off the rack.

A huge smile flashed across his face as he said, "Look mommy, the elves must have left it here for me."

I was about to say 'no', but then I hesitated and I remembered the promise I had made to myself at the shopping mall. So I had to ask myself how I could say 'no' to the little boy who never asks for anything.

I smiled back as I told him, "Nicholas we need to check the size first before we buy it."

I reached down to see the size on the tag and sure enough it was his exact size! There were no other Santa suits on the rack, only the one Nicholas had picked up. It was only twenty dollars and it looked to be a very well made Santa suit so I told Nicholas he could have it. He refused to put the suit in the shopping carriage. He carried it around the entire store and no longer even really cared what gifts I bought for the Birthday parties, which did make shopping a bit easier.

When we arrived at the register Nicholas asked the clerk, "Could you please remove the tags because I am going to put my new Santa suit on as soon as I get back to my mommy's car?"

The clerk smiled and clipped off all of the tags before she handed the suit back to Nicholas. Before we got to the toy store parking lot, he informed me he would be putting the suit on as soon as we got to the car. Sure enough as we got to the car he began to quickly take his pants off so he could put his new Santa suit on. He put the pants on, the jacket on and of course he even put the hat on. Looking at my son, I felt so proud of him. He truly did look absolutely perfect. I had never seen that big of a smile on my sons face before. In fact, I don't think I've ever seen that big of a smile on anyone's face before. He was so very proud of his new Santa suit and so was I.

As soon as we arrived at Holly's gymnastics to pick her up, Nicholas advised me, "Mommy I will not be taking off my new Santa suit and I know my sissy is going to love my new Santa suit!"

Truthfully, I didn't have the heart to tell my little Nicholas to take his new Santa suit off so I let him wear it into the gym. Nicholas was so excited. I opened the door of the gym and he confidently walked in with that big smile still on his face! Of course, everyone looked at Nicholas in his Santa suit as he walked in. He was the center of everyone's attention.

Parents started telling him how cute he looked and Nicholas simply replied, "Thanks, I am the new real Santa Claus".

I caught a quick glance from Holly showing mixed emotions so I knew she had seen Nicholas. When she was finished with gym she came over to Nicholas and politely told him, "I really like your new Santa suit." Then she turned towards me and asked, "What prize did you get for me mommy?"

I think she thought I had forgotten to get her something too. But I smiled and said, "I got you the new CD you have been begging me for." Holly smiled telling all of her friends from gymnastics goodbye and all three of us left.

As we were driving away from the gym, Nicholas looked at his sister telling her, "See I told you that I was the new real Santa Claus".

Holly looked at her brother as she sarcastically replied, "You are NOT Santa Claus now and you never will be Santa Claus. Mommy got you your suit at the toy store so it can't be the real Santa suit."

Nicholas didn't scream nor did he yell in response to his sister's comments. He simply told her, "Sissy you really better watch out or else your name will soon, yes very soon be on the naughty list."

I didn't want to ruin Nicholas's imagination and I'd been thinking to myself maybe it would be kind of fun to have Nicholas think of himself as the new real Santa Claus. I was also thinking maybe, just maybe it would help his imagination grow further and to develop even better. Besides, what would it hurt for Nicholas to think of himself as the new real Santa Claus?

So I was happy to announce, "Holly, we all have imaginations and we need to respect each other, including the imaginations of each other."

Holly glared at me through my rearview mirror as she tried to convince me to change my mind. "But mom... mom....seriously mom!" I didn't let her though. I remained firm in my decision.

Nicholas was nervously watching the entire discussion. So after a few moments, I turned to Nicholas and told him, "I think your imagination is fabulous!"

Nicholas just smiled.

I no longer wanted to put my children in the 'box' so much of society expects children to be in. I wanted to let my children be free, free to imagine, free to dream big as well as free to believe in those imaginations and dreams. I was tired of trying to make my children fit into society's 'box'. So, often as parents we try to make our children fit into the 'box' that is expected by others. We are afraid to let our children decide who and what they are going to be. Parents are so afraid to let their children try something new. Why? They don't want to see their children fail.

Unfortunately, too often we want our children to be better than all of the other children. Frankly, I was tired of the competition. Now all I wanted from both of my children was for them to be the best they can be. Not necessarily better than anyone else. All I want is for both of my children to always strive to do their best as well as to be happy and excited for the accomplishments of other's. I knew I was only having the best of intentions, but how could I suddenly incorporate this thinking into my children? Truly there was only a two word answer-Be Positive!

I woke up early the next morning to the sound of Nicholas running into my room screaming,"I just went to the North Pole....I just went to the North Pole!"

I looked at the clock on my night stand noticing it was only four o'clock in the morning. Nicholas was wide awake trying to tell me all about the North Pole.

So I tiredly told my little Nicholas, "Go back to bed."

But Nicholas continued with his story, "Mimi, Mimi it was so awesome! At first I just thought that I was dreaming, but the elves told me that I was really at the North Pole. I asked the elves why I was picked to be the new Santa Claus. And you know what? They said it was because I am so special because I have a good and generous heart. Me, Mimi I was picked because I am special, me Mimi, I am special! I always knew sissy was special, but I never knew I was special!"

What was Nicholas saying? Didn't he know he was special too just like his sissy? And wait, why was he calling me Mimi?

So I inquisitively asked, "Nicholas sweetheart of course you are special you are a very special little boy and why are you calling me Mimi?"

Nicholas didn't answer my question he simply continued to beg me to get out of bed so he could tell me all about his recent adventure to the North Pole. I was still very tired and at first I didn't feel much like getting out of bed, but I was more intrigued about his so called adventure to the North Pole as well as why he kept calling me Mimi than I was tired. I finally got up and went into the living room with Nicholas so I could listen to his story and find out why he kept calling me Mimi.

Nicholas told me about how his exciting adventure began with the elves coming and waking him up in the middle of the night because they told him he needed to get familiar with his new 'kingdom'.

Nicholas told me at first he thought he was just having the best dream ever, but when he tried to wake himself up he couldn't. He finally had asked one of the elves if he was dreaming. But the elf told him he was awake and it just seemed like a dream because the North Pole is the most magical place ever!

I asked how he got to the North Pole and Nicholas informed me that the elves arrived into his bedroom through a special porthole in his closet. Then the elves had taken him back through the porthole to get to the North Pole. I wanted to see this porthole but I didn't want to impinge on his imagination at all so I didn't ask to see it. Nicholas did tell me later on in his adventure story that the porthole is located in his closet but can only be seen and used by either the elves or himself, the new real Santa Claus.

Nicholas continued telling me all about the North Pole, "Mimi there was tons of white fluffy snow at the North Pole and it didn't freeze my fingers when I picked it up. Everything at the North Pole is covered in snow except for the candy. The candy has a little snow on it, but I liked the snow most of all Mimi and I even used the snow to build a big gigantic snowman with some of the elves. My snowman looked so real that I really thought is was going to come to life but it didn't. At least it didn't come to life when I was there maybe it was waiting or something, I don't know but it was really, really cool."

I was able to get only one word in as Nicholas paused to take a breath, "Neat."

After his short breath he continued with his story, "Mimi, there is the biggest....and I mean the biggest toy factory ever at the North Pole. I think the toy factory is probably the best thing about the North Pole. I love it!"

    Nicholas has always been so low maintenance when it comes to toys so I was a bit surprised to hear of his amazing enthusiasm for the toy factory and such a favorite of his at the North Pole. For his birthday I remember taking him to the toy store to get him his very first two wheel bike. I took him over to the bicycle section. He looked at the bicycles briefly and simply told me he didn't really want a bike. I was a bit disappointed by his little 'I don't want a bike' revelation and I was going to buy him a bike whether he wanted one or not.

    Garrett however, had told me to let him pick out any toy in the store, so we did. All he wanted us to buy him was a small tub of *Lego's*. I felt like such a horrible parent only buying him a tub of *Lego's* and I almost went back and bought him some more toys. But I didn't, instead I simply relished in the fact that my son was so happy with only a small tub of *Lego's*.

    Nicholas continued with such enthusiasm about the toy factory, "Mimi, the toy factory has real toys. You know the kind of toys that are made from real wood and the elves even hand painted the wooden toy trains, puzzles and the elves even made wooden puppets that had strings attached to move their arms and legs. Some toys are the same as in a regular toy store, but the biggest difference Mimi, is that the toys at my toy factory feel like they are really real, like they could really, really come to life at any moment!"

I sat there watching Nicholas tell me about the toy factory and it was so amazing to see how animated he was as he told me about how the trains made real train sounds and moved just like a real train. But the cutest part was when he told me about the puppets. He moved his arms, legs, head and body just as if he were a real marionette puppet!

Nicholas then went on to tell me about the so very important lists. "Mimi the most difficult but also the easiest part about being Santa Claus is the naughty and nice lists. The elves are constantly watching all of the children all over the world so Santa Claus doesn't have to. When a child is really naughty they get a mark by their name on the list. They have to do something really naughty like talking mean to their parents or being a bully to get a bad mark. But Mimi just because a little kid leaves their dirty clothes on the floor or forgets to brush their teeth twice a day is not enough to get a bad mark."

"Wow! But that doesn't mean that you can leave your clothes on the floor or forget to brush your teeth Nicholas." I added with a touch of sarcasm.

Nicholas smiled as he continued, "I know Mimi. But there's more to the lists. I am the one who has to go back and review the lists and I am the one that gets to decide if something was bad enough to keep the mark on the list or not. The elves keep track of all of the naughty things on a computer and they even showed me how to use the naughty or nice computer."

Nicholas gave me such intricate detail about each and every aspect of the North Pole, it was absolutely incredible. As Nicholas was telling me about his adventure, I closed my eyes a few times and I felt as if I were actually there at the North Pole with him.

Nicholas then went on to describe the elves. "Mimi it was so cool I was almost the same height as all of the elves, the elves were all wearing yellow pointed shoes that curled up, but Mimi, I really didn't understand why all of the elves had on the red and white stripped tights, even the boys! So I asked them, and you know what? They said that all of the elves had to wear the same tights-even the boys! I feel that as the new real Santa Claus I really should help out the boys in some way Mimi. I mentioned something about it to the head elf whose name is Jack, but he said the boy elves were actually just fine about wearing the tights. So maybe I will bring it up again later."

I was definitely enjoying my son's little, no actually big adventure story but I could not wait any longer. I needed to find out something important from my son. "Wait Nicholas, why do you keep calling me Mimi now? You've always called me Mommy. Aren't I your Mommy anymore?"

"No, you are now my Mimi". And that is all Nicholas would tell me about Mimi. He simply stated "Mimi you will find out at the end of my adventure story."

I was a bit disappointed Nicholas wouldn't tell me about the Mimi thing but I decided to try and not think about it. So I asked, "Jack, the head elf what is he like?"

Nicholas took a bit of a deep breath in as he began to speak in a loud whisper, "Jack….well….Jack is a little taller then me, he isn't big….I mean….well he is skinny and….well….jack is so overly organized. I know he is running the entire North Pole for me, it's just….well….I think he maybe a bit too uptight. He is the best dressed elf and the only elf with a red hat. All the rest of the elves have green hats. His hair looks like it's the same color brown as my hair and super, super short but I'm not sure because he hasn't taken his hat off in front of me yet. Jack's eyes are so dark blue. Kind of like the darkest blue part of the ocean. And when you look into his eyes, you can tell he is always concentrating or thinking about something. But I like Jack and I think, no I know he will relax a bit more now that I am the new real Santa Claus. I hope he like me though, I want to make him happy and I don't want to mess up anything at the North Pole."

I smiled, "Nicholas sweetheart everybody loves you! You are such a wonderful little boy!"

Nicholas smiled as he continued, "Mimi, I always thought it would be easy to be a reindeer. I thought if someday I decided to be a reindeer, I would be able to tie some sticks onto my head as antlers and then I would be a reindeer. But I found out reindeers are actually very hard working. They run and play and practice flying all day.

Because if they are not strong enough to hold the sleigh with all of the presents on Christmas Eve, then they have to stay at the North Pole and not be a part of the sleigh team. Donner told me, he was not working hard enough at last years fly practice so Santa Claus bumped him from the team last year. He also told me, he has been working extra hard this year to get back into better shape and he is hoping to be picked as the sleigh leader this Christmas Eve. As the official new Santa Claus, I told him to just keep trying his best and to believe in himself no matter what and he should never give up on his dreams."

Wow, is all I could manage to tell myself. I had never realized how mature and articulate my little Nicholas was. How could I not have noticed this side of him before? Had I been so wrapped up in Holly and every day life that I had never even taken the time to really see my son?

I cheerfully acknowledged my little Nicholas, "That was a very positive and good thing to tell Donner Nicholas. I am sure it made Donner feel very good about himself. You truly are a very special little boy Nicholas and I am so very proud of you."

Nicholas eagerly continued, "Thanks Mimi, it was so amazing to be able to encourage Donner like that. You know what though? The best part of being with the reindeers was at the end of their fly practice workout they, all go swimming. There is a huge lake with no ice and the water is so clear that you can look straight to the bottom. It's actually warm water Mimi so it kind of feels like a hot spa does. The reindeers told me, the warm water makes their muscles feel better after a hard workout. At first I watched them but then they told me to get in to the water with them. I was a little scared at first because I did not want to get hurt by their antlers. But they all told me to just jump in so I did. I had so much fun swimming in the lake with them. We all played tag in the water together and I didn't want to get out but Jack came over to the lake and told me it was time for me to go home. I was a little bit sad but I was missing you Mimi so I was excited to come back home to tell you all about my North Pole adventure."

I was so proud of his adventure to the North Pole, I gave my Nicholas a big hug but there was still one thing I needed to know, so I softly whispered, "I loved your story about your big adventure to the North Pole but why do you keep calling me Mimi?"

Nicholas pushed himself away so he could look at me as he exclaimed, "Because you are my Mimi now, you will always be my Mommy but now since I am the new real Santa Claus you are now my Mimi. I now know how special I really am and so Mimi is the special name I have given to you because you are special too. You are not just a regular Mommy anymore and Mimi you really have never been just a regular Mommy to me. You believed in me, you believe that I am the new Santa Claus. You even bought me my first Santa suit. That's what I needed Mimi. I needed you to believe in me, to believe in Santa Claus. I have given you the new name of Mimi so that every time you hear me call you Mimi you'll feel extra special!"

I felt my eyes filling up with tears as Nicholas told me how I came to be his Mimi. I was so proud of my new name. I began to get chills every time I heard him call me his Mimi. I felt very fortunate to have such a special son with such a big heart.

I tried my best to think of something wonderful that I could say but all I could manage to say back to Nicholas was, "Thank you."

Nicholas then got up onto my lap and snuggled to me, his Mimi. I stayed awake for awhile watching my new Santa Claus sleep and before I knew it, I fell asleep and dreamed of the North Pole. When I woke up my little Nicholas was still snuggled to me. I gently moved him onto the couch so I could get up to make him his favorite breakfast, pancakes and sausage. As I made breakfast, I began to wonder to myself whether or not I had just been dreaming of my son's adventure to the North Pole or had he really been there and told me about his adventure? Wait, my son is in preschool and there is no way possible my son went to the North Pole.

I began to think, I probably had dreamed up the entire adventure until my little Santa Claus woke up calling out, "Mimi, Mimi where are you?"

CHAPTER 3

There is so much in this world to be thankful for each and every day. Every night at dinner Holly, Nicholas, Garrett and I all try to find at least four things we were thankful for in that day. I started keeping a gratitude journal at the end of every day so I could keep track of all of those positive happenings. I figure if ever I have a bad day or if any of us have a bad day the gratitude journal would be there to provide us with the jolt of positive energy we would need.

Today is the official day of Thanksgiving on the calendar, which sadly is the only time the majority of the human population is thankful. I now wonder why and how Thanksgiving became so commercialized. I do still recall a time when I was one of those people who participated in the commercialization of Thanksgiving by buying everything to do with Thanksgiving and only recognizing thankfulness in connection with Thanksgiving in November.

I then began to ask myself if I was commercializing Christmas by believing my son is the new real Santa Claus and by letting him believe he is the new real Santa Claus. But I realized this was negative thinking so I stopped those little negative thoughts. How could believing in something like Santa Claus be commercializing Christmas?

Santa Claus represents imagination and believing in your imagination. Believing that dreams do come true is what comes to mind now every time I think about Santa Claus. A Santa Claus non believer may disagree with me and may think of Santa Claus as just a tool to commercialize Christmas. I could only think of Nicholas at this point and so I asked myself, 'what would Nicholas say?' However, I guess I already knew the answer. He would tell me those non Santa believers were on the naughty list and they probably had been on the naughty list for a very long time.

As far as Thanksgiving goes, I choose to make it a holiday about being Thankful nothing more, nothing less. As a family we do talk about how Thanksgiving began and all of the historical events. However, we concentrate only on thankfulness for the day. When we eat, we do as we always do and share our positive events for the day we are thankful for.

This morning when I woke up, I thought this Thanksgiving would be as the rest had been. Boy was I wrong. I was about to get the unexpected. The unexpected events that took place this Thanksgiving essentially taught me to always expect the unexpected when it comes to my little boy Nicholas, the new real Santa Claus.

We were all getting dressed for Thanksgiving as usual in order to go and share the holiday with our extended family. Garrett, Holly and I were all dressed and waiting in the living room. Nicholas was still up stairs in his room getting ready. I guess this was the first thing to let me know this would be a Thanksgiving like no other because usually he is the first one in the living room ready to go. At first, I thought maybe he didn't realize we were all waiting for him and maybe he was upstairs in his room playing.

I began to call for him, "Nicholas, Nicholas, come on we are leaving."

There was no response at all from my little boy. But as I started up the stairs, I stopped suddenly when I saw him come out of his bedroom. It was my little Nicholas in his full suit as the new real Santa Claus.

He was dressed from head to toe as Santa Claus. My new little Santa had on his new little red and white suit, his cute little red Santa hat with the white puff ball at the tip and on his little feet were his shiny new black leather dress shoes. I thought he looked fabulous!

I was about to tell him how fabulous he looked but before I could manage to speak a word, Holly came up behind me and put in her two cents. "Well, well my little brother, now we all know that you really aren't the new real Santa Claus. It's not even Christmas yet genius it's only Thanksgiving. How could you screw that one up so bad? Did you really think it was Christmas today and not Thanksgiving?"

At first my little Nicholas just stared at Holly. Then he held his head up high as he loudly and proudly stated, "I am the new real Santa Claus and whether you want to believe in me or not is your choice. However, if you would like to maintain your current status on the nice list, you should really watch your behavior, especially your behavior towards the new real Santa Claus!"

Of course my husband had to throw in "Seriously son, it's Thanksgiving and you are not going out looking like that."

I quickly interjected, "I believe..., yes I believe in you Santa. Your Mimi loves you very much and I just want to tell you that you look fabulous from head to toe."

Wow! I was so proud of myself because I was actually able to tell my little Santa how I truly felt inside when I first saw him. Garrett and Holly tried unsuccessfully to protest the fact that I was letting Nicholas be Santa on Thanksgiving. I did know now I was thankful to be his Mimi and I was also very thankful to have my son as the new real Santa Claus. I also knew I had to be the luckiest mom in the whole world to have both Santa Claus as my son and to be his new Mimi.

Of course when we arrived at our family's house, we were greeted with the expected stares as soon as they saw Nicholas dressed in his Santa suit. But as their initial shock wore off of having Santa at their Thanksgiving, everyone complimented Nicholas on his clothing choice and made him feel very special.

When we all sat down to eat, we went around the table and everyone had the opportunity to share their own positive event or thankfulness for the day.

Amazingly enough, when it came to Holly's turn she proudly stated, "I am thankful for having a brother with a big imagination."

I too was thankful for being given a son with such a big imagination. An imagination in which had finally allowed me the opportunity to let my children out of the 'box' and to be themselves. We all talked, ate way too much and were thankful for all we have each been given. However, this Thanksgiving had so much more. I feel having Santa Claus here made everyone more jolly and happy. No, it wasn't the wine! In fact I didn't even have any wine this Thanksgiving.

I felt such an awesome and natural buzz to life, I didn't even realize I had forgotten to have wine until on the way home. Garrett commented, "I guess we can just take our own wine next year. I hadn't realized my wife had become so picky about her wine recently."

At first I stared at my husband because I had no idea what he was talking about. But after I thought for a moment, I realized I had forgotten all about the wine.

I looked at my husband and smiled as I told him, "Well having the opportunity to have Santa Claus in person with me at Thanksgiving made me forget all about the wine. Honey, you could have brought my favorite reserve bottle of red wine and I still would have forgotten all about the wine."

By the time we got home tonight Santa had way too long of a day, he was sound asleep. I volunteered to carry him into the house and put him to bed. Of course this shocked my husband to no end because I am always the one trying to get out of carrying Holly and Nicholas up to their beds. I thankfully got out of my seat and opened his door. I gently unbuckled his safety belt and scooped him up into my arms.

Nicholas immediately snuggled up to me, grabbing my thumb and softly saying, "Thank you Mimi." I could feel the tears of joy begin to well up in both of my eyes.

I slowly carried him up the stairs, holding onto every moment he was snuggled to me in my arms. I laid him in his bed and as I looked down at him sleeping so soundly in his Santa suit, I didn't have the heart to put pajamas on him. I wanted him to have happy dreams full of adventure with his Santa suit on. I wanted him to wake up in the morning and run into my room wearing his Santa suit yelling, 'Mimi, Mimi you awake?' I guess those were my own selfish reasons but at least they were my own proud selfish reasons.

Sure enough the next morning I awoke to my little Santa running into my room, jumping onto the bed yelling for his Mimi which immediately put a huge smile upon my face.

Holly and Nicholas love to go to the mall at Christmas time to see Santa Claus there. I told both of them this year was going to be extra special because tonight was a fun night. Santa would be reading a story to all of the children at the mall and all of the children would be getting chocolate chip cookies and milk.

Both kids seemed excited but when their cheering ended, Nicholas simply commented, "I just still can't read very good though."

I had no idea what he was referring to so I assured him when he started kindergarten next year he would become a super reader. He simply shrugged his shoulders and went upstairs to his room.

Nicholas came down stairs for lunch but other than that stayed in his room for most of the day. Holly was a bit overjoyed knowing we were going to the mall because her best friend Mary was at the house for a sleepover. Mary would be going with us tonight for the story reading with Santa Claus.

Later on in the evening, I let the girls know we would be leaving soon so they needed to start getting ready. I told them they could even wear their pajamas to the story reading. When I went in to tell Nicholas to start getting ready, I found him already dressed and ready to go, and you guessed it, in his Santa suit. He grabbed one of his favorite books and told me he was all ready to go. I told Nicholas to go to his sissy's room to let her and Mary know it was time to go to the mall. As soon as Holly saw her brother, she immediately began to protest the Santa suit. Holly began to get even more upset at her brother when Mary began laughing at Nicholas.

Holly then began to loudly voice her protests, "No! Not at the mall. Wasn't it enough when you were able to wear the suit to Thanksgiving?"

Amidst her own laughing Mary quickly responded, "Oh please wear the Santa suit Nicholas. I think you look very cute. Holly come on it's almost Christmas, don't forget Santa is watching."

Holly still quite unhappy stated, "Fine you can wear it. But brother tonight you better be normal and for once please do not draw attention to yourself!"

I gathered all three of the kids and we piled into the car. However, I could tell by the look on Holly's face that she was not happy with her brother wearing his Santa suit. I don't quite know why. I don't know if she was embarrassed by her brother in the suit or if she was just plain jealous of all of the attention her brother received when he had the suit on.

I was very excited and pleased he had the suit on. My little Nicholas seemed to have an extra spark to him whenever he wore his suit. I remember sitting back and watching him at Thanksgiving, wondering how simply wearing the Santa suit could put such a twinkle in his eyes and he some how became more jolly. He truly did seem as if he was Santa Claus every time he wore the suit. But I knew it didn't really matter whether it was the suit or not. I was just happy that he was happier.

On the way to the mall, I let Nicholas pick his song first. I could hear him singing word for word to the music playing in the car. Wow, how did my little Nicholas know all of the words to our kids Christmas CD? I had never heard or seen anyone belt out *Jungle Bell Rock* like he did. I found myself looking in the rearview mirror over and over again to see my little Santa singing. It seemed like second nature to him.

I finally asked Nicholas, "Have you been practicing Christmas songs lately?"

Nicholas quickly responded, "Of course I have Mimi! The elves know all of the Christmas songs by heart and they told me that I needed to learn them all too. Plus Mimi, they only play Christmas songs at the North Pole. Remember when I told you about Jack the head elf? Well, he told me he would help me memorize all of the Christmas songs so he downloaded all of his songs to my *Ipod*. I never knew there were that many Christmas songs Mimi. At night, before I go to sleep, I always put my earphones in and I fall asleep to my Christmas songs. Jack told me that by listening to my songs while I was sleeping, it would help me to memorize them better and I think it really has. You wanna know something a little weird Mimi?"

Of course before I even had a chance to answer Nicholas, Holly had to speak up sarcastically, "Mommy and I already do, you!"

Trying to stop her sarcasm, I happily announced, "Holly we are all going to speak only positive words to each other, no negativity. Of course I would like to know Nicholas. What happened that was a little weird?"

Nicholas smiled and continued, "Well, sometimes I am just so tired that I fall asleep and I forget to put on my earphones. But then when I wake up my earphones are on! I asked Jack about it the other day and he wouldn't admit to it but I think he comes into my room on those nights and puts the earphones in my ears. What do you think Mimi?"

'What?' I began to think to myself. Had my son been dreaming of more times at the North Pole? Had Nicholas actually been back at the North Pole? Wait, how often does Nicholas go to the North Pole or think he goes to the North Pole? My mind began completely racing in a million different directions at this point. I knew my little Nicholas was waiting for an answer from me so I quickly tried to focus on how to answer him.

I managed to smile as I replied, "I think you could be absolutely right sweetheart. Maybe Jack does come in at night and put them on you. Have you visited the North Pole again since your big adventure you told me about?"

Nicholas began to giggle as he told me, "Of course I have been there more Mimi. I do have to get ready for

Christmas you know! I really don't have that many more days until Christmas."

"Why haven't you told me about your recent adventures? You do know Nicholas that I would love to learn more about the North Pole don't you?"

"Well Mimi, it's just that I do go quite a bit and I didn't know you wanted to know more about the North Pole."

"I loved your big adventure story about the North Pole. I would love to know about all of your adventures to the North Pole. I will always make time no matter what I am doing so that I can hear about your fun adventures," I replied.

I thought I had been making more time for little Nicholas but maybe I wasn't. To ensure I would not miss out on any of his wonderful adventures I decided I would ask him everyday if he had been on anymore adventures to the North Pole.

"I didn't know you loved my story so much Mimi. I will try and tell you about all of my fun North Pole adventures from now on. But can you please play *Jingle Bell Rock* one more time 'cause that one is my favorite?"

We were almost at the mall but I decided to drive a little slower so there would be enough time to play all of *Jingle Bell Rock* again. Luckily, Holly and Mary were so enthralled in their conversation so they didn't seem to notice all the Christmas music playing in the car.

As we parked the car at the mall, the kids began to get even more excited. For some reason Nicholas wanted to bring in the book he had brought. I tried my best to convince him to leave the book in the car but he insisted he had to take it in. Nicholas did promise me he would carry his book the whole time. Finally, I agreed to let him take the book in because I figured it couldn't hurt. Besides, I thought it maybe a good tool to use to entertain him while we were waiting for Santa to arrive.

As we were entering the mall, Nicholas repeatedly began asking me if I knew where we were suppose to go. I kept telling him of course I knew where to go. It was getting a little annoying so finally I had to ask him to stop asking me. When we finally arrived at the courtyard in the mall, I had the kids get their milk and cookie at the refreshment table while I found all of us a good spot to sit.

"Mimi, I really don't think this is where they are going to want me to sit. I don't think all of the kids will be able to see me from here. I think they would prefer me to go up and sit in that big green chair on the Santa stage."

"Umm sweetheart, that is where Santa is going to sit to read us his book. Then we can all go wait in line to sit on Santa's lap."

As I was telling Nicholas this, all he could do was stare at me, expressionless. That is when I finally began to understand. Nicholas had thought since he thinks he is the new real Santa Claus everyone was coming to see him. How could I have been so blind to what Nicholas thought? I began to realize how tricky it was going to be having a son who thinks he is Santa Claus. My thoughts were loudly interrupted by my little Nicholas.

Nicholas proudly stood up then loudly proclaimed, "I am the new Santa Claus! So I will be the one reading the story, and all the kids will come and sit on my lap!" Then he proceeded to run up on stage and was grabbed by security just as he went to sit down in the big green chair.

It all happened so fast and I had tried unsuccessfully to grab Nicholas before he got up onstage. I immediately went over to security and tried to explain that my son is little, he just wanted to try out Santa's big green chair and he truly meant no harm. After a minute of pleading with security to let us go back to our spots, they released Nicholas. But not before leaving us with a warning to not do it again. We quietly walked back to our spots trying to ignore all of the stares from the people in the audience who were patiently waiting for Santa to arrive.

Nicholas was very hurt and upset. He was trying very hard to explain his position to me, "Mimi I brought my own book to read to everyone. I practiced all day and I know that I can read it really good to everyone. I even polished my boots! I am the real Santa and they want me!"

Just then the mall Santa began his descent down the escalator and the majority of the parents began to tell their children, "Look, it's Santa."

As I looked at the children's faces, a good portion of them looked a bit confused. At first I thought I was imagining the children turning to stare at Nicholas but then

I realized they really were looking over at my son. Were they just staring because they had seen him make a spectacle of himself when he ran up on the stage or maybe they know? People have always said children can sense when they are really in the presence of Santa Claus. Maybe these kids know Nicholas is the new real Santa Claus. No, now I am letting my imagination get the better of me. Sometimes I seem to forget Nicholas is not the new Santa and I am only being supportive of his imagination by letting him believe he is. But I can't get past the way the children are looking at Nicholas with the look of admiration and belief.

I saw Nicholas looking at the mall Santa and all of a sudden he began yelling as loud as he could, "He is a fake, he is a fake, he is not the real Santa, he is not the real Santa. I am!"

Holly and Mary had quickly spotted the other members of their 'six-pack' of friends when we had gotten to the mall. They were all hanging out together in the section across the room from where Nicholas and I were at. I knew Holly could hear her brother and I was truly hopeful she would be understanding and supportive of her brother's outburst. However, as I glanced over at her, I thought her glare directed towards me was going to burn a hole right through me.

Holly mouthed the words "Mom!" and I knew then she wanted nothing to do with her brother or me right now. She turned back to look at her friends and they were all laughing. The next thing I knew Holly, Mary and security were all three coming right towards me. I grabbed Nicholas by the hand as I told him it was time to go. Security then told me that my child was causing an unacceptable disturbance. Holly told me her friends were laughing at her, calling her Mrs. Claus now. I loudly announced the fact to all interested parties that we were now leaving.

As the four us walked away, I could hear the voices of a few children behind us saying, "No, I don't want the little Santa to go."

It was a very long and quiet walk out to the car. Nicholas held onto my hand very securely. Holly and Mary on the other hand walked quite a bit behind us. I believe they were thinking the distance would help someone else think they were not with us. I seriously thought we would never get to the car.

I opened the door for Holly, Mary and Nicholas as I announced, "There will be no discussions until we have arrived back home."

I was really hoping their dad would be home by the time we arrived. On the way home, I called Mary's mom to let her know Holly and Mary would be unable to have a sleepover tonight due to an incident at the mall. I told her, Mary was just fine and we would be picking up her stuff from the house then bringing her home. I felt bad we had to take Mary home earlier than originally planned. But I knew there was a lot we would need to discuss as a family tonight. We dropped off Mary and I apologized to her mom for the early drop off.

As we drove away from Mary's house, Holly and Nicholas could no longer hold their tongues. They both began to speak at the same time and I couldn't understand either of them. I told them they needed to be quiet for now and later we would have a family discussion at home, in which everyone would have their own opportunity to talk.

As we drove up to the house, I was very relieved to see Garrett's truck parked out in the front. As I pulled the car into the garage, Garrett met us in there. He had a smile on his face that quickly faded when he saw the look on mine. Holly and Nicholas jumped out of the car as soon as I put the car into park.

As Holly was exiting the car, she loudly announced, "Family meeting in the living room, NOW!" Then she hurried into the house with Nicholas following right behind her.

As I was slowly trying to get out of the car Garrett came over to hug me as he asked me what in the world was going on.

I gave him a brief description of what had happened. After which Garrett said sternly, "Santa suit is now gone. No more of this 'I am Santa' thing. My son is NOT Santa Claus!"

I was thankful Nicholas and Holly had already gone running into the house. I didn't want either of them to know whose side their father was on. All I could think of in my head was that my husband must be on the naughty list now! Garrett went into the house right after his little anti-Santa comments. However, I did not know whether I was ready to enter the house quite yet. I looked around the garage and I saw the old blue comforter from our bed. It was lying right next to my husband's workbench and for the first time since I had sentenced it to be the dog's new blanket, it looked so comfy. I closed my eyes for a moment as I imagined myself curling up and going to sleep on the old fluffy blue comforter.

My relaxation moment only lasted about fifteen seconds before I heard Holly screaming at me. "Mom, I said family meeting NOW. Come on!"

"Okay, I will be there in just a minute. I really need to gather my thoughts after such an eventful evening." Luckily Holly did go back inside so I was able to think of what I needed to say and what I needed to do. I reminded myself of the promise I had made the day I lost Nicholas at the mall. I knew my plan inside my head of how I wanted our family to be and I needed too continue with the plan. I knew it was going to be a bit tricky in the beginning but I also knew in the end everyone would be thankful with the results. I reminded myself that nothing worth attaining in life is easy and we all just needed to enjoy the journey.

I walked towards the door of the house and I took a big deep breath in as I entered. In the living room, I saw Holly and Nicholas each sitting on opposite sides of the couch and Garrett sitting on the ottoman next to it. I could see all eyes had now fallen upon me.

I felt empowered and strong with my plan. I know both of my children are special in their own way and should be free to be themselves. I cleared my throat before I began, "Nicholas you should not have tried to run up onto the stage. I should have let you know the fake Santa would be at the mall. I am sorry I did not realize that you thought the mall people would be letting you, the new real Santa, be the one reading the story. Maybe the mall people just thought you would be way too busy for that type of responsibility since this is your first year as the new real Santa Claus. I know they would have let you be there if they had known you wanted to be there. I will…"

Holly sat there quietly as long as she could before she had to interject, "Wait, no Nicholas is not the new real Santa. His behavior tonight was completely unacceptable and embarrassing! It's bad enough all of our relatives know he thinks he is the new Santa, but now all of my friends know what he thinks! I am never going to live this one down at school."

There had been a huge smile on Nicolas's face while I was apologizing to him. However, as soon as his sister threw her thoughts into the discussion his huge smile quickly faded away.

"Sissy I am really sorry. I never asked to be the new Santa. The gift was just given to me. I was chosen because of me."

Holly quickly responded to her brother's comments, "You were not chosen. No, YOU have chosen yourself and YOU have made up this entire Santa thing! YOU ARE NOT SANTA!!"

I interjected, "Okay everyone we are going to get one thing straight here. We are a family. Do you know what that means?" There were no comments only three pairs of eyes looking straight at me. I could see the anger and embarrassment in Holly's big green eyes, the plain irritation in the ocean blue eyes of my husband and the sadness but joy in the green eyes of my little Nicholas. I was maintaining everyone's attention so I continued, "It means that we are there for each other one-hundred and ten percent, no matter what. We all need to be able to support each other no matter what. We all need to be able to dream and dream big. There are no limits and I mean no limits to our beliefs, our dreams and absolutely no limits to our imagination."

"Wait mom, do you seriously expect me to believe my little brother is Santa Claus? What if next he starts saying he believes that he is a leprechaun? Do we have to celebrate St. Patrick's Day all year long and let him wear a green leprechaun suit every day?"

Little Nicholas proudly stood up from the couch and announced, "I am not a leprechaun, I am Santa!"

I couldn't help but smirk as I continued, "Whew, I am glad we got that straightened out! Yes, Holly we would celebrate St. Patrick's Day all year long if your brother believed that he was a leprechaun. Your father and I want you both to be all you can be and we will always support you both. Please, you two never sell yourselves short. You really can be whatever you want to be. Please reach for the stars, never limit yourselves. Please! Yes, I know it maybe a little difficult Holly but the sooner you start supporting your brother the better you are going to feel inside. As for you little Nicholas, you need to understand that people may not be as accepting of you as the new Santa Claus at first. People may look at you and only see a little boy. Just remember that maybe those people who don't believe in you may never have believed in Santa. So try your hardest to not get mad or upset, especially in public. Deal?"

With that huge smile beaming back on his face Nicholas quickly responded, "Deal Mimi, I will try my best."

"Holly?"

With a bit of sarcasm in her voice Holly finally responded, "Fine, I will try my best to support my little brother. But seriously please control yourself in public and whenever my friends are over."

During the entirety of the family meeting my Garrett continued to stare at me with a bit of irritation in his eyes. I was a little happy he had let me control the meeting. I knew he had almost zero support for our son as Santa and I really did not want his opinion voiced out loud!

With a bit of calm over my children now, I told them to go get ready for bed, brush their teeth and I would be up shortly to tuck them in.

Garrett started to question me about what had just transpired in the living room. I told him, "I will explain everything later." Luckily my husband is the most mellow, understanding person so he agreed to find out about our eventful trip to the mall later on.

As I went into my Holly's room, I tried to control my excitement at what I saw. There was my little Nicholas sitting on my Holly's bed. Holly was reading Nicholas her favorite book *The Growing Tree* written by Shel Silverstein. I stood there to the side of the doorway so I would be out of both of their sights. I wanted to savor the moments of them enjoying each other as I pray they will learn to do the majority of the time. I was glad to see they were sharing a longer book together so I was able to savor this time. She was reading to him with such expression and realism. Nicholas was so into the story, asking questions as usual and Holly was patiently answering each of his questions, no matter how silly each question was. These are the times in life I am so thankful for. When the book was finished, part of me, no actually most of me was wishing Nicholas would ask for the book to be read again. Nicholas didn't though; he got off her bed and headed for the doorway. Therefore, I had to speak up and say thank you to both of them. They looked up at me and asked why I was thanking them. I explained how nice it is to see them getting along especially after a tough evening of differences between the two of them.

I told Nicholas to go pop into bed and daddy would tuck him in first while I tucked in sissy. So he skipped right over to his room. I went over to Holly, tucked her into bed and I had a heart to heart talk with her. I told her I understood how embarrassing it had been earlier. But I also told her to appreciate what a special brother she has. I told her Nicholas loves her very much and would never try to hurt her. She promised me she would try her best to understand and support her little brother as the new real Santa Claus. I kissed my Holly goodnight and once again thanked her for agreeing to support her brother even with his big imagination.

Next I was able to tell my new little Santa Claus goodnight who was of course sleeping in his suit once again.

I told Nicholas, "Thank you for taking on the huge responsibility of being the new real Santa Claus."

As I kissed him goodnight he whispered in my ear, "Thank you Mimi."

I whispered, "I love you Nicholas," as I shut off his light.

Now came time to tell my husband about the eventful night he had missed. I told him the entire story and he couldn't help but ask me how I kept my cool the entire night. He was still a bit skeptical about our son believing he is the new Santa Claus. But Garrett agreed to fully support our little Nicholas as the new Santa Claus even though he did admit that he did not believe Nicholas was really the new Santa. I accepted and I was happy along with being thankful, the entire family was on the same page for the supporting of each other. I have to say I went to sleep that night dreaming of the North Pole exactly as my little Nicholas had described it to me.

The next morning I was awakened by Holly way too early when she came running into my room asking, "Is Nicholas in here? I said is Nicholas in here?"

I was not even half awake as I answered, "I have no idea where he is at sweetheart. I think he is still in his bed, go check again I am still tired. It is very early!"

Holly rushed back into my room not even a minute later, still screaming anxiously. "He is not in his room, he is not downstairs and he is not in the house. I can't find him, where is he?"

I was trying my best to wake up enough to help Holly and to fully figure out what was going on but what can I say, I was having a fabulous nights sleep and I really wanted to sleep in on my day off. I finally gained my composure, got out of bed and walked with Holly into Nicholas's room. There he was still sound asleep in his Santa suit, just as I had put him to bed the night before.

I turned to Holly and tiredly asked, "What is going on? Don't you see your brother right there asleep in his bed?"

"But mommy, he wasn't here a few minutes ago when I was in here."

Immediately remembering the support I had promised both of my children, I let her know, "Well, maybe he had gone into the bathroom or maybe he was just hiding from you." There was a different look on her face though that told me she really believed he had not been in our house just minutes ago. Without another word, Holly walked into her brother's room, got up onto his bed and snuggled up right next to him.

I walked out of his room and I stood in the hallway for a moment and listened to Holly ask her brother where he had been. I was sure he was sound asleep until I heard Nicholas respond back to his sissy, "Shhh, I was at the North Pole."

"I believe you now. I was very worried about you. Please tell me next time. I do love you bro bro. Can I come with you one time maybe?"

"I don't know, I'll check with Jack. Thank you, sissy for believing."

Wow, I think the meeting last night did work. I was so happy my children were finally getting along so well. I went back to bed until both of my children finally came in and woke me up saying "We're starving for breakfast." While I was making breakfast, I asked Nicholas if he had gone to the North Pole last night.

"Yes, I went there last night to check on all of the toys in the toy factory. It had taken me a bit longer than the elves thought it would take me. The elves were trying to rush me back to my bed because they had seen Holly looking for me."

I really couldn't help but ask, "Nicholas how did the elves know that Holly was looking for you?"

His answer was quick and seemed very simple to him, "Their video computer of course. Remember Mimi I told you they watch kids all over the world, to keep the naughty and nice list correct. The elves that were watching Holly put out an alert to the elves that were with me and they got me back home as soon as possible. You should have seen them Mimi, I have never seen anyone move as fast as the elves did just to get me back home and into my bed!"

I had to ask, "Oh, well it's almost Christmas, is the naughty and nice list finalized yet?"

"Almost, I have a little more to review before I can finalize it for the season. So I may go back sometime this week," Nicholas replied.

"Please listen to the elves and mind them and just don't stay out too late," I reminded him.

Nicholas reassuringly stated, "I will try to get home as early as I can and I promise that I will listen to the elves. Do you know that the elves are a lot older than me, Mimi?"

"No sweetheart, I really hadn't thought of how old the elves are. How old are they?" I asked.

"Well Jack is the only elf that will tell me how old he is. He is eighty four years old. Can you believe that? He looks like a teenager and not like an old man. I try not to mention age at the North Pole 'cause some of the elves tend to be a little sensitive when it comes to their age," said Nicholas.

While I was cooking breakfast, Garrett had come in and heard a bit of Nicholas telling about the elves. He smiled at me and I knew he was enjoying his son's imagination. I knew the whole Santa thing probably wasn't easy for him either. You always want your kid to be normal and not abnormal. Or should I say you don't want other people to think your child is abnormal. You want your child to fit in with the other kids. As a parent you want your child's life as a child to be fun and carefree.

One always remembers those kids growing up who were always a bit off the 'normal'. Those kids who just didn't quite fit in and then never fit in, even in Junior High and High school. Even though you yourself never went over and befriended those kids. You could see it in their eyes, they knew they were 'different' and they knew when the mean kids were making fun of them. Even though they acted like they really weren't paying any attention to those mean kids.

I never wanted my little Nicholas to be made fun of. I knew I had to let him be himself. Who knows, maybe those 'abnormal' kids growing up may actually be very happy now. They may appreciate themselves more for choosing to be themselves versus fitting into the box of the 'normal'. I could see that Nicholas was very serious about being the new real Santa Claus and I was very happy to have my son be Santa.

I found myself always going into Nicholas's room first thing every morning when I woke up. I don't know why I began to be so afraid that my son wouldn't be there one morning. I guess I began to think he may decide to live full time at the North Pole. He always talked about how much he loved being at the North Pole. He talked about the elves as if he had been friends with them since he was born. He would mimic their voices and their actions. He would always tell me how cool it was when he saw the elves making toys at the toy factory. What if one day he got upset and never came home? I tried to put that thought out of my head but it always seemed to creep back. Needless to say I was always very excited to see my boy still sound asleep every morning when I would enter his room.

CHAPTER 4

Today started off no different than any other day. It was December 23, the day before Christmas Eve. I woke up, checked on Nicholas then on Holly, I went downstairs to make my coffee and read the newspaper. However, when I came back inside after I had gotten the newspaper, I saw Nicholas sitting on the couch looking a bit sad. At first I thought maybe he had a bad dream. But then when I asked him what was wrong. He asked me to sit down so he could tell me the entire story.

Nicholas took in a deep breath and sadly began telling his story. "Mimi, last night Jack came and got me and I went to the North Pole. This time was different though. Jack told me that I had to finalize the Naughty and Nice list. I thought it would be easy Mimi, but it wasn't easy. Jack told me that whoever was on the naughty list would just get a few presents from their parents and none from Santa Claus. No presents from Santa, Mimi? How could I do that to any kids? But Jack told me the naughty and nice list is one of the most important jobs that Santa has. There were a few kids that were kinda 'on the fence' of being on the naughty list. The elves showed me some of their video that they had on those kids and I had to decide naughty or nice. Some of the kids were real mean

Mimi so I had to keep them on the naughty list. I mean, they deserve the naughty list but still it makes me sad Mimi. I just don't want anyone to not get presents from me on Christmas!"

I wanted to make him happy but I didn't know how to make it easy for him so I said, "You know what? Maybe those kids will be nice next year then. Maybe they will be able to get onto the nice list for next year. I am proud of you for being able to make such difficult decisions sweetheart. Have you chosen the leader for the sleigh team yet?"

A smile reappeared on his face as he said, "Okay Mimi, last night wasn't all bad. I tested all of the reindeers and I picked my sleigh team for this Christmas. And guess which reindeer got the leader spot."

"Um", I responded.

"Donner Mimi, it was Donner! He was so awesome! He flew like I have never seen before. He was able to fly higher and faster than any of the other reindeer's. He even told me thanks after I picked him. He told me that I had really encouraged him that first time he had met me."

"I am so proud of you. See how great that was? Just think about the good stuff, forget about all of the sad stuff. Only concentrate on the positive and then you will be even happier all of the time," I reassured him.

"Thanks Mimi."

Then as Nicholas was walking out of the living room he ran back to me with his arms wide open and I bent down to let him run into my arms for a big hug. As he hugged me, he whispered into my ear, "Mimi you're on the nice list."

I watched as he went up to his room and looked back at me before he entered with a great big smile.

The rest of the day was fabulous as always. Nicholas seemed to know how he was going to handle his problem with the naughty list.

The next day, I awoke to Nicholas yelling the words, "Its Christmas Eve, its Christmas Eve everyone!"

It seemed as if Christmas Eve had taken so long to come this year. I don't know if it just seemed extra long because Nicholas has been wearing his Santa suit for so long and Christmas has been the highlight of nearly every conversation or was it that I actually was done with my Christmas shopping very early this year. We were all going over to my aunt's house for a Christmas Eve get together. Nicholas had requested I ask for it to be scheduled a bit earlier in the day this year. He told me he had a very busy night scheduled to deliver all of the presents to the kids all over the world. He also told me he felt very prepared but wanted to make sure he ran on time.

Luckily, everyone agreed to have the Christmas Eve get together at two o'clock that afternoon. I figured that would give Nicholas plenty of time to get home and get to bed. Holly and Nicholas were very excited about going to the family get together tonight. It gave them an opportunity to see and play with all of their cousins. As expected

Nicholas was the first one downstairs in the living room all dressed up in his Santa suit.

Nicholas was calling out, "Everyone hurry up and get downstairs."

I knew he was anxious to get out of the house so I was getting dressed and finishing my hair as fast as possible.

Once Garrett and I were all ready, I yelled down to Nicholas, "We are on our way downstairs."

Just then Holly walked out of her room. As I looked at her, my eyes began to well up with tears. She looked absolutely beautiful. She had on the red velvet dress I had bought for her last year. However, it was a bit different than when I had bought it for her. It now had soft fluffy white fur at the edges of each of the sleeves and at the bottom hem of the dress. There was also now a red sparkly belt with a shiny silver buckle attached to the dress. She was wearing a matching Santa hat with the same white fur lining at the bottom edge.

I paused for a moment before I smiled and exclaimed, "You look beautiful sweetheart! How? No wait, who fixed your dress for you?"

Holly's face lit up as she told me about her new beautiful dress, "I did. I just picked up the fur and the buckle at the craft store. I cut a little bit of material off of the bottom of the dress to make the belt. Oh and I also bought some sparkly spray to spray the dress with, so I would shine extra bright!"

I quickly replied, "And you do shine extra bright girlfriend! I think it looks fabulous. Your brother is going to absolutely love your dress as well."

"Do you really think so? I was trying very hard to surprise him with the dress. I have been staying up late every night to work on my dress. And I took money out of my piggy bank to pay for the supplies."

"Well let's go show bro bro. And Holly, thanks. Thank you for this, thanks for trying so hard to make your brother happy."

Just then I heard little Nicholas screaming, "I thought you guys were on your way down. Come on!"

"Ok, Ok we are coming." I hurried down so that I could see the look on Nicholas's face when he saw his sissy. As soon as my Nicholas saw his sissy his mouth dropped wide open. At first I was unsure if he was going to be able to say anything at all to his sissy. His face shinned so brightly with both amazement and happiness. I knew by the look on his face that he was happy.

Finally Nicholas was able to gain his composure and speak. "You look very beautiful sissy. Who made your dress for you?"

"I made it to wear for you bro bro."

"Thank you sissy, you really do look beautiful."

I knew we had to get going because Nicholas had already told me he wanted to be the first one to get there tonight, in order to greet everyone else as they arrived.

"Come on everyone lets hurry up and get into the car so we can get there," I said.

Everyone agreed to listen to *Jingle Bell Rock* over and over again all the way to my aunt's house. I think after the twelve times of listening to *Jingle Bell Rock* all of us knew every single word to the song.

As soon as my aunt opened the door she of course had to oohh and aaahh over the kids for about five minutes. Then the kids ran off to look at all of the presents underneath the Christmas tree. All of a sudden there was a knock at the front door. Nicholas practically flew to the front door in order to greet the next guest who was arriving.

As Nicholas swung the front door open widely he said in a very jolly tone, "Merry Christmas Eve."

When he saw it was his great grandma he quickly put his arms around her and whispered something into her ear. Nicholas thinks the world of his great grandma and they have always had an extra special bond. Until he started preschool, she had taken care of him one day a week.

I had always wondered why he would try and grab my coffee cup as a toddler. I soon found out it was because his great grandma shared her coffee with him. Needless to say he does still have a cup of black coffee about once a week. At first, I was worried about letting him drink any coffee but I later found out coffee is harmless and a cup of black coffee is actually recommended to help hyperactivity. Oh and his great grandma always makes him his special the attention of Holly, I called her over to me so I could find out what was going on.

Holly explained to me, "The little cousins really believe their cousin Nicholas is the new real Santa Claus and they are taking turns getting on his lap to tell him what they want for Christmas."

At first I was a bit skeptical the little cousins believed this but then as I watched each one as they were talking to Nicholas and the smiles they had on their faces, I knew they believed in him. How amazing. Nicholas had told me children are better believers than adults and this is why he thought there were more children on the nice list than there were adults. I also remembered Nicholas telling me there were some adults that didn't make the naughty or the nice list because they simply didn't believe. Their hearts were so hardened to happiness and dreaming. They had no imagination left in them. I find it so sad there are people out in the world who are so busy doing their own thing they lost their imaginations somewhere along the road of life.

I was lost in my own thoughts thinking about the different tidbits of information my little Nicholas had told me about the North Pole. All of a sudden I felt a tap on my shoulder. I quickly turned around and saw it was my mom trying to get my attention. I realized I had been totally lost in thought and I was really unsure how long I had been standing there.

My mom immediately began to question me. "Are you in another world lost in some deep thought? I have been calling your name and you never answered or are you just ignoring me?"

I quickly interrupted her questioning to answer her. "What? No mom I was watching the little cousins sit up on Nicholas's lap and then I guess I began to daydream."

All of a sudden, I noticed Nicholas and the little cousins weren't even in the room anymore. I asked my mom, "Where did they all go?"

My mom then let me know that is why she was trying to get my attention. My mom took me into the game room where the Christmas tree was at. There sat Nicholas and all of the little cousins in a tight knit circle. I approached the circle a little bit more so I would be in ear shot of what was being said. The little cousins were all listening very attentively as Nicholas was telling them about the North Pole. He told all of them he was very proud of them because each and every one of them were on the nice list so they would all be getting their presents from him in the morning when they woke up.

I continued to listen very attentively as Nicholas continued explaining that he knew which toys and stuff on their Santa lists they really truly wanted in their hearts and that is how he decided what things to bring to each of them. He then explained how looking at someone's heart is how he figures out what presents to deliver to people all over the world because the heart is what tells him what someone truly wants. Little Nicholas had already told me about most of his Christmas prep but still I couldn't help but listen to him as he told all of his little cousins about it.

Nicholas told the cousins all about playing tag with the elves as the fluffy white snow came down in beautifully shaped snowflakes. He also told them about a snowball fight, which began between him and all of the elves he was playing with. He let them know the elves were little just like them but very fast. The peppermint candy and lollipop lined streets were all explained in detail to the little cousins as was the toy factory. Nicholas asked all of the little cousins to raise their hand if they wanted to know about the reindeers as well. Like a flash of light, all of their little hands went up in the blink of an eye.

"Ok, ok I will tell you all about the reindeers then. They run really fast and they fly really fast also. They practice their running and their flying every single day. Then when it's almost Christmas they all compete and show me how good they are for this year. I have to pick out the sleigh team but most importantly, I have to pick out the leader of the sleigh team. The reindeers were all really good so it was a very difficult decision."

Little cousin Ruthie quickly chimed in. "So who did you pick? Did you pick Dancer? Because Dancer is my favorite because I love to dance!"

Nicholas shook his head no as he replied, "No Ruthie, I am sorry I didn't pick Dancer to lead the sleigh team this year. I picked Donner because he worked extra hard all year long and so he could fly faster and run faster than any of the other reindeers. But Dancer was picked to be part of my sleigh team so if you listen real hard as you sleep, you just may hear the jingle of the bells around Dancer. Each reindeer has a little bit different jingle to the bells on the sleigh. Since you are a dancer Ruthie, I know that you will recognize the jingle of Dancer right away."

Just then my little Nicholas looked up and saw me standing there. "Mimi, what time is it? We need to get home soon. I have a very busy night ahead of me. Lets all go open presents so we can get home."

Before I knew it all of the little cousins began to pass out the presents. As soon as Nicholas saw all of the presents were passed out he yelled out to everyone to open their presents. I guess everyone must have been pretty excited because everyone quickly began to open their presents. Holly and Nicholas excitedly opened their presents as well and I was very pleased to see them go and thank each person for their gift after they opened each of them. After all of the present opening was done, Nicholas let me know it was time to go. Nicholas went over to his dad to help his dad start loading everything into the car.

Nicholas and Holly gave everyone hugs and kisses goodbye and got into the car. As I was telling everyone goodbye, I received numerous comments about my little Nicholas being allowed to dress up in a Santa suit. Some commented it was cute while I overheard others say it was a bit over the top. I think the general consensus was Nicholas just has an overactive imagination. A friend of my aunt even had the nerve to comment to me that I should make sure to control my son's overactive imagination.

I calmly responded, "I let my children have imaginations and dreams," then I turned to walk out to the car where Garrett and the children were waiting for me.

As soon as I got into the car, Nicholas called out, "I call my song. I want *Jingle Bell Rock*."

I quickly turned on *Jingle Bell Rock* and we all sang it together quite a few times while we drove home. As soon as we had parked the car in the garage, Nicholas was opening the door and jumping out of the car. We helped unload all of the presents out of the car. Nicholas was quite the helper trying to get everything put away as soon as possible.

The minute everything was put away, Nicholas announced, "it's bedtime everybody and I need to pick out what cookie I want to put out for myself when I deliver the presents to all of us tonight."

Nicholas picked out a big frosted Santa Claus sugar cookie. He put the cookie on the usual Santa plate we use every year as he announced, "I feel like leaving chocolate milk out for myself too."

Nicholas poured a mug of chocolate milk in the usual Santa mug and placed the mug next to the Santa plate.

"It is bedtime everyone because the sooner we go to bed the sooner I can deliver presents," Nicholas announced proudly.

We all listened to Nicholas and got dressed and ready for bed. I went into Holly's room and I was surprised to find she was already in her bed. But as I kissed her goodnight, I caught a glimpse of what she was wearing to bed. It was her red Christmas dress.

I asked her why she was wearing that to bed but all she would tell me was, "just because". I figured that it wasn't hurting anything for her to wear the dress to bed, so I kissed her goodnight and shut her light off.

When I went to tuck Nicholas in bed and tell him goodnight, I already knew what he would be wearing to bed. He wasn't wearing any of his pajamas to bed tonight. No, he was wearing his Santa suit that some how still fit him perfectly.

He was growing like a weed. I had bought him new jeans because when he wore his old jeans it looked as if he was wearing capri's. Oddly enough his Santa suit pants weren't short on him at all. I kissed my little Nicholas goodnight and I told him to have fun but to be very careful tonight as Santa Claus.

Nicholas quickly responded, "Thanks Mimi. I will be very careful and I know that I will have lots of fun."

I shut off his light, told him goodnight one more time, then I went and got into bed. At first I was unsure if I was going to be able to sleep at all because I was a bit worried about my little Nicholas. I couldn't help but wonder about his first night as the new real Santa Claus. Before I knew it, I was sound asleep. I fell into such a deep sleep and I found myself dreaming of the North Pole. I dreamed of Nicholas getting his last minute instructions by the elves, about the reindeers, the sleigh and the actual delivering of all of the presents. It was so amazing how vividly I could see and hear all of it. I truly felt as if I was there. All of a sudden in my dream I caught a glimpse of the entire sleigh. Now I knew why Holly had worn her red Christmas dress to bed. She had gone with Nicholas. I was still not sure if it was just a dream or if somehow I was able to really see what my son was doing and where he was so I would be at ease. He was flying the sleigh perfectly. He had a huge smile on his face again and his sissy had a huge smile on her face as well. Jack had gone with them. I was assuming to make sure that Nicholas's first Christmas delivery as the new Santa Claus went smoothly. I was so thankful to get such a fabulous glimpse into the Santa Claus life of my little Nicholas.

Before I knew it I was being awakened by my two kids running into my room screaming, "Wake up, wake up. Let's go downstairs and look at our presents."

All I could manage to say was, "Okay, okay give me just a minute to wake up."

I didn't remember when or how my dream of Nicholas and Holly's adventure had ended. The last thing I remembered was Nicholas delivering presents to children all over in neighborhoods I had never even seen before. I had no idea where in the world he was at. But I remember Nicholas telling me there was an awesome computer in the sleigh that helped show him the way. It was kind of like the navigator on my cell phone. I guess maybe I was only allowed to see enough of his trip until I felt they were both safe and I could fall into a sound and deep sleep. I was trying my best to gain my composure and get myself all the way out of bed. Holly and Nicholas were still jumping up and down at the end of the bed. Garrett and I both finally managed to get out of bed. I grabbed the camcorder and Garrett grabbed the camera.

As usual we walked down first so we could videotape the kids when they first saw their presents. Garrett flipped on the lights and I tried to control my shock and amazement of what I saw through the screen of the camcorder. It was no shock the sugar cookie had been eaten and every last drop of the chocolate milk had been drunk. But what was shocking was what our family room now looked like.

First of all, the Christmas tree had more lights on it now and there was a new bright silver star at the top of the tree. Second, all of the stockings were stuffed full. Thirdly, there was a brand new two wheel bike with flames on it for Nicholas. It looked almost like a motorcycle. The bike was like no other bike I had ever seen. I had been looking for a bike for Nicholas but he hadn't found one he had liked. A brand new skateboard with a dragon on it, I assumed was for Holly. The skateboard was leaning up against a mini skateboard ramp and it was beautiful. No, I was not exactly excited that my daughter had just received a skateboard of all things but I do have to admit it was beautiful. Just like the bike, I had never seen a skateboard like this either.

Of course I had not been shopping for skateboards because I had been ignoring the fact that my daughter wanted a skateboard. But this skateboard really looked as if it had been handcrafted versus one you get at a toy store. There was a dragon on it but it didn't look like the 'typical dragon' picture. I handed the camcorder to Garrett so I could pick up the skateboard. The dragon picture looked absolutely beautiful and I could tell as I closely looked at it that it had been hand painted special onto this specific skateboard. I had never seen such beauty and detail in the picture of a dragon especially a dragon picture on a skateboard. The wheels on the skateboard were of course purple which is Holly's favorite color. I slowly put the skateboard down and as I turned around Nicholas was standing right there.

Nicholas eagerly told me, "Come on Mimi, you have to look in your stocking."

I can't say after seeing the bike and the skateboard for the kids that I wasn't a little, okay a lot excited. I found myself running with Nicholas over to look into my stocking. When we got over to my stocking, I think Nicholas was even more excited than me. He suddenly dumped out all of the contents of my stocking. He showed me the socks he had put in there and told me they were suppose to be extra soft for my feet when I run on the treadmill. Next he handed me a CD from my stocking. I looked at the front of the CD and there was a picture of Nicholas on the cover and it was entitled, *Jingle Bell Rock*.

"Mimi, I did this CD just special for you. I know you love it when I sing you *Jingle Bell Rock*. So, some of the elves recorded me singing *Jingle Bell Rock* for you. You will love it Mimi. You can even download it so you can listen to it while you run on the treadmill. But come on Mimi you haven't opened the best one yet."

Just then he handed me a little box wrapped in silver paper with a big red ribbon tied around it. I slowly pulled the end of the red ribbon and peeled away the silver wrapping. I looked around to see everyone quietly watching me open the box. I fought back the tears as I lifted the silver chain out of the box. There was a heart locket on the silver chain engraved with the word 'Mimi' and inside the locket was a picture of my Nicholas dressed in his Santa suit with that huge smile on his face I love so much. I reached over and grabbed my Nicholas onto my lap and I held him.

This time it was my chance to whisper into his ear, "Thank you Santa, I love it. It is truly the best present I have ever been given." I sat there for a moment hugging my little boy not wanting to ever let go.

Finally, he jumped up and told me, "Put it on Mimi....put it on!"

Garrett came over and helped little Nicholas put the necklace around my neck. I got up and looked into the mirror so I could see how beautiful it looked on me. It looked perfect, more beautiful than I thought it would. We all finished looking at the intriguing gifts we had received from Santa. Garrett made all of us an incredible breakfast, then we opened our presents from each other. We never spend a lot on our gifts to each other. We try to be creative and to make whatever gifts we can as an expression of love. We each gave thanks for the presents and we got ready to go over to my parent's house. I was still a bit puzzled where all of the extra Santa presents under the tree and in the stockings had come from. I guess I assumed Garrett went out shopping and had bought a few extra things, even though Garrett absolutely hates going shopping. I thought maybe he was in the spirit of Christmas a bit more this year because of our little Nicholas.

    Holly chose to wear one of her new outfits she had received. Nicholas on the other hand decided to once again wear his Santa suit. Garrett voiced his concerns because he was afraid Nicholas was going to start smelling in his Santa suit. I wasn't so concerned. I smelled the suit and it smelled just fine. There were no stains or spills on the suit so I let him wear it. Plus, Nicholas had taken a bath this morning before putting his suit back on so he smelled nice and clean. I went into Holly's room while she was getting ready and I asked her how she slept last night. She told me she hadn't gotten much sleep so she was still very tired.

I asked Holly, "Why?"

Holly simply stated, "I just didn't sleep well because I was so excited."

I looked at Holly as I nodded my head agreeing with her.

Holly paused for a moment before she hesitantly asked me, "How long are you going to let Nicholas wear his Santa suit?"

I hadn't really thought about it so I replied, "I really don't think I should control how long he wears his Santa suit for."

Holly graciously stated, "It is great my brother is the new Santa Claus but I really hope he only wears the suit at Christmas time because I don't want any of my friends to find out about him."

I understood Holly didn't want her friends to make fun of her about her brother but I still didn't want to impinge on Nicholas's imagination.

When we all arrived at my mom's house, Nicholas was still very full of energy. He thoroughly enjoyed hearing how happy everyone was with what Santa had brought for them. His great grandma thanked him for the necklace and earrings she had on. Then she turned and asked me when I had put them in her stocking at her house. Unsure what to say, I just smiled.

At dinner, Nicholas continued to tell everyone his stories about the elves and the reindeers. He also let everyone know how tired he was from working all night.

Halfway through dinner he went over to his grandma and asked if he could go lie down on her bed. She scooped him up in her arms and carried him off to put him in her bed. Someone had to comment how tired some kids are because they stay up so late on Christmas Eve and then get up so early on Christmas morning.

Garrett and I decided to leave shortly after we ate because the conversation had turned to what an overactive imagination little Nicholas had. I was a bit annoyed my family had nothing better to do than to talk about my son's imagination. But hey, at least he has an imagination and at least he has fun in life. I didn't let on to anyone that I was the least bit annoyed. I was proud of my son and so I left it at that. I politely told everyone I should have made sure Nicholas had gotten more sleep the night before and I needed to take him home so he could get some good sleep in his own bed.

Garrett carried Nicholas out to the car, put him in his car seat and drove us all the way home without Nicholas waking up. Garrett and I put him up in his bed when we arrived home and he was still out cold. I tucked him in bed and he was in such a deep sleep I actually watched for his chest to rise and fall. I even felt for air coming out of his nose to make sure he was still breathing. He was still breathing. I think he was just overly tired. While I was tucking Nicholas into bed, Holly had already crawled into her bed and fallen asleep as well. I thought they had the right idea so I told my husband I thought it was time we went to bed too.

As we were lying in bed talking about what a perfect holiday season it had been, Garrett told me we needed to talk about Nicholas and 'the Santa thing'. I on the other hand was not ready to discuss Nicholas as Santa. I was thoroughly enjoying how everything was going but I knew things would be different now that Christmas was almost over. My husband told me we really shouldn't let little Nicholas wear his Santa suit anymore since Christmas was over. I wasn't really on board with the idea but I just agreed because I didn't want to discuss it any further. I guess I also thought maybe Nicholas would wait until the next holiday season to start wearing it again. I am just fine admitting when I am wrong and boy was I wrong. Little did I know Nicholas thought the Santa suit should be his year long attire.

CHAPTER 5

It seemed like it was just Christmas Eve and here it was already New Years Eve, another year gone. We had all been invited to a very formal New Years party at the Froman's house. We've known the family for years and now our kids go to the same school together. I was excited and I had been looking forward to dressing up for New Years Eve. I was wearing my favorite little black dress that Garrett absolutely loves. Garrett was wearing my favorite outfit of his, which I had bought for him on Madison Avenue when we visited New York together earlier that year.

I went into see what Holly was wearing. I was so excited to see she was dressed in her stylish little black dress I had bought for her in New York as well. I was sincerely relishing in the fact I have been given such a perfect and wonderful family. My fabulous thoughts however were abruptly interrupted by my husband. All of a sudden I heard Garrett telling Nicholas he had to change because it wasn't Christmas anymore. I rushed into my little Nicholas's room to see what was going on. There he was sitting on his bed dressed in his Santa suit. I looked at Garrett and he was simply shaking his head 'no'.

Garrett and I briefly had a conversation outside Nicholas's room in the hallway. I told Garrett it really wasn't hurting anything or anyone by letting little Nicholas wear his Santa suit for one last time this year. After a bit of debating, I won and went in to tell Nicholas it would be just fine to wear his Santa suit to the party. I left his room with a smile on my face because I thought I had won. I did begin to doubt I had really 'won' when I saw the look on Holly's face.

Holly looked at me and I knew she could no longer hold her thoughts in. "Mom, my friends are going to be there tonight. I am happy to be the sister of Santa Claus but can't we just leave that at Christmas. I don't want to be made fun of. My friends don't understand Nicholas. They think he is weird."

I was about to comment on Holly's statements when I saw little Nicholas hiding behind the corner. I was really hoping he hadn't heard what his sister had just said. But then I looked at him and I saw the tears in his eyes. Then he ran back into his room.

I decided to loudly proclaim, "There is NO dress code for tonight. Everyone can wear what ever they want and I mean what ever they want!" Well I knew my proclamation would cover the situation at least for tonight. Seriously, I thought how bad could it really be, letting Nicholas wear his Santa suit?

Little did I know, people think when Christmas is over then it is over! I guess this is why so many people take down their Christmas trees the day after Christmas. In my opinion, it took me so long to decorate the house and the tree, I think the decorations should be up at least until New Years day. Garrett and I choose to keep the tree up at least until New Years day, since Christmas trees are so expensive now. Truthfully, there have been those few occasions we actually left the tree and the decorations up until the end of January. Of course we only did in those situations because we had somehow picked out trees those years that stayed green.

As we were walking up the walkway of the Froman's house, I realized these were some of those people who must take down their decorations early. There was absolutely no sign of Christmas left at their house. Of course that was about to change. Nicholas quickly noticed there was no longer any sign of Christmas. He asked me why they had taken down all of the decorations already. I remember trying unsuccessfully to explain to him the possible reasons people take down their decorations early. I finally felt as if I was rambling on because even I had no idea what I was saying.

Luckily, Nicholas proudly interrupted me and told me, "Well, I guess I will be their Christmas decoration tonight."

I couldn't help but smile at his announcement. In fact I looked over at Garrett and I even saw a smile flash across his face. Holly tried to hide her smile but I saw it shinning through.

We rang the doorbell and Nancy Froman greeted us with a genuine smile that quickly turned into a fake smile as she looked down at Nicholas.

I guess she simply couldn't keep her little comments to herself. She sarcastically commented looking right at little Nicholas, "Oh my. I thought Christmas was over. Did your mommy and daddy forget to tell you that this was a New Years party and not a Christmas party?"

I was oh so proud of my little Nicholas. He simply smiled that huge smile of his and walked into the house. Holly and Nicholas quickly found their friends and went their separate ways to enjoy the night.

After Nancy Froman's snide little comment, I suddenly remembered the reason we didn't socialize much anymore. Nancy is tall and slender with quite a bit too much plastic surgery. Sometimes I stare at her to see if I could find a body part of hers she hasn't had plastic surgery on. Garrett always makes jokes about her lips and begs me never to get lips as big as hers. I know some women become obsessed with plastic surgery and I definitely feel Nancy is one of those obsessed women. When we first met her, she was very pretty but now she looks as if she is a completely different person. What strikes me the most is she becomes more negative with each surgery. It's almost as if she dislikes herself more and more with every nip and tuck.

Garrett and I on the other hand went into socialize with the other adults who were there. I was trying to stay with Garrett because I can't stand it when we go to an event together and all of the women feel the need to sit on one side of the room and gossip while the men go to their own side of the room. This little scenario has always annoyed both my husband and I so we made a pact to always stick together at the events we go to.

    Garrett and I have had numerous extensive discussions trying to figure out why the men and women don't all hang out together at the majority of the events we attend. I always dread attending the weddings of people my husband works with. Why? Well because at those weddings the women always clump up together. Sitting there like lumps on a log drinking their little cups of hot tea and coffee. Me on the other hand, I don't fit in with those types of women. I like to have at least a glass or two of wine and I love to get up and dance. I remember this one wedding Garrett and I had attended that was way too much fun. I was up dancing with Garrett and all of the other guys were up dancing as well. Yes, of course all of the women were just sitting there. I was really hoping I had not been too over the top but the next day I remember feeling that I probably had definitely been way too over the top. I had apologized to Garrett because I really hoped I had not embarrassed him. He was fabulous as always and told me not to be sorry because he had a blast that night.

    Garrett was so excited when he came home the next day because one of the guys he works with had come up to him and told him, "You're lucky, I wish my wife loved me that much."

So I guess those weddings aren't so bad after all because now I know those guys are just sitting there wishing their wives weren't such prudes.

This party tonight however wasn't so bad. There was a little bit of gender segregation but not much. For the most part the women were staying with their men. I was actually enjoying all of the conversations with the people there. Then wouldn't you know it, little Ms. Nancy had to come up to my husband and I to give her stupid, non important opinions about my little Nicholas.

She just started right in with her unwelcome comments. "Is Nicholas ok? I just don't think he should wear a Santa suit after Christmas time. That just isn't healthy to let a child's imagination run wild like that."

I of course being the type of person to not let any type of negative comment about my children nor about my husband go by, had to respond. "Well, I didn't know there was a dress code for tonight. Besides he is getting ready for next year. And actually it's been shown that parents should never impinge on their child's imagination. A big imagination is actually a sign of an above average intelligence."

I could see she really didn't know how to respond back to me so she simply smiled and walked away. I felt a nudge from Garrett which made me well aware he was a bit uncomfortable about the entire conversation. I personally don't understand what the big deal is about the Santa suit. Why does everyone make such a big deal about Nicholas wearing the Santa suit? Do people really feel the need to be judgmental about a child? After all he is just a child with a fabulous imagination and I guess I may never understand the negative judging of some adults. I love it when my little Nicholas wears his Santa suit. I can't help but smile when I look at him in his Santa suit.

The rest of the night, the party went almost without a hitch. Garrett and I had a very nice time. There was a live band at the party so there was dancing and just a plain old good time. Yes, there were a few people who came up to Garrett and I trying to tease us about Nicholas in the Santa suit. But, amazingly enough when we would just blow off their comments they stopped with the teasing.

I would always respond by telling the person trying to tease us about Nicholas, "You better watch out or else you'll end up on the naughty list."

They would chuckle and walk away. It worked for me, although Garrett never said anything about the comments but I did catch the occasional 'told you so' look from him.

Everyone at the party did the traditional countdown to midnight and I was happy to start off the New Year with a kiss from my husband. I do have to admit I did avoid Nancy the rest of the night. I really didn't feel like hearing anymore of her negative comments. I remained quite successful at avoiding her, until we went and told her and

Mr. Froman thanks for the invite to the great party. Her husband is very nice and wished us a Happy New Year. Nancy on the other hand gave us one of her fake smiles.

We gathered the kids and let ourselves out. I was completely shocked Holly and Nicholas had stayed awake the entire night. I remembered how nice it was to have them right next to Garrett and me as we counted down to the New Year.

Of course Holly and Nicholas were out cold within minutes of leaving the party. When we got home, Garrett carried Holly up stairs and put her to bed. I carried my little Nicholas up to bed and tucked him in. I kissed Nicholas goodnight then I went and kissed my Holly goodnight too. As I closed her bedroom door, I realized I am so truly blessed to have two such wonderful children. I went and crawled into bed and had a very peaceful sleep to start the New Year off. Never did I even imagine though how eventful my New Year would be.

I was up before anyone else the next morning so I decided to make breakfast to start the New Year off right. While I was cooking, Nicholas first, then Holly came strolling down the stairs. When breakfast was almost ready, I told the kids to go wake up their father. Holly and Nicholas love to wake up their daddy so they went running up the stairs.

Next thing I heard was both of them yelling, "Wake up daddy, wake up!"

Then all that could be heard was the three of them giggling. A few minutes later I heard the footsteps of all three of them racing down the stairs. Nicholas and Holly set the table while Garrett poured coffee for us and juice for the kids. We all sat down, Holly sang her prayer for us and we all must have been very hungry because we practically dove into the food.

Nicholas of course began the breakfast conversation. "You know what Mimi? Remember when I told you that it was hard deciding about the naughty and nice list because I didn't want anyone on the naughty list?"

I remembered the conversation perfectly. My little Nicholas had been a bit distraught because he truly wanted to take everyone around the world presents. I guess he was also a bit distraught because he has always tried so hard to be good so he would make it onto the nice list. He has always known of the naughty list and has always tried to avoid the naughty list at all cost.

I replied, "Of course I remember our conversation about the naughty and nice list. It was right after you had finalized it for the year."

"Well Mimi, I think it is going to get easier!"

I had no idea what he was talking about but I had a sneaking suspicion it had something to do with last night at the New Years Eve party. I was suddenly very curious.

I couldn't help but be very curious so I asked Nicholas, "What do you mean sweetheart? Did something happen last night at the party?"

Nicholas calmly paused, closed his eyes and took in a big deep breath before he began his story. "All I did was walk into the room. All of the kids were staring at me. They asked me why I was wearing a Santa Claus suit after Christmas. So I told them, I told everyone that I am the new Santa Claus. Then for no reason at all, everybody just started laughing. At first I didn't know why everybody was laughing so I decided to just start laughing too. But then Holly pushed me a little bit to get my attention and she told me that everybody was laughing at me. So of course, I stopped laughing and I asked everybody what they were laughing at. And you know what they said? They told me it was because I think I am the new Santa Claus. I started to get really mad inside but then sissy's friend JJ made everyone stop laughing and it was ok the rest of the night. JJ made sure he was with me and sissy all of the time. He was really nice so I told him he was definitely on the nice list for the New Year. I did warn all of the other kids they better watch out or else they will stay on the naughty list. Yes, I mean stay on the naughty list. I am telling all the elves, well maybe just Jack that those kids are all starting off on the naughty list and that maybe, just maybe, I will move them to the nice list. But last night was a lot of fun too. We played games in the game room and we watched movies. It was so cool they have one of those tables called……..um…..foosball, yah it was called a foosball table. How was yours and daddy's night at the party?"

Wow, I was still trying to digest everything my little Nicholas had told me, and I was trying to think up an appropriate answer to his question about how the adult side of the party had been.

Finally, I turned to Nicholas and answered, "Well Nicholas it was very nice. Your daddy and I were able to talk to some of our old friends we don't see very often, we danced and we ate probably a bit too much! But we did have a nice time. Thank you for asking."

I noticed Holly seemed to be a bit distant, in a different world, day dreaming so I turned to her and asked, "So, how about you Holly? Did you have a nice time at the party? Oh and who is JJ?"

I did catch Holly shoot her brother a quick glance before answering my questions. "It was good and I was ok with Nicholas wearing his Santa Claus suit. So yes, thank you Nicholas, I think it was the best thing for both of us that you wore your Santa suit. Oh and JJ is just a guy in my class this year at school. His family just moved here from New York. I told him he should have stayed in New York but he said he was glad to be here."

We finished our breakfast amid just 'normal everyday discussions'. When everyone was done, I told everyone to stay seated and I cleared all of the dishes. I returned with a pen and a piece of paper for all of us. I had everyone make a list of what they wanted to leave behind in the last year and not bring with them into the New Year. After everyone made their lists, we each took them to the fireplace where Garrett had started a fire earlier in the morning. One by one we each took a turn to burn up those things written down we did not want with us in the New Year. None of us shared our lists so I don't really know what was on anyone else's lists. But I did know we were all eager to jump right into the New Year.

No, Nicholas did not stop wearing his Santa suit. He in fact wore it all of the time. It really didn't bother any of us anymore. At least I thought it didn't bother any of us anymore. I thought we had all become so use to it. The Santa suit seemed as if it was a part of Nicholas now.

CHAPTER 6

It's only January and Holly has been so busy since New Years. We really haven't had anytime to focus on Nicholas and the Santa suit. Between gymnastics, karate, horseback riding, school and church group, Holly was over the top busy. Last year, I tried to cut back on her activities but Holly couldn't choose between them. She loves to be busy and to constantly be doing something. She is a confident and independent little girl. Generally speaking, she doesn't really care what other people say or think about her. So I guess I don't really understand why she gets so annoyed and irritated sometimes when friends and acquaintances see her brother in his Santa suit. I think about this quite often and I wonder if it is because everything else in her life is so perfect and normal so to speak. Maybe I have made her life too normal and perfect. As a parent though, it's hard not to try to make our children's lives perfect. We want our kids to always feel loved and happy.

Holly had been excited there was no gymnastics this Friday because she invited her friend Mary over for a sleepover. The last time Holly had a play date was back in December when Mary had come over and we all went to the mall to see Santa. I was a bit nervous so I was sure

Holly was a bit nervous about what her brother was going to do. I had tried to get him a sleep over at his grandparent's house but they were already planning to go out to dinner with some friends. Even my sister was busy. So I had ultimately run out of options. I was going to try to keep Nicholas as occupied as possible so he would stay out of his sister's way. And I did try my best but in the end I found myself unsuccessful at my goal.

I picked up Holly and Mary from school first. I thought I would take them home and let them have some fun alone before Nicholas got there. Garrett was getting off work just a little early so he could pick up Nicholas from preschool. The girls went right up to Holly's room and turned on the stereo. I smiled to myself when I heard the two of them up stairs singing and dancing to their favorite songs. They stayed upstairs the entire time. I finally took them up some milk and cookies. They were very polite but I knew I wasn't really welcome, so I excused myself and went back downstairs.

As soon as I got back downstairs, I heard the back door fly open and Nicholas was yelling, "Mimi, Mimi I'm home!"

I rushed over to Nicholas as he ran and jumped up into my arms. He was in an excellent mood and I definitely knew he must have taken a nap at preschool today. He is in such a better humor when he actually gives in and closes his eyes to take a nap at preschool. Little Nicholas insists he hates naps and they are not good for him.

However, I think he hates naps because he always thinks he is going to miss something. Miss what? I have no idea. But he has so much energy. I think it must be so hard for him to actually calm his entire body down enough to take a nap. Usually when he has expended his full day of energy, he simply goes to sleep. He could be on the floor, at the table or even at a restaurant. But when he is done, he is done and out cold.

    I truly treasure all of the times when I am fortunate enough to watch my baby boy as he sleeps. He has these beautiful long eye lashes that seem even longer when he has his eyes closed. I love watching his lips most of all. His lips are the only part of his body that usually moves when he is sleeping. They are always smiling. I know this sounds absolutely absurd but it's true. As you watch him when he sleeps, you know he is happy because of the smile on his face. Sometimes it's a little smile with his lips barely curved upward and other times he'll have the same barely there smile, then all of a sudden he will get the biggest smile ever on his face. His entire face lights up and I feel like he must be awake knowing I am watching. I remember when I first started to watch him I would say his name while he was asleep because I didn't really believe he was asleep. But over time, I did eventually begin to believe he actually was asleep because he never answered me when I would say his name. Nicholas is a child who always answers if he hears his name being called. As a parent this does make me count myself fortunate. My son may have possibly not been given the selective hearing gene so many men seem to have.

Garrett has not yet exhibited the selective hearing gene either so I guess I am lucky all around. I can't remember a time Garrett has not listened to me, he always hears me. I have always known I was lucky to have the best husband in the world because he truly does hear me. By this I don't mean he only hears all of the words I say. I mean, he actually listens to me and knows what I want and need without actually saying exactly what I want or need.

Garrett and I are truly soul mates. I still remember the first day I met him. He was wearing a pair of infamous black acid washed jeans, his football jersey and he had long hair. Well today one may not consider his hair long but compared to his short military style haircut he has now, his hair was long. He introduced himself to me and I immediately knew I was going to marry him someday. I was only sixteen so I definitely tried to put that thought out of my head. However, you can't escape fate and I truly believe it was fate that we met. We did end up getting married young because we knew we were meant to be together. We have been married for sixteen years and I have truly enjoyed every minute we have been married. Of course today as I look at other nineteen year olds, I am still amazed we got married so young. But I am definitely thankful we did get married young because we have always been each others 'rock' and 'other half'.

Our children are so fabulous and I feel are an equal part of Garrett and myself. I guess Nicholas got the extremely imaginative side from me though. I am always the over the top dreamer. I never see any limits in this world for myself. I have always felt the world is there for the taking so why not.

"Mimi, Mimi I'm home. Don't you wanna know about my day?"

There I was lost in thought again and Nicholas was trying very hard to get my attention and to bring me back into the real world.

"So sorry Nicholas, sweetheart I was just reminiscing in my head," I replied.

Nicholas smiled as he asked, "You were remin... what in your head Mimi?"

"I was reminiscing in my head, which means remembering fun memories," I replied with a smile.

"Mimi what were you membering?" he asked.

"I was remembering about when I met your daddy and how much I love your daddy and you and Holly. But Nicholas how was your day at school today?"

"Well Mimi I had a very good day today! Ms. Meg told all of us that we are going to start having share day on Friday. We can take anything we want as long as it isn't scary or violent. Did you hear that Mimi? Teacher told us anything!"

"Yes sweetheart I heard you. That is so exciting, I am so happy for you," I replied a bit unsure as to why he was so excited.

"Well I told Ms. Meg that I already know exactly what I am going to take to share. Do you know what I am going to take to share Mimi?"

I stood there for a moment before I answered trying to think of every possible thing Nicholas could be planning to take to preschool as a share item. Quite a number of things came to me but one thing did definitely stand out to me in my head. At first I thought he would want to take one of his dinosaurs but then I knew he would want to take his favorite belonging, his Santa suit. I didn't know whether or not I should let Nicholas know I had actually guessed in my head what he would be taking. But then I decided he would be honored I knew him so well. "I bet that you are going to take your Santa suit to show everyone."

Nicholas wrapped his little arms around me as he exclaimed, "Mimi you are right! I knew you would know what my bestest thing in the world was to me 'cause you're my Mimi!"

After seeing he was so happy that I had guessed correctly. I was happy that I had actually told him what I had guessed. I was excited he was so confident and sure of himself. But I couldn't help but be a little bit nervous about him taking his Santa suit to share. I didn't want any of the other children to make fun of him. I know he is only in preschool but still kids can be bullies to each other at any age. I know kids are usually only bullies to each other because they aren't confident enough in themselves and they actually like the person they are bullying and want what the child they are bullying has. But still as a parent you want to protect your child from bullies and even from potential bullies. Because children don't really understand the meaning behind bullies until they are much, much older. I did have an idea of how the situation would unfold though and I needed to let Nicholas know how supportive I was about him taking his Santa suit to school for share.

"Well Nicholas I think that taking your Santa suit is a fabulous idea. I bet nobody else will bring anything that could even compare to your Santa suit. I know Ms. Meg and all of the kids will absolutely love your Santa suit."

"Thanks Mimi. Where is sissy?"

"Sweetheart, she is up in her room with her friend Mary--." Before I could finish my sentence, Nicholas was already half way up the staircase. I had wanted to warn Holly Nicholas was home before he barged into her room, but I guess now it was too late. Yep, too late I just heard Nicholas open Holly's door and now both girls were screaming for Nicholas to get out of the room. I went running up the stairs to try and intercede before things got out of hand and I truly feel like I arrived just in time!

"Okay, okay girls I will get Nicholas out of here in a minute. Okay Nicholas, tell the girls hello and goodbye because daddy and I have a surprise for you." Well of course the word surprise perked Holly's ears right up and she looked at me but I quickly gave her the leave it alone glance so her and Mary went right back into her room and shut the door.

"Mimi, Mimi what's my surprise?" Nicholas asked as soon as we left Holly's room.

"Well sweetheart, daddy bought you something." I had barely gotten the words out of my mouth when Nicholas ran back down stairs to his father.

"Daddy, daddy what did you get me?"

Garrett told little overly eager Nicholas to close his eyes and count to thirty. Nicholas closed his eyes and eagerly began counting to the magic number thirty. While Nicholas was counting, Garrett went over to the coat closet and came back with a present wrapped in Christmas wrapping paper.

"Open your eyes," shouted Garrett way too excitedly.

Wow, I think Garrett was as excited to give Nicholas the present, as was his little boy to get the present. Garrett was at the store last week and he had called me to see what I thought about the game *Candy Land*. I told him I loved it and for some reason we had never bought the kids the game yet. He told me he was getting the game because he had loved it as a child too.

Garrett never ceases to amaze me. He never buys random things. In fact everything he buys always has some sort of meaning. He had snuck the game into the house one night after the kids went to sleep. I remember he had brought it up into our room and had gone to our wrapping paper closet and when I looked over he was using Christmas wrapping paper to wrap it. I didn't question his wrapping it at all. I just kissed him and told him 'thanks'. I thought it was so special he had bought the game and he was taking the time to wrap it up. Come to find out he had actually bought two games. He had bought *Candy Land* and had wrapped it in Christmas wrapping paper for Nicholas and he had bought Holly the game *Dogopoly* and had wrapped that game in pretty sparkly purple wrapping paper for her.

As soon as Nicholas saw the present all wrapped up in Christmas paper, he got one of his huge smiles on his face as he started jumping up and down squealing. I didn't have the heart to tell Nicholas to calm down. He was so over the top excited and I enjoyed seeing the big smiles on the faces of my two favorite men.

Nicholas tore the wrapping paper off and I don't know how but he got even more excited when he saw it was the *Candy Land* game.

"Daddy, did you buy this for me? How did you know I always wanted this game?" Nicholas asked.

Garrett quickly and proudly stated, "Yes Nicholas, I got you this game and I thought you, me and Mimi could all play it together since sissy is busy with her sleepover."

Nicholas answered his dad quite quickly and without any hesitation. "That sounds awesome daddy. Can we order pizza and pop some popcorn too daddy?"

"Well of course we can pop some popcorn but we have to ask Mimi what she and the girls have planned for dinner."

I already knew Holly and Mary wanted cheese pizza for dinner so I let Nicholas know we could order pizza for dinner. Of course, I knew however Nicholas would only want his favorite pepperoni pizza. I assured my little guy that Mimi would order him his special pepperoni pizza. I would order the girls their cheese pizza and I would order a combination pizza for daddy and me. I never keep soda in the house because we try to minimize our sugar intake as much as possible but I had already decided to splurge tonight and order the kids some soda with their pizza. I was trying very hard to make tonight special and fun for Holly and Nicholas.

The night was going so well and I was so relaxed and happy. We all ate our pizza downstairs together at the table. Tonight we switched it up a bit though. We went around the table and each of us had the opportunity to read a question out of the question box for everyone to answer. We were all having a lot of fun. I was a bit sad when dinner was over because I was truly enjoying how perfect our lives were at the moment. After dinner was over, the girls went back upstairs to Holly's room while Garrett and I cleaned up all of the dinner stuff. Luckily, we had only ordered pizza and we hadn't actually had to cook anything so there wasn't much of a mess to clean up. Garrett and I were so enthralled in our conversation while cleaning. I hadn't even noticed or even wondered where my Nicholas was at. Until I heard both of the girl's screaming extremely loudly upstairs!

As soon as I heard the girl's screaming, I knew Nicholas must be in Holly's room bugging the girls. I had no idea how bad it was until I arrived in the doorway of Holly's room. Nicholas was jumping up and down in the middle of Holly's bed with of course his Santa suit on and a big smile upon his face. It was a special kind of smile though, one that just melts anyone who sees it. Well, melts everyone except for obviously Holly.

As I looked away from Nicholas and back to Holly, her look said it all! She wanted Nicholas out of her room as soon as physically possible. I knew Nicholas loved his sissy very much so he always wants to be around her and I knew he wasn't really hurting anything. However, I respected Holly's unspoken request because her friend was over and I wanted her to have a fun time with her friend.

I quickly told Nicholas, "Get down right now mister. You need to come out of sissy's room and leave the girls alone."

Nicholas quickly jumped off of his sissy's bed still with a huge smile on his face. As soon as the two of us were walking down the hallway, I heard Mary start laughing and ask Holly, "Does your brother seriously still think he is Santa Claus? He is such a dork."

I was truly hoping my little Nicholas had not heard what Mary had said, but I knew in my heart he had. I was not going to say anything, I just wanted the two of us to go back down stairs and continue our fun with Garrett.

But midstream in my thoughts, Nicholas abruptly stopped in his tracks. I looked down at my little guy and said, "Sweetheart just brush it off."

However, as I looked down at my Nicholas, I saw the hurt in his big green eyes. Somehow, when I became a parent, I could feel my children's hurt. Whenever I see the hurt in their eyes it hurts me as much, if not more than it hurts them. I call it the 'Parent Protection Mechanism' or the PPM. As a parent, you never want your child to be hurt physically or mentally. Then when they do get hurt the parent protection mechanism kicks in and you can feel their pain and hurt by simply looking into their eyes.

I wasn't quite sure what my little guy was going to do. He just stood there. I was hoping maybe he was taking a little time to calm down by standing there. Then all of a sudden he took off running back down the hallway. I quickly reached out to grab him but not quickly enough.

Not even a second later, I heard my Nicholas screaming at the top of his lungs in Holly's room, "Just to let you know I am the new real Santa Claus. I was going to put you on the naughty list but you are my sissy's best friend so I will give you a warning. But know that I am watching you very closely and I will be telling the elves to watch you very closely as well. And if you do anything else that is mean, then I will have no other choice but to place your name onto the naughty list."

I stood there listening to my little Santa amazed at his confidence and his composure. Unsure of exactly what I should do next. Yes, he was screaming at the top of his lungs. But he was speaking appropriately and from his heart and I found myself feeling very proud of him. After he was done making his statement, he simply turned around and walked away. Holly slammed her door as soon as he had walked out.

The rest of the night went off without a hitch. Garrett, Nicholas and I continued to play games downstairs. We made popcorn so I took up popcorn and drinks to the girls. The three of us had fun downstairs with our popcorn and our games. I think Nicholas loved our popcorn fight the best when we all started throwing popcorn at each other. The fun came to an end when the popcorn bowl was empty. Garrett and I looked around the family room, realizing we had quite a mess to clean up.

After cleaning we decided it was bed time. It wasn't a school night so I told the girls they could stay up as late as they wanted. I let them know we were going to bed so they could have free reign of the rest of the house. Nicholas put his sleeping bag next to my bed in my room. I knew as soon as I fell asleep though, my little Nicholas would sneak up into my bed to cuddle up next to me.

The next morning Nicholas was of course the first one up and waking me up. I reluctantly crawled out of bed to go downstairs to make breakfast. Fortunately, Garrett heard me getting out of bed so he got out of bed as well. I knew this meant I didn't have to make breakfast because Garrett is the expert pancake maker/designer. Holly and Nicholas love it whenever their dad makes them pancakes because he can seriously make them whatever design of pancake they want. Garrett makes every design of pancakes. He makes every thing from alligator pancakes, to pirate hook pancakes and every design in between, including Nicholas's favorite Santa hat.

    Breakfast went well but I could feel just a slight tension between Mary and Nicholas. Holly was in a good humor and I figured I would ask her later today, after Mary went home, what else was said after she had closed the door. Holly had her dad make her a bobcat pancake, Mary ordered a tiara pancake and Nicholas ordered a Christmas tree pancake. The rest of the morning went quite well and after lunch, Mary's mom came to pick her up.

    Nicholas was in his room quietly building his *Lego's* so I went into Holly's room. Holly was actually cleaning up her room, which she usually hates doing. She knew I was going to eventually have to talk to her about the events with her brother from the day before. So I decided this was as good of time as any.

    "Hey Holly are you busy," I asked.

    "Well just a little, I am trying to clean up everything from last night mom."

"Okay that's fine. I'll just sit here on your bed and we can talk while you are finishing cleaning up," I replied.

Holly paused and reluctantly answered, "Well, okay, I guess that will be fine."

"Good. So I wanted to tell you sorry that your brother escaped and came upstairs yesterday, bugging you and your friend. But he wasn't hurting anything was he?"

Holly took a deep breath in as she walked over to the bed and sat next to me. "Well no…..not really. It's just….why does he always have to wear his Santa suit mom? Don't get me wrong….I….well….I believe….I really do believe…..you know….that, that Nicholas is Santa and all. I mean, I was there….well I think I was there. It's just that sometimes it all seems like a dream. I guess I see how people look at my brother whenever he wears his Santa suit. They think he's weird….that something is wrong with him. I don't want people to judge me because I am…...you know Santa's sister."

Wow, I realized I hadn't even thought of things in that way. I had been so worried about people not judging my little Nicholas and concentrating on how our family needed to support Nicholas. I hadn't even thought about how people judge the family members of important figures. I didn't want anyone to judge my Holly either. I wanted her to be accepted and loved as well. I was not even remotely prepared on how to respond to what Holly had just said to me. I quietly sat there on her bed thinking for a few moments as to how I should respond.

"Sweetheart, I am so sorry, I did not think about your feelings in the Santa situation. I was so worried about people not believing in your brother that I didn't think about people not believing in you. All that I can say is you need to have confidence in everything about yourself. You are full of confidence about everything else in your life. So just be confident about this as well. Have no doubts in yourself. You were at the North Pole with your brother. You did spend Christmas Eve night delivering presents with him. Don't doubt you were there. Don't let what other people may think fog your memories up at all. Embrace your memories and enjoy your memories."

Holly came and sat down on the bed next to me and gave me a nice tight hug, "Thanks mom."

CHAPTER 7

The weekend had flown by and I could hardly believe it was already Monday. I went in and woke up Holly and told her to get ready for school. I was about to go in and wake up Nicholas when he opened the door first and came out of his room in his Santa suit.

I quickly told Nicholas, "Honey you need to get ready for school today. Did you forget you had preschool today?"

My Nicholas quickly and confidently responded back to me as he smiled, "No, I didn't forget about preschool today Mimi. But obviously you forgot it is share day today at preschool. Remember, I told you when I got home on Friday that Ms. Meg was starting share days this week."

Our conversation together on Friday quickly came back to me after he refreshed my memory. "Yes, now I do remember our conversation. But Nicholas, I also remember share day is on Friday and not on Monday."

Nicholas stood there for a few seconds before responding back to me, "Well I just see that as a technicality. Ms. Meg did say share days were going to be starting on Friday but she didn't say we couldn't bring something to share on Monday."

I knew Nicholas wearing his Santa suit to preschool today really wouldn't hurt anything. But I also knew the teachers were really trying to set up specific rules for the children to follow at preschool in order to get the children all prepared for Kindergarten next year. I wanted Nicholas to follow all of the rules in preparation for next year. I knew I had to make him wait till Friday to wear his Santa suit.

I bent down to his eye level and explained, "Sweetheart your share day is Friday so we have to wait until then for you to wear your Santa suit. Let's go pick out a different cool outfit for you instead."

Nicholas reluctantly followed me into his room and helped me pick out different clothes for today. I was pretty sure this was going to be the longest week for my little Nicholas. I was definitely correct. Everyday he was counting down until Friday. All week he reminded all of us what he was going to be wearing on Friday for share day. On Thursday night, he nicely set out his Santa suit in his room.

Boy, did five o'clock come early on Friday morning. Nicholas was up and ready with his Santa suit on and in my room waking me up. I told him to go back to bed but he replied, "I'm too excited and I can't sleep".

I did successfully convince him to get into bed next to his dad and me to watch cartoons. I was satisfied at least Garrett and I were able to get a little more shut eye before it was time to get up.

The three of us finally got up out of bed at seven o'clock. Nicholas quickly ran into his sissy's room to wake her up. After successfully waking up his sissy, he ran downstairs and was pouring himself his cereal and a glass of lemonade as I walked into the kitchen. It was nice to see my son being so self sufficient. I think Fridays are actually going to be great days. Actually they will be great as long as Nicholas learns to sleep in just a little bit longer because I really hate to be woken up at five o'clock in the morning.

Holly finally came downstairs and ate some breakfast too. Nicholas was rushing poor Holly through breakfast, overly encouraging her to eat faster.

I could see Holly was starting to get a bit annoyed to say the least so I finally told Nicholas, "Stop rushing your sissy, we will leave at fifteen minutes after eight o'clock like always, not a minute sooner."

Nicholas saw I was serious so at least he did stop bugging his sissy for a little bit. I couldn't help but laugh a little when I realized how 'like a hawk', he intensely continued to watch the clock on the kitchen wall.

The moment the clock struck eight fifteen, Nicholas grabbed his school stuff while he announced, "Okay everyone, it's time. Everyone in the car, now! Come on, we are going to be late, it is time to go now!"

I think Nicholas must remember it always takes his sissy a few minutes to actually grab her stuff and get into the car. He grabbed his sissy's back pack, my purse in addition to his school stuff. It was quite humorous to see his little arms carrying everyone's stuff.

He was our morning encourager today, standing at the back door yelling to Holly and myself, "Just get into the car. Come on sissy and Mimi! I have your purse Mimi and your backpack sissy so just come on and get into the car!"

Holly and I made our way to the back door where our encourager Nicholas was standing. Holly grabbed her back pack from him as she gratefully stated, "Thank you bro, bro for grabbing all of my stuff."

I grabbed my purse from him, kissed him on the cheek and said "Thank you Santa," which of course, caused a huge smile to appear upon his face.

"I call my song." Nicholas shouted as soon as we were all in the car.

Holly politely smiled as she replied, "That's fine bro, bro because we are dropping you off first today right mom?"

I quickly replied, "Yes sweetheart. Nicholas wanted to be dropped off first today."

Earlier this week Nicholas had begged me to drop him off first because he wanted to get to preschool early in order to be there as all of his little buddies arrived. I knew my little Santa had called his song and truthfully, I really didn't even have to ask him what song he wanted because I already knew. I put the CD in and played his favorite song.

As soon as he heard it start to play, a huge smile appeared on his face as he cheerfully told me, "Thank you Mimi, you just knew didn't you?"

"Yes Santa, I just knew," I replied.

Preschool really isn't far from the house so we were able to listen to *Jingle Bell Rock* two full times through and part of the way through the third time. I am still so amazed at how Nicholas loves this song. He sang word for word the entire time it played. He knows all of the words perfectly. He doesn't stumble or pause for any of the song. He sings it with a special realm of confidence as if he had written the song himself.

As soon as we pulled into the parking lot at preschool, Nicholas was already unbuckling his seatbelt and ready to jump out of the car. I had to remind him the car was still moving and he needed to stay seated. I also had to remind him we do not unbuckle our safety belts until the car is parked and turned off. He quickly apologized for breaking rules. It's not like him to break rules. I know he only did because he was extremely excited for today.

Holly announced, "I am just staying in the car mom while you take bro, bro in."

This was unusual. Usually Holly enjoyed taking her brother in with me and checking him in whenever we take him to school first. But there was no need for an argument about whether or not she had to come inside. I told her to lock the doors. The parking lot is right outside the check in area anyways so I knew I would be able to see her in the car the entire time.

I went over and opened the car door for Nicholas as he practically flew out the door. Nicholas gets a bit upset with his father and me sometimes because we keep the child lock on his door so he can't open it while we are moving. But Garrett and I won't budge on the child lock issue. I remember the day when Nicholas had reached the door handle as we were driving down the street. He was able to open the door slightly and fortunately it had not flown open too badly. Thank God we were able to pull over right away to fix the door before anything bad happened. He wasn't even a year old and Holly had never even attempted to open the door when the car was moving as a child. Therefore, the thought of a child not even a year old opening the car door as the car was moving had never even crossed our minds. Garrett and I pretty much felt like completely incompetent parents when that had happened. It still, to this day a very touchy subject with us.

    I probably could have stayed in the car with Holly this morning and Nicholas could have signed his own self into preschool today. By the time I was shutting his car door he was already opening the front door into his preschool. I found myself running up the walk trying to catch up to my little Santa. This was definitely unusual as well. Nicholas usually always likes to walk into preschool with me. Sometimes he doesn't even want to stay at preschool and he begs me to take him to work with me. But today is definitely different, he is so excited he gets to be Santa at preschool.

At least he had left the front door of the preschool open for me. As I walked into the door, he was already with Ms. Meg telling her all about his Santa suit.

Ms. Meg obviously taken a bit off guard by Nicholas in his Santa suit looked at him and a bit timidly replied, "Umm....Nicholas I love your Santa costume. I'm....umm....I am so happy you have your Santa costume to share with everyone today."

I could tell Nicholas didn't like Ms. Meg using the word costume in reference to his Santa suit. Nicholas only liked and actually always made everyone refer to his Santa suit as a Santa suit, not a costume. And yes, my little Nicholas is always actually very good at politely correcting everyone who mistakenly says costume instead of suit. What came next, I guess I totally should have expected my little Nicholas to say.

Nicholas proudly announced, "You know Ms. Meg, I am the new real Santa Claus."

Ms. Meg shot me a quick glance then returned her eyes to Nicholas to say, "Oh really Nicholas, well I think that is great."

I was positive Nicholas could feel Ms. Meg really didn't believe what he had just told her because of the way he was staring at her. And I knew he was going to respond by saying something else. I wasn't sure what he was going to say in reply. I also knew Ms. Meg's reference to his suit as a costume must still be bugging Nicholas at least a little bit.

With a very serious but stern tone and a very serious face, Nicholas looked at Ms. Meg as he stated, "No, Ms. Meg, I am serious about this! I am the new real Santa Claus and this is NOT a Santa costume, it is a Santa suit."

Ms. Meg is always such a happy go lucky, energetic and sweet person but I really don't think she was prepared as to how she should appropriately respond back to my little Nicholas. The goal of the preschool was to keep a positive atmosphere for all of the children and to appreciate all of the children's individuality and creativity. However, I think the idea of Nicholas being the new real Santa Claus was a very different idea than any other child had ever presented her with. I was unsure as to how it would be handled. My first instinct was to scoop up my little Santa and take him to work with me. But I knew Nicholas had to stay here at preschool and I was very confident he could and would handle himself quite well today at preschool.

Ms. Meg took a moment before replying with a nice positive reply, "Well I am so happy we have Santa Claus here with us and I am sure that all of your friends here at preschool will be happy too."

Nicholas came running over to me with his arms opened wide, giving me a great big hug as he jumped up into my arms. I gave him a kiss on the cheek as I whispered into his ear, "Santa, remember that you rock and I love you. Don't get upset if there are any nonbelievers here today."

Nicholas kissed me on my cheek as he whispered back into my ear, "Thanks Mimi, I love you."

I waved goodbye as I turned to walk back out to the car. As soon as I got back into the car, I could tell Holly was a bit frustrated at something.

Holly took no time at all telling me exactly what was on her mind. "Gosh mom, that took long enough. I thought you only had to sign him in not spend part of the morning here. I don't want to be late for school today."

I knew something else must really be bothering Holly because it generally takes a bit more than a ten minute drop off to irritate her. I calmly replied, "Holly, first of all you are not going to be late for school and second of all, you could have come in with me to drop your brother off. You usually like to come inside when we take brother to school first. Is something bothering you sweetheart?"

Holly sat there quietly before finally responding. "Well, I decided that I am not talking to Mary anymore, at least for right now."

Now I was going to have to interrogate Holly for a bit because something must have happened. "What happened?"

Obviously it must have really been bothering Holly because all of a sudden she began blurting out the entire incident. "Well after she stayed over last weekend, she went to school this week and told everybody about Nicholas dressing up as Santa Claus and what a weird brother I have. Most of my friends just blew it off and ignored Mary but there are a few kids in my class that I can't stand and now they have been teasing me all week about Nicholas. I try to ignore them and I don't act like it bugs me but mom it really does bug me."

In response, I knew I could only respond as my little Nicholas would. "Holly we both know there is only one thing to do." Holly stared at me a bit oddly as I continued. "Tell your brother and he will put them on the naughty list. I think one year on the naughty list would teach them a good lesson. Besides, your brother already gave Mary a warning."

Holly looked at me for a moment before a big smile appeared. "Thanks mom. I will tell Nicholas after school. Can you pick me up first so I can go with you to pick up bro, bro?"

"Sure sweetheart, not a problem," I replied as I noticed we were already at Holly's school. I drove into the driveway and pulled right up to the drop off curb. Holly reached over and kissed me on the cheek before opening her door and jumping out of the car.

Since little Nicholas wasn't there, I had to tell Holly myself what Nicholas tells her everyday. "Don't trip and fall sissy."

Holly looked at me with a smile as she closed the door and walked off into the crowd of kids at school.

Poor Holly had tripped and fallen in a huge mud puddle last year at school. She had gotten completely wet and muddy. Holly called her dad because he was home.

He had to bring her dry clothes and dry shoes to school. Since little Nicholas had been home from school that day hanging out with his dad, he helped get the clothes for Holly and went with his dad to take them to her. At first Holly was very irritated with her brother when he started telling her everyday not to trip and fall. But I told Holly, her 'bro bro' had been very concerned about her and it was his way of telling her everyday to be safe. So now every day when he tells her not to trip and fall she tries to appreciate it by politely telling him 'thank you' when he says it to her.

I still remember one time when Holly had gotten out of the car before he had told her to not trip and fall. Nicholas was so concerned he convinced me to pull back into the parking lot and park the car so the two of us could walk over to where Holly was. I pulled her aside from her friends so Nicholas could tell her it in private out of ear shot of her friends. I think, actually going up to her at school with Nicholas was a bit too much for Holly because now she always makes sure to stay in the car until Nicholas tells her 'not to trip and fall'.

I hadn't actually told the kids I was off work today. I had the day to myself and I was very much looking forward to having a 'me day'. There were a lot of errands I needed to get done and I wanted to deep clean the house. I also wanted to make sure to squeeze in my workout for the day so I could spend the evening with the kids and Garrett.

My 'me day' had definitely flown by way too quickly. I could hardly believe I was already at the school waiting for

Holly. I was waiting outside her classroom holding her backpack I found outside the classroom door when the bell rang. She smiled as soon as she saw me. I found myself giving Mary a smile, hoping she understood my smile was saying 'don't mess with my kid'. She wouldn't look me in the eyes after she saw my smile. I was pretty sure Holly caught me giving my 'don't mess with my kid' smile to Mary because her own smile did turn up a bit more into a smirk when she saw me.

We walked hand in hand to the car as she told me about her fabulous Friday. She had finished the book she was reading so she had gotten a special Popsicle treat from her teacher and she was still beaming about it. Once we were in the car and both doors were closed, Holly quickly wanted to know if it was time to go and pick up her brother yet. I assured her picking up Nicholas was our next stop. She smiled as she leaned back into her seat and continued telling me all about her fabulous Friday. I was so happy and excited about the wonderful mood Holly was in and how excited she was about picking up her brother. It was so nice to see Holly so happy. I secretly thought maybe, just maybe it was okay her friends had teased her a little bit because it was making her appreciate Nicholas a bit more.

As soon as we drove into the parking lot, I was seriously feeling like it was the morning all over again. I quietly asked myself 'had Holly not just heard me this morning tell her brother he had to keep his safety belt on until the car was completely stopped?' I really did not feel like repeating that same question again this afternoon and besides I know Holly must have heard me this morning. So I decided to look at her and say her name, "Holly?"

She immediately buckled her safety belt back up as she quietly responded, "Sorry mom, I'm just a little excited about picking bro, bro up and I do still feel a little bad that I didn't walk him into preschool this morning. I know it was a bit selfish of me because I did know how excited he was about today."

I was touched. Holly was actually so aware of how she had behaved this morning. "I know sweetheart, but please don't beat your self up so badly about this morning. We all make mistakes and you had a lot on your mind. I am sure your brother will understand when you talk to him about it later."

As soon as I was fully parked, Holly was already unbuckling her safety belt, opening her door and jumping out before I had the opportunity to let her know she could unbuckle.

Holly must have seen all of the kids playing outside because she was running straight towards the playground yelling out, "bro, bro we're here to pick you up."

Nicholas must have had his sister radar on because he heard her and ran straight toward the gate on the playground with a huge smile on his face with of course his Santa suit still on.

He appeared to be very excited his sissy was there. I could hear Nicholas loud and clear saying, "Sissy, sissy you came to pick me up!"

Holly was standing at the gate trying to patiently wait until I got there to open it for her. Holly knew it was against the rules for anyone to open the gate except for an adult and she did always follow that rule quite nicely. She had told me once that she did not want any of the little preschoolers to escape because they are little and they could get hurt or lost very easily.

As soon as I opened the gate, Holly ran in and gave her brother a big hug and the two of them just started talking to each other a mile a minute. I stood there for a moment soaking in the fact of how my two children are absolutely awesome. I knew though, they both wanted to get home so I quickly went inside to sign Nicholas out and to grab his stuff. I was about to walk back out the door when Ms. Carrie stopped me.

Ms. Carrie seriously should learn how to smile. If I had met Ms. Carrie when Garrett and I were considering this preschool, we probably would have crossed this preschool right off of our list. But no, we didn't meet her until well after Nicholas started attending preschool here. I have always thought there was a big possibility she scares the children by how awful she looks. Her lips always seemed to be pursed in a fashion making me think she had sucked on one too many lemons. Her hair is always so over sprayed with hairspray. I am truly glad she has short and thin hair or else her hair could very well possibly injure one of the children at the preschool. I guess if she actually had even an inkling of niceness inside, it would make her look better on the outside. But oh no, she looks like she sucked on a lemon on the outside and she acts like she is full of sour lemons on the inside. I always try to smile at her whenever I see her. I made sure Nicholas never had to be in her class and I always encourage him to smile at her but to ultimately stay away from her.

Ms. Carrie quickly ran up to me and started talking to me in her annoyingly high pitched voice, "Um, before you leave the teachers had a meeting today and they wanted me to talk to you."

I knew this didn't sound like it was going to be good just by the tone of her voice. I try to follow all of the preschool rules and so I replied, "Sure, is there something wrong?"

She was quite hesitant in her reply. "The....umm the teachers and I....umm....well I just feel that Nicholas was a bit disruptive by wearing a costume to school today. Share day was really meant to bring a toy to school and not a costume. So we would appreciate it if he did not wear the costume next share day. Maybe you could encourage him to bring a non violent toy or something instead."

Okay, yes this comment immediately infuriated me but I did swallow and took a deep breath before responding. I wanted to make sure I responded in an appropriate manner and in a way to not get my preschooler expelled from preschool. I politely responded the only way I possibly could have right then.

In the sweetest tone possible I stated, "Well, I am so sorry you were under the impression little Nicholas had worn a costume to school today. He actually wore his Santa suit. Also, if a simple Santa suit was disruptive to any child or adult, more than likely there is an issue with that person, which needs to be dealt with and should not be considered a problem with my son. The Santa suit follows all of the rules of share day as far as it is neither violent nor scary. So I do truly hope the preschool will be able to deal appropriately with the person who has a problem with the Santa suit." I simply smiled at Ms Carrie as I turned to walk back out to the playground to let Holly and Nicholas know it was time to go.

Both of the kids were playing nicely together outside and usually I would let them play for a few more minutes but today I really wasn't in the mood to let them play any extra here. I wanted to get both of them out of here now.

As soon as I called for them, they both came running over to me and we all three walked over to the car together. Holly helped Nicholas get into his booster seat and even buckled her brother up. Holly sat in the back seat right next to Nicholas and buckled her safety belt. The two became immersed into their own conversation as we drove away. I was able to catch bits and pieces of their conversation while I drove us home, but it was enough for me to know they had planned a fun night for all of us.

Holly asked what was for dinner and they were excited when I told them it was taco night. I was trying to concentrate on the fact my children were so happy in the backseat and not on the fact someone had a problem with my son's Santa suit. But I couldn't help but ask myself why somebody would be judging a little four year old. What would posses a person to be upset by a mere Santa suit? I thought maybe something had happened at preschool with the Santa suit. So I decided we would have a discussion at dinner about how Santa suit share day had gone at preschool.

We arrived home and unloaded the car, which was my new car rule at home. I have been getting a bit irritated lately because I was always finding toys, papers, crayons and just plain junk the kids would bring into the car and then leave it there until my car looked like a big messy pile. Therefore, now you must take everything of yours out of the car or it gets thrown away. Amazingly enough both Holly and Nicholas seem to not be bringing very many of their belongings into the car when we go places now.

After we unloaded the car, the three of us decided to work on a puzzle together until it was time for Garrett to come home. We had put almost half of the puzzle together when I saw it was almost five o'clock. We decided to take a break and start making dinner. While I started cooking dinner, the kids went into the dinning room and set the table. A short time later, I heard Garrett walk in. As I turned around to kiss him, he set a Margarita bucket on the counter. I had told him it was taco night and I had secretly been hoping he would get stuff for margaritas. Sometimes I think he can actually read my mind and I was sure happy he had read my mind today.

As soon as Holly and Nicholas heard their dad come into the kitchen, they both came running in, giving him a simultaneous bear hug. My husband gave them a bear hug right back and Holly and Nicholas ran off to finish setting the table. Garrett kissed me and asked me if everything was okay. I told him everything was fabulous. He gave me a strange glance so I knew he could tell something was bothering me a bit. Once again, I think he was reading my mind.

I looked back at him and told him quietly, "I'll tell you later." He shook his head yes as he turned and ran upstairs to change before dinner.

Garrett and I sort of have an unspoken rule between us about 'I'll tell you later'. If ever either of us tells the other one the phrase, 'I'll tell you later' we respect it knowing there is a reason why we will be told later and not right then.

The kids had finished placing our dinner plates, utensils and glasses quite nicely on the table. Holly and Nicholas were back in the family room trying to finish putting the puzzle together, while I was placing dinner on the table. Garrett walked down the stairs as I was finishing. I think he must have known I really needed a hug because he followed me back into the kitchen and gave me a nice big hug.

"Thanks sweetheart. I will tell you later, but I did need a hug." As I told him this, he looked at me and smiled.

Seeing my husband smile always makes everything ok again. He quickly poured the drinks for everyone as I rounded up the kids to get them seated at the dinner table. We were all immersed in a wonderful conversation about our day.

Holly excitedly told us, "I got the best books ever at the book fair today. I bought five dog books. Oh....wait can I go get something really quick?"

It appeared to be quite an emergency what she needed to go and get so I smiled and said, "Of course Holly, not a problem."

She quickly ran upstairs and came back with something hidden behind her back.

Holly looked at Nicholas as she told him, "Okay close your eyes bro, bro and hold out your hands."

Nicholas got very excited so he quickly closed his eyes and held out both of his hands. Holly placed the book into his hands she had bought for him at the book fair.

As soon as he felt the book in his hands, he opened his eyes to look at the book. It was a Christmas book with Santa Claus on the front cover. Nicholas smiled as he gave his sissy a nice big bear hug. "Thanks sissy, I always wanted this book."

Nicholas set the book down on the table right beside his plate and I assured him one of us would read the book to him later in the evening. All of a sudden Garrett asked Nicholas how the Santa suit share day had gone. It got really quiet for about thirty seconds although it seemed as if it had been quiet for an hour. Nicholas took in a big deep breath before he began his story about his day as we all listened intensely to every detail.

Nicholas began, "Well daddy, I am just not quite sure how to start the story about my day. I was so excited at home and I know I was rushing Mimi and sissy at home to get out of the house because I was so excited about my share day today. I was so excited to show Ms. Meg, me in my Santa suit this morning but then I was a little hurt when she called it a costume. She acted like I was just dressing up as a Santa Claus or something. I don't think she really knows I am the new real Santa Claus. Most of the kids thought my Santa suit was really cool. I....I....well I just don't think all of the kids understand I am the new real Santa Claus. I am the one who decides if they are on the naughty or the nice list and I am the one who decides what presents they will get on Christmas morning. I loved wearing my Santa suit all day though because I am so comfortable in it. But I....well, I guess I wish all of the kids would have understood I am the new real Santa Claus. It was great though talking to the kids who did get it and do know and believe I am the new real Santa Claus. I can tell you this. All of those kids will be on the nice list this year just for believing. I guess I really thought all kids at least believe in me. I know quite a few adults don't believe in me but I wish at least all kids believed in me."

I had to interrupt my little Nicholas's story because I needed to ask him an important question. "So Nicholas, what did you say to the kids who didn't believe?"

Nicholas looked at me straight in the eyes as he continued. "Well Mimi, I was forced to tell them they were now going to be put onto the naughty list."

"Nicholas honey, don't you think that putting those kids on the naughty list was a bit much?"

Nicholas thought for a moment before he quickly responded. "Of course I don't think it was too much Mimi. I gave each of them two warnings. I didn't want to put any one on the naughty list but I really had no other choice. Mimi, they laughed at me. But I told them they could still get onto the nice list if they changed their attitudes. Mimi, I just want everyone to believe in me."

I knew from the look in his big beautiful eyes he was telling the truth and all he truly wanted was for everyone to believe in him. Unfortunately, this was one thing I couldn't fix for my son. I couldn't force people to believe in him. All I can do is love my Santa and fully support him, which includes supporting all of his dreams and his imagination.

I didn't quite know how to respond to Nicholas so I did the best I could. "Well sweetheart, all of us know you are the new real Santa Claus and all of us support you. But none of us can control what someone else believes. Just like I don't think you would want anyone controlling what you could or could not believe in. Nicholas honey, you have to be you. Remember what you told me, you were chosen to be the new real Santa Claus because of your heart. You are special and that is all that matters. Remember to always be jolly and happy, never letting any of the bad stuff get you down."

Okay, now I was actually done lecturing myself, I felt totally better about my day picking up Nicholas from preschool. I guess it could have been worse. Everything can always be worse. I was suddenly so thankful for my husband and my children and I really don't care what anyone else thinks. My main goal is protecting my kids. Especially my little Nicholas as he has found himself as the new real Santa Claus. I have to keep reminding myself to stay positive so I can help Nicholas and even Holly stay positive.

After dinner was over, I really wanted to leave the dishes for the morning, so I did. All four of us finally finished the puzzle we had been working on and we decided to watch a movie together. Holly let Nicholas pick out the movie so we all got to watch *How the Grinch Stole Christmas*. I know Nicholas has always loved this movie but I thought now, since he is the new real Santa Claus, he would somehow not like this movie so much. I was wrong. He still loves the movie and knows almost every line the Grinch has. All of us had a fun time watching the movie and munching on our popcorn. When it was time to go to bed, Holly and Nicholas asked if they could set the tent up in the living room to sleep in. I gladly agreed because I was sure they would have fun sleeping in the tent together.

Garrett and I went upstairs to go to bed but I had forgotten my toothbrush downstairs. As I quietly went back downstairs, I heard Holly and Nicholas talking in the tent. I was sure Holly would tell her bro, bro about what had happened at school so I decided to stay really quiet in order to listen to their conversation.

Holly quietly told Nicholas, "Bro, bro...there is something...that....well that I have to tell you."

I couldn't see my little Nicholas but I could tell from his very quick response he was very eager to know what his sissy had to tell him. "What sissy...what's wrong sissy?"

Holly paused for a few seconds before answering, "Well bro, bro....I really don't know how to say this but Mimi told me I should tell you what happened...and....well...."

Then Nicholas whispered, in the quietest of whispers, so quiet that I had to get a bit closer to their tent. "Sissy you can tell me anything. Remember I am your Santa Claus too."

On the tent wall, from the shadow caused by the flashlight, I saw Holly reach over and give her Santa Claus a great big hug as I felt a warm tear roll down my cheek.

With a bit of hesitation in her voice Holly stated, "Thanks Santa I needed to hear that because....well because....well I don't want this to hurt you too but Mary went to school after she stayed the night last weekend and told everyone I have a weird brother. She also told everyone about you dressing up as Santa Claus while she was at our house. Most of the kids at school blew her off but there are a few kids who have been teasing me now. I just didn't want to tell you or mom or dad because I didn't want to hurt your feelings. But when I told mom this morning, she told me you would fix everything."

I couldn't see my little Nicholas but some how I sure could feel his face getting very, very red and hot. It was taking him a minute to respond but I knew he must be trying to gain his composure, to answer in a calm Santa Claus way and boy was I right.

Nicholas took a long deep breath in before he responded. "Well sissy I know that Mary is still your friend, even if she does say bad things about me because I am the new real Santa Claus. Sissy, I know you know I already gave Mary a warning about putting her on the naughty list and I feel she needs to be put onto the naughty list for this year. Now sissy, if she improves her attitude and starts being nice to you and stops making fun of me as the new real Santa Claus, then I will consider putting her name back onto the nice list. I hope this doesn't sound like I am being too harsh sissy but I think, no I know little Miss Mary needs to be taught a lesson this year. Do you remember Jack the head elf from the North Pole?"

Holly quickly responded, "Of course I remember Jack. He was actually my very favorite elf."

Nicholas sounded a bit shocked as he responded, "Well I am glad you remembered Jack but I really didn't know he was your very favorite elf. Anyways, Jack told me a lot of kids learn their lesson just by being put onto the naughty list one time. So maybe Mary will learn her lesson by being put onto the naughty list this year. Please don't worry sissy, be strong and remember you are the lucky one because your brother is the new real Santa Claus. You know what? I know I am the luckiest Santa Claus ever because I have you as my sissy."

With a bit of spice in her voice, Holly happily said, "Thanks bro, bro for making everything ok and I do know I am very lucky to have you as my brother. Now let's watch our movie."

I quietly crept back up the stairs not wanting Holly and Nicholas to know I had been ease dropping on their entire conversation. As Garrett saw me walk into our bedroom, he quickly shut off the television. I knew he had patiently waited all evening to find out why I had been upset earlier. For some reason, what I was going to 'tell him later' seemed so unimportant. Garrett, Holly, Nicholas and I were all healthy and happy, which is truly all that was important. Those negative comments and feelings of others really weren't important. I knew I needed to tell Garrett what had been said about Nicholas but strangely, I no longer felt mad about those comments. No, I felt more sorrow for those people than anything. I realized those people obviously had nothing better to do than to put a little four year old boy's imagination down. Amazingly enough, the anger was completely gone.

Even though the anger was completely gone, I still told Garrett the entire story about my eventful day. He didn't interrupt me at all during my story. He sat there intently listening to me talk.

When I was all done with telling the event, Garrett asked, "Aren't you upset about what happened today?"

I quickly responded without a thought, "Strangely enough, I'm not upset. Honey, I'm happy I have you, Holly and Nicholas. You are the three most special people in the world to me. And I refuse to let any negative comment of others put a damper on our family. We are strong and we will remain strong as long as we stick together and stay positive."

Garrett paused for a moment and I could tell the whole Santa thing was still bothering him. He finally responded with a bit of hesitation, "I don't know why my son has to think he is the new real Santa Claus. Why can't he be into sports or something else? I don't want my son to be different. I want a regular son. I mean, I appreciate he has such a good imagination and all. But I would rather he only be imaginative at home and not around other people."

I knew Garrett was still struggling with the thought of his son being the new real Santa Claus. It was still hard on me at times. But I continue to remind myself, Nicholas is special and he has always been special. He has never and will never be the average kid. I know he may never 'fit in' but it's ok with me. I enjoy watching my little Nicholas so full of life and loving everyday of life. Watching Nicholas always puts a smile on my face. I watch other people around Nicholas and somehow he manages to get a smile on the faces of those people as well. I want my son to be himself. I don't want him to be who I want him to be or who anybody else wants or expects him to be. I know Garrett really doesn't understand my whole 'let your kid be free' philosophy still. But I am trying to show Garrett how good it is for our kids and how much happier our kids are by not trying to put them into an expectation box.

    I desperately wanted Garrett to understand my new found philosophy but I knew it was going to take some more time before he 'got it'. I continue to hold onto the positive thought that he will 'get it' once he sees more results of how happier our kids are. I pray my little Nicholas can stay strong and persevere through the negative judgments of others. I know my Holly can stay strong and I know she will always continue to support her brother as the new real Santa Claus. A part of me still wanted to try once again explaining my 'let your kid be free' philosophy to Garrett, but I refrained and I tried to be more diplomatic with him instead.

    I closed my eyes and I took a nice long deep breath in before I responded back to Garrett. "I know having a son with a fabulous imagination is a little bit difficult. But we need to love and support our son and his imagination.

Honey, Nicholas is special and we have always known there was something extra special about Nicholas. We need to embrace how special he is. I know it's hard, but please try not to let what other people say or think affect what you think about your son. Just love him whole heartedly. That's all I ask."

    Garrett looked at me for a moment before he smiled and kissed me goodnight. I knew he would think about what I had said about our little Nicholas. However, I was happy he hadn't voiced any objections as to what I had told him. I wanted all of us to continue living each day to the fullest, which is exactly what we did, of course not without a few bumps or so during our journey down the road of life.

CHAPTER 8

Here it was Sunday again and we had nothing in the cupboards for lunches so once again we needed to go grocery shopping. I really don't enjoy going grocery shopping. There is so much junk food on the shelves these days and they package the junk food in attractive packaging to draw the children in. Even food labeled 'healthy' isn't necessarily 'healthy'. It takes forever reading the labels and buying the healthiest food possible for your family. If you have to take your kids shopping with you it takes even longer. They see everything in the store they want. You feel like the mean mom because you keep saying 'no' to everything they want. Oh well, Market here we come. I walked out of my room all ready to go shopping and I see my little Nicholas walk out of his room. As I see my little Nicholas, I feel an immediate smile come across my face. Suddenly, I knew I was going to have a fun time grocery shopping today.

I ran up to my little Nicholas giving him a great big hug. "Yes, yes, yes Santa Claus is going grocery shopping with me!"

My little Nicholas got a huge smile on his face as he hugged me back saying, "Thanks Mimi! I am all ready to go. Are you ready?"

With a huge smile still on my face, I answered, "Yes sweetheart, I am all ready. Let's go see if sissy is all ready to go."

Nicholas grabbed my hand as he replied, "Sounds good Mimi, let's go get sissy."

Holly was outside in the backyard playing basketball, not really excited to go shopping. She really wanted to stay home and play basketball. Reluctantly she came into the house to put her basketball away so the three of us could load into the car.

Nicholas eagerly yelled, "I call my song first. I want *Jingle Bell Rock*."

Holly tried to put a half smile on her face before putting her two cents in, "I know bro, bro, but I get my song second."

Holly turned to me asking, "Mom why does Nicholas always remember to ask for his song first? Can't we just alternate having the first song since I always forget to ask first?"

Before I even had the chance to respond back to Holly, Nicholas took on the authority to answer for me, "No sissy, the first song choice goes to whoever asks first. I guess you have to start remembering to ask first."

Holly glared over at her brother as she responded back to me instead of responding back to her brother, "Mom, fine I will start remembering to ask first."

Holly looked straight into her brother's eyes telling him, "Game on bro, bro. So you should be afraid, no very afraid."

Nicholas didn't respond back to his sissy. He simply stated, "*Jingle Bell Rock* please Mimi."

I turned on *Jingle Bell Rock*, which we listened to once and we listened to Holly's song once before arriving at the grocery store. When we arrived, I told Holly and Nicholas I had already made a shopping list so they were not to ask for anything at the market. They looked at each other and then back at me as they each agreed not to ask for anything at the market. As we walked up to the doors of the market to grab a cart, they both ran to a cart with the car attached to the front of it. Before I even had the opportunity to say yes or no to the cart with the car, they were already inside and seated. Of course I had to let my Santa Claus and his sissy ride in the car.

I really never have a problem with my kids riding in the car attached to the cart. My only problem is actually pushing the cart with the car attached to it. I seriously have to wonder if the person who invented those carts with the cars attached to them actually ever used them with kids in the car while trying to push the cart in an actual market while shopping for groceries. I think not. Yes, the whole car attached to the cart seems like a good idea and they even look cute but they are pretty impossible to maneuver in a market with kids in the car while trying to shop for groceries. I always have to remind my kids of the rules while in the car attached to the cart, which is exactly what I did once again today.

 I didn't want everyone outside the market to hear me so I bent down to the door of the car, quietly reminding Holly and Santa Claus the rules of the car. "Okay kids remember to always keep arms, hands, feet, legs and most importantly your head fully inside the car at all times. If I have stopped the cart then and only then may you ask to get out of the car and you may only proceed out of the car if I give you the okay. Are these rules fully understood? Do either of you have any questions before our trip through the market begins?"

 With both sets of their eyes glued on me, they quickly shook their heads 'no'. They knew I was very serious when it came to the rules of the car attached to the cart. I think the only reason for their serious faces was they knew their safety depended upon what I said. Of course there was also the possibility they may not fully trust my driving so much, even if it's only the cart I'm driving through the market. We were on quite a roll through the market. Nicholas and Holly were quietly playing in the car as I was trying my best to drive the cart without crashing into too many displays.

 I was on my way to the last item on my list which was cereal. I hate going down the cereal isle because I know I will have to fight the kids to get them to pick out a healthy cereal. I try to make Holly and Nicholas always pick out a cereal which is good for them, without too much sugar but still a cereal they are actually going to eat. Of course cereal companies try to entice kids to get their cereal with the promise of a toy inside or a toy after you buy five boxes, which tends to put me in a dilemma with Holly and Nicholas. We needed cereal though so I decided I had to make the stop at the cereal aisle.

After I was sure I had brought the cart to a complete stop I announced, "Okay if you want to pick out your cereal you better get out now or forever hold your peace."

In a split second, Nicholas and Holly were out of the car. They seem to relish in the opportunity of each being able to pick out their own cereal. They were quite intensely looking at all of the different cereal up and down the cereal aisle. I didn't mind them taking their time. It was cute watching how intense they were focused in picking out a cereal they wanted. Nicholas suddenly grabbed his box of cereal and ran back to me for approval.

I was a bit surprised by his choice so I had to ask, "Cheerios?"

He looked at me for a moment before he responded. "They are healthy right Mimi? It says so on the box and aren't we all trying to be healthy right now?"

It's always nice to know your child actually pays attention to what you say. And I do have to say it was also nice to see my son wanted to be healthy as well. So I just smiled and said, "You are very right my Santa Claus. Thanks for picking a healthy choice. Are you sure you will eat them though?" He walked right up to me and had me bend down so he could whisper into my ear, "Mimi on Saturday mornings when you and daddy sleep in, sissy helps me sneak daddy's *Cheerios* for my breakfast and I found out I really do like *Cheerios*. But don't tell daddy I sneaked his Cheerios Mimi."

I smiled and agreed to keep his little *Cheerios* secret. Besides he has his own box now. I guess Nicholas had been fairly quick in picking out his cereal but his sissy couldn't decide on one. I finally had to give Holly a two minute warning, just to try and speed up her cereal decision making. Usually, Holly is such a decisive person but when it comes to cereal she obviously feels one must make the cereal decision without any haste. I was watching my watch and giving her ten second updates on her remaining time. Nicholas must have been feeling the pressure as well because he ran over to his sissy to try and speed her up. As soon as I started the final ten second countdown, Holly ran over to a box of cereal, picked it off the shelf and ran back to the cart with Nicholas. As I held Holly's cereal choice in my hand, I was a bit shocked at her cereal decision as well.

I looked at Holly and I had to ask, "Oatmeal? It took you all that time Holly to pick out oatmeal?"

Holly eagerly and confidently responded back to me, "Why shouldn't I pick oatmeal Mom? Didn't bro, bro pick out a healthy cereal too? Remember mom we are all trying to be healthy now."

Well, I guess the cereal aisle hadn't been as bad as I had expected it to be. I was proud both of my kids had made such healthy choices with their cereal picks. I was about to tell the kids to get back into the car attached to the cart when somebody had to comment on Nicholas's Santa Claus suit.

A man, which none of us even knew, came right up to the three of us and sarcastically said, "Well, well it looks as if you are quite a bit early for Christmas this year little buddy?"

I could tell this little comment irritated all three of us. I was trying to figure out in a split second how to appropriately respond to this rude man. However, obviously Holly was much more prepared to respond to a sarcastic comment than I was.

Holly quickly piped up, "Sir, obviously you don't realize who you are really talking to. My brother is the new real Santa Claus and I am pretty sure you just bought yourself a place on the naughty list this year with your little comment. Come on bro, bro lets go."

I pushed the cart away and none of us even looked back. I could feel my face was very hot though. All I could think to myself was how some people have no common sense at all. Suddenly, I could feel my face cooling down as I thought to myself how well Holly had stood up for her brother. I knew it must have taken a lot of strength for her to stand up to an adult who was making a comment about her little brother as the new real Santa Claus. But she did stand up to the rude man with quite a bit of confidence and quite eloquently, I should add.

On the way to the check out line, I could hear the two of them playing in the car like nothing had happened, which put a smile on my face. I paid for my groceries and we headed out to the car. The moment I stopped at our car, Holly jumped out of the cart.

"I call my song first", yelled Holly.

"Okay", Nicholas responded without even a pause.

I opened the car door for the kids to get in as I loaded the groceries into the trunk. While loading the groceries I kept thinking to myself either Holly really had her game on now or possibly Nicholas had let his sissy win the first song because she stood up for him in the store. Either way I was happy to see Nicholas had the full support of his Mimi and his sissy as the new real Santa Claus. I also knew the full support from his daddy would be there soon.

As I turned the car on, I was still unable to clear all of the thoughts from my head about the incident inside the store. I was hoping today at the market hadn't affected my little Nicholas too much. Way too many thoughts kept filling my head as I began to back out of my parking space. Boom! The car shook as I realized I hit something. I quickly looked in the rear view mirror to see what I had hit this time but I couldn't see anything.

Holly sighed as she quietly stated, "No, not another yellow pole."

Nicholas on the other hand began to giggle which quickly turned into hysterically laughing. As I looked at Holly, I could tell she was trying her best not to laugh. But the temptation from Nicholas's laughter was too great. Holly joined in with Nicholas as they both began to laugh hysterically together.

I was not amused. Garrett would be so upset if I crashed my car again. Hesitantly, I opened my car door to see what was hit and how much damage I had caused my car this time. There it was another yellow pole. Yes, I hit another yellow pole. Why would someone put a two foot high yellow pole next to the cart return? I had never noticed the yellow pole right there. My entire body was frozen as I stood there staring at the newest yellow pole I had hit.

Nicholas was still laughing as he poked his head out the window to ask, "Well Mimi, was it another yellow pole?"

I wasn't in the mood to discuss the newest yellow pole. I abruptly told Nicholas, "Get back in your seat and buckle up now mister."

Holly and Nicholas were laughing so loudly that I could hear them from where I stood at the back of the car. However, I was relieved as I looked down at the back bumper. No major damage this time, I think I must be destined to have a yellow mark on the back of my bumper. Thinking to myself, maybe the yellow ads a bit of character or maybe not.

Listening to the laughter all the way home was not my idea of fun. I refused to let the laughter continue. In a very serious tone I stated, "Ok Holly and Nicholas you both need to stop laughing now."

Neither Holly nor Nicholas could answer me, although I did glance at them through my rear view mirror. I could tell they were trying very hard to stop laughing. However, every few minutes I could hear a loud giggle.

As we arrived home, I told both kids, "Please go into the house, I will unload everything myself."

Holly and Nicholas did as I had asked and they where nowhere to be found as I unloaded and put away the groceries. I was still unsure as to how I would explain the latest yellow pole incident to Garrett. Once again I was completely lost in my own thoughts when I heard a strange sound.

"Beeeeeeeeeeeep, beeeeeeeeeeeeep, beeeeeeeeeeeeeep." I looked around and noticed it was Nicholas hiding up on the stairs trying very hard to get my attention without upsetting me.

I wasn't really mad or upset any longer so I smiled as I said, "Nicholas sweetheart, you can go ahead and join me downstairs if you would like."

In a flash Nicholas rushed down the stairs and stood next to me. Nicholas reached around me giving my legs a nice big hug. As I bent down to hug him back, he ran into the family room. He must have known I would follow right behind him.

Nicholas sat down on the couch and quietly asked me, "Mimi can you please sit down next to me?"

Sitting down next to Nicholas I worriedly asked, "Are you okay? Is everything okay?"

Nicholas just smiled as he cheerfully said, "Mimi….I….well….I didn't want to upset you so I never told you about something funny that happened one time when I was at the North Pole."

Why was he telling me this now I thought? Suddenly, I found myself very curious as to why he felt the need to tell me now. Nicholas kept staring at me motionless with a big smile on his face. Somehow I knew this was going to be a fabulous story.

I tried to tone down my excitement as I asked, "Okay Nicholas what happened at the North Pole that was funny?"

In a quite serious tone Nicholas replied, "Mimi, I will tell you what happened but only if you promise not to be upset."

Now I really needed to know what had happened at the North Pole. I quickly answered, "Just tell me Nicholas."

"Mimi, you have to promise," Nicholas replied.

In as nice of a tone as possible, I answered, "Fine Nicholas, I promise."

Nicholas smiled as he began, "Not long after New Years, Jack came and took me to the North Pole again. Jack told me he had come to get me because there was a party at the North Pole. Mimi, I was very excited because it was my very first party there."

A bit shocked, I interrupted my little Nicholas to ask, "What? You went to a party at the North Pole and you didn't tell me about it?"

As Nicholas shook his head he asked, "Mimi, didn't you promise you wouldn't get upset?"

I sighed as I answered, "Yes, I promised not to get upset. I promise to sit here and listen quietly."

Once again Nicholas smiled as he continued, "Okay Mimi, Jack did tell me it was a party at the North Pole but I didn't understand he meant at the actual real pole at the North Pole. After he picked me up he took me to my house so I could get ready for the party. Jack gave me a really cool Santa suit for parties only. It isn't as nice as my real Santa suit though, the shirt is almost like a regular t-shirt and the pants are kind of like jeans but it almost looks just like a real Santa suit. Anyways, after we got ready, Jack took me in his golf cart to the pole."

Nicholas paused as he began to laugh as I patiently waited for him to continue. Finally, Nicholas closed his eyes in order to gain composure before he continued with his story, "Okay, sorry Mimi....it's just that....well....it's just the real pole of the North Pole is yellow with big red stripes. As soon as I saw the yellow pole, I started laughing because I remembered when you hit the yellow pole when we went through the drive through. Also the time when you hit the yellow pole, almost hitting the statuary man.

So, I told Jack it was a good thing my Mimi wasn't at the North Pole party. Jack was curious about why I was laughing at the yellow pole so I had to tell Jack the whole story. I hope you don't mind Mimi. But....well....Jack was laughing so hard that....well....the rest of the elves at the party wanted to know what was so funny. So, we told them....actually Jack told them all about you and the yellow poles."

By this time I had almost completely forgotten all about the negative man at the market. It seemed as if the negativity at the market hadn't really affected my little Nicholas much at all. However, I do think the day at the market must have made Nicholas start realizing some people out there just don't believe in him. I did like seeing how much Nicholas tried to remain positive about the incident as he chose to only concentrate on the yellow pole incident.

The comment didn't seem to affect Nicholas wearing his Santa suit at all. Nicholas simply continued to wear his Santa suit everywhere he went except for preschool.

CHAPTER 9

    I do always try to be a safe driver but I know I am not always the best driver despite my safe driving efforts. There is only one thing impinging on my effort to be a good driver, the yellow pole. Nicholas now refuses to go through any type of drive through restaurants with me because of the stupid yellow pole.

    I rarely take my kids to fast food restaurants but I mixed up the date of a bridal shower. I felt bad that Nicholas rode thirty minutes in his car seat all the way out to his grandparent's house, only to discover his Mimi put the wrong date down. I drove us back into town and Nicholas told me he was very hungry. Still feeling bad, I promised Nicholas we would pick up some food before we went back home. The drive through lady was telling me I had to move forward to wait for the rest of my food and Nicholas was in the back complaining about the toy in his bag. There was a huge yellow pole to the right of me. I was driving Garrett's coveted pickup truck. I must have turned the corner too sharp and I felt the truck hit the pole just a little bit and I remember I had thought to myself 'how bad could it be, I was only going maybe 5 miles per hour when the stupid yellow pole jumped out and hit the truck?'. When the drive through lady brought out the rest of the food, I should have known by how she looked at the side of the truck then at me, that it was bad. But I didn't, no I was trying to keep a positive attitude.

I still remember the five minute drive back home with Nicholas like it was yesterday. I have seriously never seen a time when he was so absolutely quiet. I think Nicholas must have been thinking the entire five minutes of what exactly he should say to his Mimi.

Finally, as I stopped the truck, Nicholas gave me his words of encouragement. "Mimi maybe daddy won't even notice or maybe daddy will just be happy because we are both okay."

I turned around and smiled at my little Nicholas as I said, "Maybe."

I went around the side of the truck to take Nicholas out of it. I couldn't force myself to look until I let little Nicholas out of his car seat. Nicholas jumped down from his seat, staring at the dented truck. As I saw the damage, I froze right in my footsteps amazed at what hitting one yellow pole in the drive through can do.

Nicholas then grabbed my hand and said, "Come on Mimi let's go inside and see sissy and daddy."

I knew I couldn't stand out there all day staring at the truck even though I wanted to. I don't know why. I think I thought maybe if I stared long enough it might make the dented side magically be fixed. But I knew I should go inside the house with Nicholas. So I did. Garrett saw the look on my face and he immediately knew something was wrong. I confessed quite quickly as I took him outside to show him the damage. Luckily, he is a very calm, cool and collective person who doesn't scream or yell. I saw his mouth move a few times as if he was trying to say something but the words were not coming out of his mouth.

With my positive thinking, I thought maybe it really wasn't bad so I asked, "You think we could just pop the dent out?"

Garrett laughed as he said, "No, we can't just pop out the dent. The entire side of the truck is a dent. Look above the tire it's dented almost all the way into the tire. It's okay though at least you and Nicholas are fine. Don't worry we'll get it fixed."

Wow, was all I could remember thinking. I am so happy I married such a great man. Garrett was right, we got the truck fixed and it was back to 'normal' within three weeks. Unfortunately, Nicholas and Holly still remember the yellow pole incident. Even though Holly wasn't there, she still somehow remembers the drive through yellow pole incident. Besides Holly and I had an entirely different pole incident together just about three months later.

I remember I woke up on a Saturday morning knowing I was going to have an accident. I told Holly on the way to her Saturday morning Drama class that I felt like I was going to get into an accident that day. I asked Holly to be sure her buckle was nice and tight and to please stay seated. We made it the entire way to class and we were safe and sound. We were a bit early so I decided to press my luck so we drove down the street to the donut store. After we bought our donuts, I simply put the car in reverse and began backing out of the parking space. The radio was on and we were both singing to the song playing on the radio. Yes, maybe it was my mistake to sing and drive at the same time since I can't carry any type of tune whatsoever. I accelerated out of my parking space and BOOM! We abruptly stopped without me hitting the brake. I knew we must have hit something. I looked before I backed out of my parking space. At least I was pretty sure I looked.

    After the big BOOM, I began to doubt and wonder if I really did look. I remember looking in my rear view mirror, praying I hadn't just hit the statuary man. The statuary man has a little statue stand with statues for sale at the edge of the parking lot. Most of his statues are small garden style statues but it seems as if he has hundreds of different styles crammed in the small little stand. After my silent prayer, I looked in the rear view mirror and saw all was well with the statuary man. I was relieved I hadn't hit anyone. There was no car there, no one on the ground, what could I have hit? I quickly put the car in drive and I sped my car out of the parking lot still not seeing anything I could have hit. I screamed about five times or so just to get any anger in me out.

    Holly was very quiet for about a minute or so until she was sure I wasn't going to scream anymore. Trying to make me feel better she quietly said, "Mom, at least the air bags didn't go off."

I tried to keep a serious face because I was still a bit mad. I wasn't quite sure how much damage there was yet. From the force and sound of the BOOM, I had a feeling my car would be going into the repair shop on Monday. Holly was really trying to help make me feel better, she was politely not laughing at me and she did have a good point, the airbags had not gone off. I began to imagine what would have happened if the airbags had gone off. Once the image came into my head, I really couldn't help but laugh. This was a great thing because as soon as I started laughing, Holly began to laugh as well. The laughing took the scared look right off of poor little Holly's face.

We arrived at drama class a couple of minutes later and unfortunately there were no spots left in the parking lot. I was forced to parallel park my car on the street. To say the least, I am very under talented when it comes to parallel parking. I always have Holly get out of the car to stand on the sidewalk so she can help direct my parking efforts. This day though, I asked her to look at the back of the car first so she could see the damage. I found I could not resist looking in my rear view mirror. I wanted to catch a glimpse of Holly's face of her first impression as to what the damage on my car looked like. As I sat there watching her, I saw her face become somber as she began shaking her head. I guess I had been trying to convince myself there really wasn't much damage to the back of my car.

But after a loud BOOM like we just experienced, how could there not be any significant damage to my car? Holly walked over to the passenger window so I rolled it down.

I no longer even cared about parking my car. All I needed was for Holly to tell me how bad it was. I asked, "So Holly, I looked at your face as you looked at the damage. How bad is it?"

Holly began to laugh hysterically and I was getting a bit annoyed she thought the damage to my car was so funny. She saw me glaring at her a bit so she began trying very hard to gain enough composure to respond back to me. "Okay mom, I really don't know how, but there is no damage to the back of your car. There is just one little yellow mark that I think will come off when we wash the car. So I guess you must have hit another yellow pole."

Holly couldn't resist laughing again as I put the car into park and got out to see the damage for myself. I seriously thought she was kidding me. How could there be no dent or major damage after a big BOOM and sudden stop like that? I so wanted Holly to be right. I was ecstatic when I saw for myself there really was no damage to the back of my car except for a little yellow mark.

Holly saw the amazed look on my face and couldn't help stating, "I told you mom, there is no damage but I am going to tell daddy as soon as I talk to him that you hit another yellow pole."

I knew Garrett was really going to be wondering now about my driving with this latest yellow pole incident. I was certain he would do much better with the news of another yellow pole after a few glasses of red wine. I calmly told Holly, "Sweetheart, I think it would be best if mommy told daddy about this and besides the yellow mark on the bumper we aren't entirely sure it was even a yellow pole I hit. I never saw a yellow pole in the parking lot."

I could see Holly wanted to be the one to tell her father about the incident and she did stop laughing just long enough to give me her input on the incident. "Well mom, I will respect the fact that you want to be the one to tell dad. But I really, really think it was a yellow pole you hit. So, after class I want you to drive by the parking lot so we can see what you really did hit."

"Holly, just please get back up on the sidewalk to help me parallel park so you won't be late for class and I promise to think about your suggestion while you are in class. Deal?" I watched Holly's face thinking about my proposition as she walked back up onto the sidewalk.

Holly hesitated for a moment before finally agreeing, "Okay you've got a deal."

By the tone in Holly's voice, I could tell she really didn't want to agree to it until I promised to go back and see what I had hit. But I was a bit hesitant to go back to the parking lot twice in one day. However, I did think about it while Holly was in her drama class and I finally decided there really wasn't any harm in going back to the parking lot to see what I had indeed hit.

After drama class Holly got into the car and she began to tell me what a great improv class she had today. I was enjoying the fact she was sharing with me about her class but I did have to interrupt her just for a moment. "Okay Holly, I have decided there is probably no harm in going back to the parking lot so we will stop by there on our way home."

Holly smiled as she continued telling me about her class. At first I was unsure whether or not to drive into the parking lot or drive by the parking lot. I guess I was a bit indecisive because I didn't want to hit anything 'hiding' in the parking lot again. I obviously was lucky this morning with no damage but I didn't want to press my luck today by going to the same parking lot twice but I knew Holly really wanted to know what we hit. I also thought maybe she would drop the incident and possibly forget about the whole thing if she knew exactly what it was we hit. As we pulled into the parking lot, I was making extra sure to drive very slowly. We both looked around the parking lot but at first we didn't see what it was I hit.

"Mom, it's over there, right there mom that's what you hit. See I told you it was a yellow pole!" Holly exclaimed.

I was so surprised she actually spotted what I had hit. It wasn't big or tall in the least. No wonder I hit it. I couldn't have even seen it out of my rear view mirror because of how short the pole was. "Okay Holly, that thing is so small there is no way we can justify calling it a yellow pole. Maybe I will let you call it a yellow stick but that is it."

Holly started laughing, "No mom it's a yellow pole. It may be short and not so big around but it definitely is qualified to be called a yellow pole."

I did eventually agree to it being called a 'small yellow pole' and Holly did agree to let me tell her daddy about it first. We went to lunch then we went shopping, luckily with no more yellow pole incidents. We both had a great rest of the day but to this day Holly does continue to remember the 'small yellow pole' incident.

CHAPTER 10

Nicholas loves to go shopping at *The Grove*. Spring was coming and it was getting warmer outside. So, I decided to go summer clothes shopping at *The Grove*. Nicholas of course jumped at the opportunity to go shopping when he found out where we were going. Holly hesitated a little but then jumped at the opportunity as well when I told her I was going clothes shopping for her. She likes to pick out her own clothes even though I am the final authority when it comes to what clothes we actually buy. Both kids hurried to their rooms to get ready and it was no surprise when Nicholas came out of his room wearing his Santa suit. Even Holly didn't say anything about Nicholas's Santa suit. Garrett was working today so it was only the kids and I going shopping together.

Of course while we were walking through *The Grove* shopping, some people did stare at little Nicholas a bit but he was really good now about people staring at him. He smiles and waves.

We looked at some of the stores until we finally made it to the end of *The Grove* to shop at *GAP*. Holly loves *GAP* clothing so she walked quite a bit ahead of us on the way to the store. We found way too much stuff to buy at *GAP* as always. All three of us made our way up front to purchase all of the goodies we had found. As I was waiting for the checker to come to the register, I instructed Holly and Nicholas to stay right close while everything was getting rung up, which they did very obediently. The checker arrived to the register a bit grumpy. I decided to try and be as good of a customer as possible.

Even though she hadn't greeted me, I decided to greet her, "Hi, how are you doing today?"

She gave me an odd look before responding, "Not one of my best days. I just want this day to be over so I can go home."

I watched as the checker took a glance at Nicholas. The glance turned into intrigue as I saw she was now watching little Nicholas dance around the store in his Santa suit. I didn't want to mention I saw her watching little Nicholas but I did want to respond back to her. "Well I hope you have a better rest of the day."

She didn't immediately respond back to me, instead she continued to watch little Nicholas before finally responding. "Do you know who that little boy is?"

I quickly stated, "Yes, why?"

I could tell she didn't quite know how to say what she wanted to say. "Well….well…..is he your little boy?"

"Yes, he is my little boy." I wasn't sure where she was going with this so I didn't really know how much to say at that point.

She was still a bit hesitant but I could tell she was in awe of little Nicholas. "I...well...I was just wondering why he....well....why he has a Santa suit on."

I smiled and decided to tell her the truth. "Well my son Nicholas believes he is the new real Santa Claus. So we let him wear his Santa suit whenever he wants."

She continued to ring up the items I was buying with most of her attention on Nicholas though. It appeared he was absolutely oblivious anybody was watching him. I was happy to see the checker was actually smiling now. Little did I know how much my Nicholas had influenced her entire day. The checker put all of our items in bags, all the while continuing to stare at Nicholas. There were no other customers waiting behind me so I truly had the distinct feeling she had taken her time ringing up my items.

When all was bagged and paid for she slowly handed me my bags commenting, "Thank you. Thank you so much for bringing your son in today. He has truly brightened my day. Thanks for letting him be himself. I believe."

I grabbed my bags trying to find the right words to respond back with. I managed to say, "Thanks for believing."

I turned to I walk away from the register as I grabbed onto little Nicholas's hand. I looked for Holly and I saw she was already at the elevator. Nicholas squeezed my hand and looked up at me with a smile so I knew he had been paying attention the entire time.

When we stepped outside the store, Nicholas turned to me smiling again. He took about four steps before he commented, "Mimi, another believer. Today was a very good day."

I had to smile back at Nicholas before I agreed with him, "You're right sweetheart, another believer."

The walk back to the car was pretty uneventful except for the fact Nicholas had an extra special skip in his step. When we got into the car, Nicholas immediately told his sissy she could pick her song first. Holly looked at him at first, she was unsure of what to think but she knew she couldn't pass up the offer so she gladly accepted it.

Garrett was already home and waiting for us by the time we got home. He came out to the garage to greet all of us at the car. As I parked the car, Garrett opened my car door and gave me a nice kiss on the lips. All of us were in a great mood and Garrett appeared to be a little out of the loop.

He looked at all three of us for a moment before he had to ask, "Okay why is everyone so happy and in such great mood?"

Nicholas quickly piped up before Holly and I had a chance to say anything. "I have another believer!"

Garrett was a bit confused and obviously still out of the loop. "Huh? Another what?"

Nicholas looked right back at his dad to once again respond. "You know dad, another believer in me. I am the new real Santa Claus!"

I could tell by the look on Garrett's face he was a bit unsure of what to say in response. "Oh....well congratulations Nicholas, you must be very excited."

I quickly interjected to try and take the pressure off of my husband. "Yes honey, Nicholas is very excited about this. The new Santa Claus believer is the checker at the *GAP* at *The Grove*."

Garrett was truly trying to share all of our excitement as he stated, "Okay then how about we order pizza tonight to celebrate Nicholas having a new Santa Claus believer."

Holly didn't hesitate to respond to the possible pizza night. "Yes! I vote for pizza night. How about you Nicholas, did you want pizza tonight too?"

Nicholas quickly responded as well. "Of course I want pizza sissy. Pizza sounds great daddy and can we have a game night tonight too, daddy?"

Garrett smiled as he responded, "Of course we can have game night tonight as well. I think that sounds like a great idea. Thank you Nicholas."

We all had another wonderful family pizza and game night. I ended up telling Garrett all about our day and the new Santa Claus believer after we put the kids to bed. Garrett was happy we had such a wonderful day but I wish he could have actually been there to see the lady staring in awe at our little Nicholas. I am not sure why, maybe just so Garrett would better understand how important our little Nicholas is to other people and how much joy he brings to them by being Santa Claus. But life goes on and boy did it!

Holly was so excited about her upcoming gymnastics performance. She had been working very hard lately in gymnastics. I am so proud of how much Holly has improved on her floor routine as well as on her trampoline routine. She has been going to gymnastics three to four times a week lately to work on her routines and her coach has been phenomenal with her.

It's Saturday and Garrett was getting all ready to go out to do something. He obviously forgot I was taking Holly to her last gymnastics practice before her big gymnastics performance on Monday night. I reminded Garrett almost everyday last week that he had to take care of Nicholas today. But now it's finally Saturday and it seems he may have forgotten his most important Saturday chore, taking care of Nicholas.

As I saw Garrett go and get his truck keys, I figured I obviously needed to remind him of his most important Saturday chore. "Um sweetheart you do remember you are in charge of Nicholas today don't you? It's Holly's final gymnastics rehearsal today for her performance on Monday night!"

Garrett oddly responded, "No, why can't you take Nicholas with you. Nicholas will be fine at gymnastics waiting for Holly. Besides you're only going to be sitting there. It's not like you are going to be performing back flips on the floor or something. So why can't you watch Nicholas while you are watching Holly?"

I was a bit annoyed to say the least so I tried very hard to gain my composure before I replied, "Well, first of all Nicholas has been waiting to spend the day with his daddy. He has been looking forward all week to spending the day with you today. Second of all, if I take Nicholas, I will only be watching him and I won't be able to watch Holly's practice. So no, Nicholas can't go with me to Holly's practice. Nicholas is staying home with you and the two of you are going to have a great 'guy's only day' today."

Garrett was sure on his toes today. He quickly replied, "But that's just it. I am not going to be home this morning. I have to go to the hardware store right now and get a bunch of supplies so I can finish everything on our backyard patio project. You keep telling me you want me to finish the project and so my plan today was to finish it."

I was no longer annoyed, instead I decided to be matter of fact, "Well then you are going to have to figure out how you plan to include your son into your day so the two of you will be able to have a great 'guy's only day' because Holly and I are leaving in about ten minutes and it will only be her and I."

Just then I heard someone walking down the stairs. I turned around in time to see my little Nicholas walking cheerfully down the stairs. He ran up to his daddy and gave his daddy a great big hug asking, "What do we get to do today daddy?"

Garrett saw the absolute excitement on his son's face at the opportunity to spend the entire day with his daddy. Excitement does usually tend to cause a chain reaction as did it in this case. Garrett got a huge smile on his face and replied to Nicholas, "Well son, today we get to have a 'guy's only day'! We are going to go to the hardware store first and then we are going to work outside on a project. How does that sound?"

Nicholas eagerly replied, "That sounds awesome daddy. I'm all ready so let's go now."

Garrett hesitated for a moment before he continued, "Okay son just go get dressed and then we can go."

Nicholas looked at his daddy a bit strangely. "But daddy I'm already dressed."

I knew what Garrett was going to say next and I so desperately wanted to stop him from saying it but I wasn't fast enough. "Son, it's a guy's day not a Santa day. Besides Nicholas it is a long time till Christmas."

Nicholas dropped his head and his huge smile quickly disappeared. Luckily, Garrett noticed this so I am pretty sure out of guilt tried to make Nicholas happy. "Hey buddy, I just thought you would be more comfortable in jeans and your boots. Plus I didn't want anything to get on your Santa suit because I would be sad if it got ruined." Nicholas still didn't respond so Garrett continued. "You know what Nicholas, I would love it if you would wear your Santa suit today for our 'guy's only day'.

That's all it took. Nicholas popped his head right back up and his huge smile quickly and magically reappeared. "Thanks daddy. I'm ready to go then. Are you?"

Garrett hesitantly replied, "Yep, I'm ready to go."

Nicholas eagerly said, "Great, then let's get going."

Garrett gave me a 'thanks a lot look' before he kissed me. Then they both said, "Goodbye," and walked out the front door to the truck.

I watched them through the living room window and I really thought they would have a great day together. I was definitely looking forward to spending the day with Holly and I know she had been counting on a mommy daughter day. I was planning on taking Holly shopping at the mall after gymnastics practice. I noticed she has been getting a bit taller so her jeans seemed to be getting a bit shorter on her. Plus, it's always nice to go shopping for new clothes. I knew she would have fun especially because we were shopping for her.

Holly came down the stairs with a skip in her step. As soon as she heard the front door close and from the tone in her voice I knew she was happy it was a 'girl's only day' today. "Hey mom, are the guys gone?"

I looked at Holly and I couldn't help but giggle as I answered her, "Yes, the guys are gone. Our 'girl's only day' has now officially began."

Holly quickly replied, "Good, I thought they were never going to leave."

"Well Ms. Holly, I need to get you to gymnastics very soon. Are you all ready to go? Do you have all of your stuff?"

Holly looked at me for a moment, I think because she was probably wondering why I had gotten serious all of a sudden. "Come on mom, chill out. The guys are gone! We need to have a little bit of fun at home with them gone before we go to gymnastics!"

I did realize I had gotten a little too serious all of a sudden. I took a deep breath in and I 'chilled out'. "Okay Holly what 'fun' do you have in mind for us?"

With a bit of a sly look on her face Holly replied, "Just wait mom, I will be right back."

Holly ran upstairs and before I knew it, our favorite songs were playing quite loudly on her stereo system. She came running down the stairs with a big smile on her face and a microphone in each hand. "Here mom, I got a microphone for each of us."

"Thanks Holly!" I took the microphone out of her hand as we both started singing and dancing to our favorite song, You *Belong with Me* by Taylor Swift. We sang about five more songs including *Ain't No Mountain High Enough*, and the *Cha Cha Slide*. We were truly having so much fun I didn't want our singing and dancing time to end. But I caught a glance at the clock on the stove and I saw we only had five minutes to get to gymnastics.

I quickly gave my microphone back to Holly. "Holly, quick! Go shut off your stereo. We only have five minutes to get to gymnastics."

Holly didn't run upstairs right away but I didn't mind at all. Why? Because she quickly reached her arms around me giving me the best hug ever. "Thanks mom, I had a lot of fun." She turned to run up the stairs but stopped half way. "Mom I really mean it! I really needed some fun time with just me and you!"

I smiled and quickly replied, "No Holly, thank you! I really needed that too!"

Holly smiled as she finished running upstairs to turn her stereo off and put the microphones away. She came back downstairs, a smile still on her face. She grabbed her gymnastics bag and we ran to get into the car. Since it was only Holly and I, she didn't have to call her song. She turned on her pick right away. We sang all the way to gym and we made it right on time. I don't know how but we did.

I enjoyed sitting there watching Holly practice her routines. She was doing a phenomenal job. Every now and again, I couldn't help but wonder how the guy's were doing. I was really hoping the day would go off without a hitch. But I felt a knot down deep in my stomach telling me the guy's were having a very eventful day. Every time those thoughts about the guy's came into my head, I tried to quickly get them back out because I really wanted to concentrate only on Holly today. Today was our 'girl's only day' together and I didn't want any distractions.

I was truly amazed at how quickly the four and a half hour practice had gone. They had taken a quick half hour light lunch snack break. They worked extremely hard the entire practice. I was so proud Holly practiced full out for the entire four hours. I was getting tired just watching her practice. I was hoping she still would have enough energy left to go shopping.

Holly still looked perky and peppy but I decided to ask, "Holly do you feel up to going shopping for some new clothes at the mall or would you just like to go home?"

Holly had absolutely no hesitation as she replied, "Of course I feel like going shopping! Come on mom let's get out of here. I am so absolutely and thoroughly done with gymnastics for today!"

Holly grabbed my hand as we walked out to the car together. Holly didn't even turn on any music on the way to the mall. Instead she talked the entire way, telling me all of the stores she wanted to go shopping in and even where she wanted me to park because the parking spot put us closer to the store she wanted go into first. As soon as we drove into the parking lot of the mall she let out a loud squeal, which just about scared me half to death. I thought I hit something again so I slammed on my brakes. Of course Holly must have known exactly what I was thinking because her squeal turned into a loud laughter. I quickly but of course not too quickly went and parked in the exact location Holly told me to park in.

Holly and I had so much fun shopping together and spending way too much money we totally lost track of time. I looked down at my watch and I saw it was already five o'clock in the evening. At first, I felt relieved and once again assumed everything must have been going great with the guys because I had not received any phone calls or text messages from Garrett. I reached down to grab my phone out of my purse to call and let Garrett know Holly and I would be home shortly. My relieved feeling ended abruptly as I looked at my cell phone. I saw I had five missed calls, eight unopened text messages and two unheard voice messages. I suddenly remembered, I had turned the ringer off on my phone so my 'girl's only day' with Holly would not be interrupted. I guess I figured Garrett could handle anything that would have and could have happened. But obviously the guy's had an eventful day and Garrett was obviously trying very hard to get a hold of me.

I couldn't wait until we got out to the car. I needed to listen to my voice messages and see the unopened text messages now. A million bad thoughts started running through my head. Why had I turned the ringer on my phone off? What if my little Nicholas had gotten hurt? Or worse yet what if both of them were hurt?

Holly was a bit annoyed and began to question my sudden obsession with my phone. "Come on mom you can check your messages later. What's the rush? Dad is a competent adult, he can handle whatever problems he and Nicholas are having on their 'guy's only' day. Plus there is one last store by the exit I want to go into."

I totally understood Holly's annoyance. Truthfully, I would probably be more than a bit annoyed if Holly was obsessing about her cell phone messages right now. But the knot deep down in my stomach was continuing to agitate me and I wanted the knot to go away. I thought maybe if I sat down for a moment to look and listen to all of my messages, I would feel better.

I turned to Holly and stated, "No Holly, I can't wait to listen to my messages. There are a ton of voice messages, missed calls and unopened text messages I need to check. Please let's sit down for a moment and then we will finish our shopping. And I promise we will go into that last store you want to go into."

Holly looked at me and she must have known by the look on my face I was truly worried about how the 'guy's only day' had gone today. "Okay fine mom. But please can you hurry?"

I was already sitting down on the bench when I answered Holly. "Yes sweetheart I will hurry as fast as I can. Besides once I see and hear my messages I will feel much better and we can finish our shopping."

Holly sat on the bench next to me and pulled her phone out of my purse. I was definitely relieved I had actually remembered to put Holly's cell phone in my purse today. As I began to check all of my text messages, I saw all of my text messages were from Garrett requesting and then demanding I call him back as soon as possible. I could definitely tell the more recent text messages were a bit more intense. The more recent text messages were done in all capital letters and the most recent had quite a number of exclamation marks on them. I also saw, all of my missed calls were from my husband so I hesitantly decided I should probably listen to all of my voice messages. The voice messages were all pretty generic as well. Garrett was stating I needed to call him as soon as possible because we needed to discuss Nicholas. I was praying my little Nicholas hadn't gotten hurt or something. At first I thought, I was going to wait and discuss whatever Garrett wanted to discuss about Nicholas when I got home. But I couldn't help but wonder if my little Nicholas was okay. I decided to call my husband right away.

    I don't even think the phone rang a full ring before Garrett answered it. "Geez... where are you and Holly at? I thought gymnastics practice was only four hours."

    I could tell from his tone he had not had the same easy and fun day with Nicholas as I had with Holly. I tried to respond back to him with the sweetest voice possible. "Is everything okay with you and our little Nicholas?"

    Garrett rarely, if ever screams. So I was quite taken a back when he screamed his reply back into the phone. "No, everything is not okay!"

    There was a brief moment of silence from him and I could hear he was taking a long deep breath in. I knew since he screamed, he must be very upset right now. I was almost positive by the tone of his voice, nothing was wrong physically with my little Nicholas and he hadn't gotten hurt.

After the brief moment of silence and the long deep breath, Garrett finally finished his response. "I am just a bit tense from everything that happened today. Please don't worry, Nicholas did not fall or get hurt. It's just....well...it's just... I have had a very long day today and I haven't been able to get a hold of you and talk to you about it. It's just...well....you always seem to make everything better. I can't wait until you get home. Can I call a babysitter for the kids so we can go have a nice long talk over dinner?"

I really wanted to spend a nice evening at home with my husband and the kids but I could definitely sense Garrett needed to get out of the house tonight so I happily agreed. "Okay sweetheart that would be just fine. Holly and I just have one more store to go into and then we will be on our way home. So arrange for the sitter to come around seven o'clock or so if possible."

I looked over and I saw Holly staring at me, so I knew she had heard at least a little bit of the conversation and she wasn't excited her and her brother would be having a sitter tonight while her parents went out. I didn't really feel like talking about it until we got into the car. I decided to act like I didn't see Holly staring at me. I ended the conversation with Garrett and put my phone away in my purse.

I casually asked Holly, "Okay girl are you ready to go to the last store you wanted to go into?" Holly just sat there. "Well come on let's go so we can see if there is anything you like."

Holly continued to stare at me before she finally quietly got up and walked next to me to the last store.

Thank goodness Holly likes to shop because as soon as we walked into the store, she got a smile on her face. We looked around and I was glad we went there. They had a lot of cute clothes and accessories. They even had a few cute pairs of shoes. I loved everything Holly was picking out to try on. She had an entire arm load full of stuff to try on by the time we made our way over to the changing rooms. Luckily this store had no limit to the number of items in the changing rooms. As Holly tried on outfit after outfit, I began to realize this store was going to be the most deadly store to my pocket book. I really hated making Holly limit how many items she could buy. But since I was the one buying the items, I knew I had to. Holly picked out all of her 'very favorites' as she put it and then we narrowed the amount from there.

Holly was definitely happy with how many clothes, accessories and shoes she got today. As we were walking out to the car, Holly reached her arm around me and gave me a hug. "Thanks mom, I had a really great and fun day with you today."

I hugged Holly back and I let her know I had a great day with her as well. We got into the car and made our way out of the mall parking lot. Holly once again didn't turn on the radio. But I think this time it was because she really wanted to find out about my conversation with her daddy.

We had only been out of the mall parking lot for maybe thirty seconds before Holly asked, "Okay mom, so what happened that made the 'guy's only day' so bad? Do Nicholas and I seriously have to stay with a sitter tonight? I thought we were going to have a fun family night at home, just the four of us?"

I knew Holly really would not understand why her daddy needed a break after his long day. So I decided to respond back to Holly with a sweet positive attitude. "Holly, your daddy has not given me any details about what exactly happened today. All I know is he needs to go out to dinner with only me so we can talk. So yes, you and your brother have to have a sitter for tonight so daddy and I can go out for a really nice dinner. Please, I need you to get along with your brother extra good and please try not to mother him too much."

Holly was still not so pleased her parents were going out to dinner without her and her brother. But after a moment, she replied in a nice tone, "Fine mom, I will behave and I will be nice to brother. Don't worry, just go out and have a nice time with dad. I just had so much fun with you today....I didn't want our day together to end. But I do understand daddy needs to talk to you about his 'guy's only day' over dinner."

I looked at Holly and I smiled at her. I knew it must have taken a lot out of her to understand her daddy and mommy needed a night out together. I just wish I had known a little sooner Garrett would want to go to dinner tonight. If I had known sooner, I could have possibly arranged a sleepover at one of her girlfriend's houses. But I realize there is always a reason for everything so there must be a reason the kids needed to stay home with a sitter tonight.

I hadn't responded back to Holly, I guess because I wasn't really quite sure exactly what I should say in reply. But she deserved some sort of reply so I said, "Thanks Holly, your support is greatly appreciated. I promise to have my cell phone on during dinner so you can call me if you need anything at all."

Holly was still in a good mood so she looked over at me and said, "Thanks!"

We finally arrived home, as I opened the garage door much to my surprise there was Nicholas sitting on the steps in the garage. His elbows were on his knees and the fabulous huge smile of his was no where to be found but most importantly, I noticed little Nicholas no longer had his Santa suit on. Poor little Nicholas looked like he needed a great big hug so I parked the car as fast as I could. I unbuckled my safety belt, swung my car door open and leaped out of the car. The next thing I knew, I was sitting on those steps in the garage holding my little Nicholas. He didn't say a word. He clung to me as we sat there on the steps together. I am still not sure exactly how long I sat there quietly rocking my baby boy. I do know I could feel his pain. Even before he started crying, I could somehow feel it. When he started crying, I started crying as well. We both cried together on those steps until Garrett came out into the garage. When Nicholas looked up to see his dad, he wiped the tears out of both of his eyes and he glared at Garrett for a few seconds. He gave me great big hug before getting up off my lap and running into the house.

I was still unsure of all of the events, which had taken place today but I did know feelings got hurt. I try to always stand a firm ground jointly with Garrett. But for some reason in this case, I felt as if I was probably going to end up on the side of my little Nicholas. I did want to hear both sides and make no decisions or verdicts until I had fully evaluated everything. Therefore, I wanted to watch the words I uttered out of my mouth. I wanted to make sure my words maintained an impartial judgment for now.

I hadn't looked at Garrett since he had come out into the garage. I continued looking down at the ground while I was thinking. I finally looked up at him and saw the hurt in his eyes as well. At this point now I was totally thrown off. Obviously, whatever had taken place today had affected both my husband and our child significantly.

I softly asked Garrett, "Are you okay honey?"

He sat down on those garage steps right next to me and gave me a hug before he replied, "No...no...I am not okay. I had a really tough day today. I know Nicholas did too though. I called Sara from the church and she told me she could baby sit for us tonight. She will be here a little before seven o'clock. That is if you still want to go out to dinner tonight with me."

I gave Garrett a hug before responding, "Of course I want to go out to dinner with you tonight. You can tell me what happened today over dinner. But right now I really think I should go and talk to Nicholas about what happened today so I can get his thoughts and feelings about all of the events, which transpired today. I just don't think we should leave him with a sitter until he talks about his day."

I could tell by Garrett's look he really wanted to tell me about his day first. But I knew there would be ample time over dinner for him to tell me his side. I got up and I went inside the house to look for my little Nicholas. I finally found him sitting in the corner of his room behind his door. I closed his bedroom door and sat on the floor next to him. Nicholas snuggled right up next to me. I wanted him to tell me his side of the events, which had transpired today but I wanted him to tell me when he was ready to. I didn't want to force him to tell me. I hoped he would tell me when he was ready.

We sat snuggled next to each other until he began to tell about his day. Luckily it didn't take too long before he was ready to talk.

"Mimi, I had a really....no really, really bad day today. I was so excited I was going to get to spend the day with just daddy. But now, I really wish you had let me go with you to Holly's gymnastics practice. Right now Mimi, I never ever want to have a 'guy's only day' with daddy again. Okay, I heard daddy calling a sitter for me and sissy so you and him can go out to dinner. So I know daddy will tell you his side of the story at dinner. I wish just me and you Mimi could go out to dinner but it's okay for you to go to dinner with daddy 'cause I will have fun with the sitter and sissy. So here is how my bad, very bad day went today. When daddy and I left the house we went to the hardware store first. I like the hardware store so I was excited. When we got out of the truck someone in the parking lot said, 'Hi Santa', so I said 'Hi', I looked at daddy and I saw his face getting red. I knew he was embarrassed. I thought maybe daddy was just embarrassed I had said 'Hi' to a stranger. I guess I should tell you Mimi, I had to put a lot of people on the naughty list today.

When we got into the hardware store, first we went over to where all of the nails were and there was already a man looking at nails when we walked up. Daddy told me what nails we were looking for so I could help him look. Daddy and I were just looking at the nails and minding our own business when a mean old man had to say something to us....well actually he said something to me."

Nicholas paused as he remembered the event from earlier. "That mean old man said, 'Son it's almost Easter not almost Christmas. So why don't you have your Easter bunny costume on?' So, I just looked at that mean old man. I know I am the new real Santa Claus and I know I really have to watch what I say to people. So I did just what you told me to do Mimi."

At this point I was really praying Nicholas had followed one of my good pieces of advice in the appropriate way and not vice versa. I calmly said, "Okay Nicholas, so what did you do?"

Nicholas continued, "Well Mimi, I looked at him square in the eyes and I said, 'You don't know who I am do you?' Then the mean old man laughed and said, 'Son, I have no idea who you are except that your daddy lets you wear a Santa costume in the spring.' I continued to stare at him and I said, 'Well, bad for you. I am the new real Santa Claus and you just earned a top spot on the naughty list.' The mean old man just laughed and walked away. Do you know what daddy did?"

I could completely and vividly picture all of the events Nicholas had described. I did know my husband still wasn't so completely sold on the whole idea of his son being the new real Santa Claus. So I could definitely picture the embarrassment he had. I think Garrett probably really didn't know quite what to say or do. After Nicholas asked me if I knew what his daddy did, he continued to stare at me so I figured I should probably diplomatically answer him. "No sweetheart what did your daddy do?"

Nicholas continued to stare at me as he shook his head and continued. "Nothing Mimi, that's what daddy did....absolutely nothing! Some strange mean old man was talking to me and being a big fat meany and daddy did nothing! After the mean old man walked away daddy just reached down, grabbed his nails and said, 'come on Nicholas we need to get some paint now.' And daddy walked away."

Nicholas was mimicking his dad's voice and body movement. He paused at one point to take a little minute break before continuing on with his version of the day's events. I didn't quite know what to say yet so while he was taking his minute break, I gave him a hug before he continued.

Nicholas took in another long deep breath before continuing with his story. "I just....well....Mimi....I just didn't even know what to say to daddy. I knew he had heard what the mean old man had said to me and I also knew daddy had said nothing back to the mean old man. Daddy went to grab my hand before we walked over to the paint and I just grabbed my hand back. There was no way Mimi that I was going to hold onto daddy's hand." Nicholas paused again in his story.

This time when Nicholas paused in the story, I felt I needed to ask, "Nicholas honey, what did you want daddy to do in the hardware store to that mean old man?"

Nicholas thought for a moment before responding to my question and continuing with his story. "You know what Mimi, I really hadn't thought of that. I guess I just really wanted daddy to stand up for me. I think it would have been funny if daddy had punched that meany but all daddy really had to do to make me happy was tell that mean old man, I really am the new Santa Claus. That's it Mimi….that really isn't asking much. I guess I just needed a little bit of support as you would put it Mimi."

Well it seemed as if we were making a little progress, which made me happy. "So Nicholas was the rest of the day okay?"

Once again Nicholas stared at me and shook his head 'no'. "You really have no idea about the day do you?"

I was a bit taken aback by the question but I guess Nicholas was right. I truly did have absolutely no idea about the 'guy's only day'. "Well Nicholas, to tell you the truth daddy hasn't told me anything about the day yet. I told daddy he had to wait and tell me his side of the story over dinner. So the only things I know about the day so far are the things you have told me."

"I know Mimi. But the mean old man was only the start of a bad….no very bad day. Next we walked over to the paint aisle. Daddy grabbed two cans of paint and he let me help him pick out the color of the paint."

I noticed there was a positive event, which occurred so I felt the need to interrupt little Nicholas, "So that was nice of daddy. He let you pick out the color of the paint. So Nicholas what color did you pick out?"

After my little comment Nicholas once again paused before he continued on with his story. "Well Mimi....you....you are right it was nice daddy let me pick out the color. But you know what Mimi? Daddy didn't buy the first color I chose. After daddy said no to my first color, I had to choose one from the five colors he chose."

I couldn't stop my curiosity from getting the best of me. I had to once again stop Nicholas in the middle of his story. "So Nicholas what color did you really want? What color was your first pick?"

Nicholas didn't take a moment to think at all this time. No, he answered me quite quickly. "Mimi, do you really have to ask? What color do you think I chose?"

I truly hate guessing games. I like to know the answer. I guess because I am not really good or I should say not good at all when it comes to guessing games. I didn't want to disappoint Nicholas so I closed my eyes as I took a moment to concentrate on what color my little Nicholas would have wanted to paint our new backyard patio. As I closed my eyes, all I could see was the North Pole. No matter how hard I tried to concentrate, all I could envision was the North Pole. As I opened my eyes, I was ready to make my guess. I didn't know if I was right but I was hopefully at least close to the right answer.

I didn't want to say my answer too loud in case I was wrong so I answered very quietly, "Nicholas, did you pick Santa Claus red?"

I knew I was right by the huge smile magically appearing on my little boy's face. His smile reached its maximum smile capacity as he happily exclaimed, "Mimi you are a hundred percent correct! I really think you underestimate yourself when it comes to guessing games. You really do guess well. Yes, I picked Santa Claus red. I love that color Mimi. You should see the North Pole Mimi, there are so many buildings and almost all of them are painted Santa Claus red."

I understood why Garrett had not bought the Santa Claus red color. He has worked very hard on the backyard patio project and he generally tends to pick more subtle colors.

Nicholas continued with his story, "Well Mimi, I did pick the color from daddy's color choices. I picked some light brownish color. I think it's kind of a boring color so please don't give me any credit for choosing it. I wanted a fun color but I guess its okay because it's not a play ground for me and sissy. I think the new patio is more for you and daddy and for any big people you invite over."

I did feel a little bad I kept interrupting Nicholas from telling me his version of the day's events. But this time, I interrupted him because I really felt it was necessary to interrupt. "Nicholas sweetheart, the new backyard patio project daddy has been working on is for all of us. It's not only for adults. I want all of us to be able to enjoy it. Okay?"

Nicholas looked at me a bit strangely before asking, "Well Mimi thanks for trying to include me and sissy but if it's really for us too, then why does it look so neat and perfect?"

I thought for a moment about what Nicholas had asked. And I realized I had never looked at it that way. "You know what Nicholas you are right. I think daddy and I may have planned the project a bit too grown up. I guess we should have included you and Holly in the planning of the project. How about tomorrow, we see how we can make the backyard patio a little more fun for you and sissy. How about I mention it to daddy over dinner, deal?"

Nicholas smiled at me as he responded, "Deal, thanks Mimi for always trying your best to listen to me and sissy and our ideas."

I couldn't help but smiling as I told my little Nicholas who somehow had such a grown up way of thinking now, "You're welcome Nicholas. But whenever you and sissy have a problem or feel you are being left out by either daddy or I, then you need to speak up. I would much rather you tell me sooner than later. As soon as something bugs you or irritates you please come and tell either daddy or myself. Now enough of getting side tracked, finish telling me about your day."

Nicholas once again took a long deep breath in as he continued his version of the events from the day. "After I had picked the color from daddy's color choices we took the color paper to the man at the paint counter. Daddy handed the man the paper and told him which color we had picked. The man put the paint color in and put the paint cans on those shaking machines. Daddy and I were standing there and the paint counter man said to daddy, 'Um....is that your son?' Daddy told him I was his son and then the paint man asked daddy, 'What's wrong with your son? Why is he dressed up in a Santa Claus costume?' Daddy just leaned toward the paint man as if I couldn't hear him or something and said, 'my son just has a big imagination.' Mimi, a 'big imagination' is all daddy said. Daddy could have told him the truth about me being the new real Santa Claus. But oh no, daddy just said I have a 'big imagination'. This really made me mad at daddy Mimi. Plus daddy let the paint man get away with calling my Santa suit a costume. My Santa suit is not a costume. It is a very important suit. Nobody in the whole hardware store was nice. But don't worry Mimi, I put all of them on the naughty list. And the next time I am at the North Pole, I am going to review the naughty list to make sure the elves put all of those naughty people on the naughty list, especially the big old meany man and the mean paint man."

Nicholas paused as I asked, "Did you say anything sweetheart?"

My little Nicholas tried to smile as he continued, "No Mimi, I didn't say anything 'cause I didn't know what to say and when the paint was done in the shaking machine, daddy just hurried up and got the rest of the stuff he needed at the hardware store. We went to the check out stand and I was really hoping our check out person would be a really nice believer so daddy would know I really am the new real Santa Claus. But instead it was a mean and grumpy lady. When she finished ringing everything up and daddy was getting out his wallet she asked daddy, 'Why the Santa costume?' You know what daddy said the same thing to this mean and grumpy lady he had said to the weird paint man. Daddy said, 'oh sorry my son just has a big imagination.' I know one of my duties as the new real Santa Claus is to always be jolly. But Mimi, I was having a very tough time being jolly today. I did keep a smile on my face but inside I wasn't smiling. I was biting my teeth together really hard. But the mean and grumpy lady just couldn't help but to say one more thing. She said to daddy, 'You should really watch your son's imagination. It seems like it may be a little out of hand.' Daddy smiled….Mimi he actually smiled at that mean and grumpy lady and said, 'Thanks I will keep that in mind.' What….what will daddy keep in mind? Will he keep in mind that I have a big imagination? I thought having a big imagination is a good thing! Mimi, I tried….I really did try very, very hard to keep my teeth bitten down together so I wouldn't say anything to the mean and grumpy lady. But all of a sudden, before I knew it, I was responding back to her little comment, 'You will be wishing you hadn't said that about me because I am the new real Santa Claus and you are now only going to get coal this year in your stocking if you are lucky....and....just to let you know you are now officially on the....' But before I could finish telling the mean and grumpy lady she was now on the naughty list, daddy grabbed my hand and pulled me out of the store. I didn't talk to daddy the whole....whole entire way home. I was really mad at daddy Mimi. And just when I thought that it couldn't get any worse Mimi, you know what happened?"

Nicholas just stared at me waiting for an answer but this time, I had the distinct feeling it would be best if I didn't try to guess the answer. I thought it would be best if Nicholas answered his own question he had asked.

I did give a small and quiet reply, "No."

Nicholas hastily continued with his story. "Fine Mimi, I will tell you what happened. As soon as daddy pulled up to the house, he told me I was to go inside the house and change out of my Santa costume. I really don't know if daddy was saying costume because everyone at the hardware store today had used the word costume or if daddy really thinks my Santa suit is just a costume. Mimi, I know sissy and I aren't suppose to correct you and daddy but I thought it was very important to correct daddy this time. I did NOT want his little costume comment to go unnoticed so I did say, 'Santa suit daddy, it's a Santa suit not a costume.' Daddy just said, 'fine call it whatever you want to, just go and change out of it as soon as you get into the house.' But I really thought that daddy was being mean so I went into the house Mimi and I ran upstairs to my room and I locked the door. Then after a little while when I could hear daddy outside working, I went out into the backyard so I could talk to him about my Santa suit. I really didn't want to be mad at daddy and all I really wanted was for daddy to just believe."

"So did you go and talk to daddy?" I asked.

Nicholas hesitated before he quietly continued, "Mimi....I....I know I shouldn't say this but I really don't care about any other believers if my own daddy doesn't believe in me. So yes, I went into the backyard to talk to daddy. I didn't know...I really am serious.....I didn't know daddy's friend from his work was coming over to help him with the backyard patio project. So all I did was walk into the backyard to talk with daddy. I didn't see daddy at first. All I saw was his friend. Daddy's friend saw me and said, 'Hey aren't you a little early this year.' I guess I was just still upset about everything that had happened at the hardware store. So I told him, 'Well you are going on the naughty list too!' Then I ran back into the house and up to my room. All of a sudden a few minutes later daddy came running up the stairs and in to my room. He made me change out of my Santa suit and he took my Santa suit and he won't tell me where it's at! As if taking my Santa suit wasn't bad enough, he made me come back downstairs after I had changed to apologize to his friend. Daddy sent me to my room and he told me I had to stay there the rest of the day. I knew daddy was really, really mad at me and I was really mad at him so I stayed in my room. When his friend was leaving, I heard him teasing daddy about me and my Santa suit.

Daddy came into my room and told me I was going to be in big trouble when you got home because I had embarrassed him at the hardware store and in front of his friend from work. I was super....really super mad at my day with daddy. I spent the rest of the day in my room until I overheard daddy talking to you on the phone. Then I knew you were going to be home real soon so I spent the rest of my time sitting out on the steps in the garage."

"Wow," was all I could manage to say after listening to my son's version of events of his 'guy's only day' with his daddy. I had so wanted both Nicholas and Garrett to have a great day together, which obviously hadn't happened. I grabbed Nicholas, tightly hugging him for a few minutes. Finally, I looked down at my watch and realized I better get ready to go out to dinner with Garrett because the sitter was going to be there very shortly.

"Okay Nicholas," I said. I paused as I looked at him for a moment before I continued, "Look at me, please look at your Mimi. I will fix everything. At least I will try my very, very best to fix as much as I can. But I need you to have a fun night with sissy and Sara. You and sissy love it so much whenever Sara gets to watch the two of you. So please.... pretty please don't you worry about a thing. Okay?"

Nicholas looked into my eyes for a moment as if he was able to read all of my thoughts. "Okay Mimi, I will have a fun night with sissy and Sara and I will try my best to not worry about anything."

I was definitely happy Nicholas was so willing to have a good night tonight. "Thank you Nicholas."

As I opened Nicholas's bedroom door, I heard someone on the other side of the door trying to move away real quickly but not quick enough for me to not see who it was. I think she had probably been outside of the door the majority of the time. At first, I started to get a little upset Holly had eavesdropped on a personal conversation I had been having with her brother. But on second thought, I was kind of glad she had eavesdropped because then she was already up to speed on what was currently going on in our immediate family. But I did feel the need to go into her room to discuss that with her.

I didn't even have a chance to say a word before Holly started pleading her case. "I am so sorry mom. No....okay....I'm not sorry. I was listening to almost....well....most of....okay all of your conversation. It's just that....well it's just....I try to be very careful with my brother now. I believe....yes I am a believer....I've seen my brother in action as the new real Santa Claus. I just don't want him to be hurt by anyone. Bro, bro is just so sweet. He is always nice to everyone....and I never want him to get hurt. So yes that is why I felt the extremely urgent need to be on the other side of his bedroom door eavesdropping."

I was a bit taken back by her strong support of her brother. Like Nicholas, I felt this was a moment when I needed to pause and take a long deep breath in before responding, so I did. "Holly I was just going to tell you it was okay you were eavesdropping on the conversation between Nicholas and me. I completely understand why you were eavesdropping. And yes it is very important to keep you in the loop about what is happening in our family. But I do have to say, I truly appreciate the over the top support you have for your brother. Please don't get mad at your daddy though. We need to all understand it's taking your daddy a bit longer than the rest of us to become a true 'believer' that your brother Nicholas is the new real Santa Claus. We also have to realize maybe daddy has never really truly believed in Santa Claus. But don't worry Holly your daddy will come around. I just know he will. So you, Nicholas and I must continue to have our positive attitudes about everything. Your daddy will see the truth, I just know he will. I do know you're aware your daddy and I are going to be going out to dinner tonight and since you heard the entire conversation I had with your brother, the same applies to you. I need you to get along with your brother and have a fun night with Sara. Okay?"

Holly eagerly replied, "Of course okay mom. We will have a blast so don't worry. And mom I will try my best to get Nicholas to think about something other than his awful day with daddy. So don't worry, just go out and have a fun night with daddy."

I kissed Holly on the top of her forehead before walking out of her room. Each day I continue to be so proud of how well Holly has been handling the fact her brother is the new real Santa Claus. I'm sure it hasn't been entirely easy for her but she has done a phenomenal job. Holly has such a high level of never ending support of her brother now. I have also appreciated the fact, Holly is no longer so self absorbed. She realizes the world doesn't completely revolve around her and how special her brother is as well.

Suddenly, I heard a knock at the front door so I quickly ran into my room to get dressed and ready for dinner. I heard Holly and Nicholas running down the stairs to answer the front door. I was really hoping Garrett was downstairs as well so the kids wouldn't open the door if it wasn't Sara. I was relieved when I heard Sara, Holly, Nicholas and Garrett all downstairs talking to each other. I threw my clothes on and fixed my hair as quickly as possible.

As I started walking down the stairs, there was my little Nicholas at the bottom waiting for me with a compliment, "Wow Mimi you look beautiful!"

I quickly hugged my fabulous son and whispered into his ear, "Thanks Santa," then I kissed his cheek.

Seeing Garrett was ready to go I asked, "Honey did you call for the pizza delivery?"

Garrett was obviously feeling at least a little bit better because he grabbed me and hugged me before he replied, "Yes, all done. The pizza should be here any moment."

Just then the doorbell rang and of course it was the pizza delivery man. Garrett paid the delivery man as I took the pizza into the kitchen. We both kissed the kids and told them goodnight. I had also told Sara, since it was a Saturday night the kids could stay up until we got home so she wouldn't have to worry about putting them both to bed. Holly and Nicholas squealed when they heard they could stay up. However, I knew they would more than likely both be crashed out on the couch or the floor by the time we got home.

On the way to the restaurant, Garrett and I tried making casual conversation together, which to say the least was a bit odd. Usually we talk about everything. Garrett and I have always had such a connection with our thoughts, we seem to know what each other is thinking without having to say a word. But I really didn't want to start an intense conversation about our son in the ten minutes it would take us to get to the restaurant. The much needed conversation about our son was without a doubt going to be a nice or maybe not so nice conversation, which would definitely take longer than ten minutes to complete.

I was so excited though when Garrett had told me which restaurant we would be going to. Garrett knows I absolutely love the food at *The Bistro* and he also knows they have the best wine selection in town. I still don't know how he was able to get a reservation on such short notice though. I didn't ask him because I was happy he had been able to get the reservation for the two of us. Truthfully, I really didn't care how he had been able to get the reservation, only that he had gotten it.

I was also happy we were going to *The Bistro* because it's an upscale and quiet restaurant so I knew we would be able to have a nice long conversation about our little son Nicholas. I became more excited when we finally drove into the parking lot of the restaurant and Garrett handed the keys to our car to the valet.

Garrett came around to my side of the car, opened my door and helped me out. Usually I don't let him open my car door and I always tell him I'm a big girl. I guess the strong and independent female side of me doesn't like to think I can't open the door for myself. Garrett and I use to have a great debate about the whole opening the door for a woman thing, until he finally graciously gave up about it. He respects my preference of opening the door for myself. However, I do have to say even after sixteen years of being married, he still always asks me if I would like him to open the door for me. I guess he was feeling the extreme need tonight to go ahead and open the door for me without asking, which was fine by me.

When we checked in inside *The Bistro*, I was happy they took us back to the second room which was always extra quiet. I didn't want to be seated too closely to any nosy people. I wanted to have an intimate conversation and dinner with only Garrett.

I knew after the waitress brought us our wine, it would definitely be time to begin our in depth conversation about the 'guy's only day' and about our son Nicholas as the new real Santa Claus. Since I had already heard Nicholas's version of the day's events, I thought it was only fair to listen to Garrett's version of the day's events before I came to any conclusions.

I had the distinct feeling Garrett really didn't want to even bring up the events of the day so I had to initiate the conversation. "Okay honey I understand you had a very difficult day to say the least but I have heard Nicholas's side of the story and now I need you to tell me your side of the story."

Garrett started off and his version of the story varied a little. He claimed he had been embarrassed by the mean old man by the nails. He even admitted to not saying anything to the mean man because he really didn't know what to say. Garrett claimed he was trying his hardest to grab the nails he needed and to get out of there. Garrett also admitted he refused to paint the backyard patio Santa Claus red.

He stated, "Santa Claus red are you kidding me? It was the brightest and just about the worse color ever. And no, we will never have any part of our house painted Santa Claus red."

I simply replied, "One should never say never."

Garrett shook his head as he continued on with his story, which continued to stay pretty similar to Nicholas's version of events. The next discrepancy came though in the description of the paint man.

Garrett stated, "It really wasn't that bad. The paint guy just didn't understand why Nicholas was wearing a Santa suit in the spring time."

Of course the next discrepancy came in the description of the clerk. Garrett claimed, "I just disregarded what the clerk was saying and I wasn't even acknowledging her."

Garrett did admit to demanding Nicholas go inside and change out of his Santa suit as well as to the fact he was very embarrassed Nicholas had come outside in his Santa suit and told his friend he was on the naughty list. Well, I have to admit, I sat there for a moment trying to digest once again the series of events my son and my husband had experienced on this day.

I drank a nice large sip of my red wine before I finally responded, "Okay honey what it sounds like to me is that you're embarrassed your son is the new real Santa Claus and tha-..."

I found Garrett rudely interrupting me before I even had the opportunity to finish my initial voicing of my opinion of the days' events. "Okay, I think I have been more than a little patient with our son believing he is the new real Santa Claus. I don't really care how often he wears his Santa suit around the house or how often he wears the Santa suit during Christmas time. But we seriously can't let him wear his Santa suit out and about all year long. I want my son to be 'normal' and I...."

Okay now it was definitely my turn to rudely interrupt Garrett because I was seriously getting more than a bit frustrated with him. "Okay, first of all we need to be on the same page. This is about our son. This is not and I stress the word NOT about what I want and this is NOT about what you want. This is only about what our son wants. And by the way yes...yes....our son is not normal and neither is our daughter. No they are both extraordinary children we both love very much. I think you first need to look at yourself to find out why you want a 'normal' child! Why the hell would you want to put one of our children in a 'box' of standards created by the world. We were wrong when we did that with Holly and when our little Nicholas became the new real Santa Claus, I chose to let Holly come out of the 'box' of standards, which have been set by the world. I truly had thought we both agreed upon that decision together. But obviously I was the only one who let Holly out of the 'box'. And now here you are trying to put both of our extraordinary children back into the 'box' of standards set by the world. Haven't you noticed our children are both so much happier since we let them be themselves without trying to make them the people we expect them to be?"

I had said my peace at least so far so I decided to let Garrett continue. I assumed by throwing in my opinion mid stream to him, he would have a change of heart as to how he was talking about our extraordinary children.

Garrett quickly began, "Okay sweetheart, yes I do know we have extraordinary children. It's just I don't understand the whole Santa Claus thing. I have tried....I really have tried to understand but I can't....I just can't seem to understand why our son thinks he is the....the new real Santa Claus. Just like I don't understand why Nicholas insists on playing *Jingle Bell Rock* and all of the other Christmas songs year round. And I guess, I never know what to say back to people when they make comments about Nicholas when he has his Santa suit on."

The waitress came to our table just in time to take our order. I guess the waitress had good timing. At least Garrett and I had an opportunity to have a little breather and to take a little break from our intense conversation about our children. Luckily, since *The Bistro* is our favorite restaurant and also since Garrett and I are creatures of habit, we knew right away what we were ordering. The waitress took our orders, refilled both of our wine glasses and left Garrett and me alone once again.

As soon as the waitress had left our table and was out of earshot distance, I decided to be the one to continue our discussion. "Honey, I totally understand how you feel. I do understand it's not the easiest thing to have a son who is the new real Santa Claus. I believe and I am proud to be a Santa Claus 'believer'. Everyday I wake up feeling as if I am the luckiest person in the world because I was chosen to be the Mimi of Santa Claus. I use to question why and how I could be the Mimi of Santa Claus. But I don't anymore. I have chosen to gladly and graciously accept my role as the Mimi of Santa Claus. You have to embrace your new role and love your new role as the daddy of Santa Claus. You are so very right that some people don't understand. But that's okay. Make it their loss and not your loss. I see people all around us and all over the world every day that aren't happy. But I never want to be unhappy like them. I never told you but I had a strange epiphany the day our little Nicholas became the new real Santa Claus. My epiphany was that I wanted to live a fabulous life. Not just sometimes, no, I wanted to start living a fabulous life every day of my life. So I do....I do live an absolutely fabulous life with you and the kids. I know and I understand you may not understand my positive thinking and my fabulous thinking. I just need you to see how great it has been with the kids. I help them to ignore the negative thoughts of others and to try their best to only surround themselves with positive people. But I do need you....actually....Holly, Nicholas and I all need you to be on board with the fabulous life and positivism. I understand you may not be able to do it overnight like I did. But I...we need you to be on board in the same positive ship we are on and not to think we are all absolutely crazy."

    I wasn't really sure how Garrett was going to respond or even if he was going to respond. We sat there in silence for awhile drinking our wine. I was happy to say in the least, the waitress finally appeared with our dinner. The waitress left our table after delivering our eloquently prepared meal and once again refilling our wine glasses.

However, the silence between Garrett and I continued. I wanted to say something….I really did want to say something….anything to break the dead silence presently at our table. But I unfortunately for once in my life didn't know what exactly to say to him. At first, I felt like saying forget it, I won't ever let Nicholas put his Santa suit on again and agree to put our kids in the 'box' of standards set by the world around us. But I knew that would be the worst thing to say because I would be so very unhappy, living a life like that. I also knew living a life like that would be the furthest thing from living the fully fabulous life I so desire. I love my fabulous life and I want Garrett to want a fabulous life as well.

We ended up eating about half of our dinner before Garrett finally put his fork down to respond to my earlier statements. "I….I….just don't know how to live a fabulous life everyday. I do see you and the kids living a fabulous life everyday. Truthfully, I guess I am a bit jealous by how well you deal with having our son as the new real Santa Claus. I don't know how to accept our son as the new real Santa Claus. Did Nicholas tell you I took his Santa suit away from him and hid it?"

I quietly replied, "Yes, Nicholas told me you took his Santa suit away from him. Honey haven't you ever noticed how the Santa suit still fits him as perfectly as the day we bought it for him. I have given pants and shirts away he has grown out of but for some reason he hasn't grown out of his Santa suit. Haven't you ever wondered why his Santa suit still fits him so well?"

Garrett looked at me for a moment and then continued, "I want to live a fabulous life with you, Holly and Nicholas but I need your help. I don't understand the whole positive thinking thing. The thing is....well....I find it very hard when Nicholas wears his Santa suit all year round. He is going to be testing soon for school so he can get into the same private school as Holly. I don't think....well actually I pretty much know the school and the parents there will not want a child attending the school who thinks he is the new real Santa Claus. I think it is very important for Nicholas to attend the school because of its academics and because of its activities. Plus it's the only private school in the area."

Great, I thought to myself. I really hadn't thought of next school year yet. I did know Garrett was right about the Santa suit in relation to the school. Now I needed to think about how I could help my little Nicholas to incorporate his Santa suit and being the new real Santa Claus in with Elementary school.

I quietly answered, "Honey, I really haven't even begun to think about school next year for Nicholas. But now since you mentioned it, I think we did get a paper in the mail to schedule his testing date for admission. How about this, I will agree to try my very best at finding a solution on how to incorporate Nicholas's Santa suit in with Elementary school. And could you agree to try to do your best in supporting our son as the new real Santa Claus?"

Without hesitation Garrett responded, "Agreed. But I am not ready to give Nicholas back his Santa suit."

Wow, how do I respond back to no Santa suit for Nicholas? I can't agree to 'no' Santa suit. Nicholas needs his Santa suit. I will feel like a big failure to Nicholas if I don't get his suit back.

I sternly replied, "No, that will not work. Nicholas needs his Santa suit. I can't go back home and tell him he is not getting his Santa suit back."

Once again without hesitation Garrett responded, "Well the Santa suit is hidden and fortunately for me, I am the only one who knows where it is hidden. I need a little more time to get use to Nicholas being the new real Santa Claus."

I didn't want to be too irrational and I definitely wanted to make sure I maintained a positive attitude so once again I took a long deep breath in before I replied, "Fine, you can keep the Santa suit hidden. But only as long as you agree to start living only for the positive and to try your very best to start ignoring the negativity in life. You also have to agree to try to believe Nicholas is the new real Santa Claus."

I knew I had put a lot out there on the table for Garrett to agree to. He definitely was taking a bit more than a moment to respond. "Okay, I agree. But I will need all three of you to help me."

I was about a hundred and ten percent positive Holly and Nicholas would agree to help their daddy in a positive way. I also knew I wanted to help Garrett as well so I quickly agreed.

The rest of dinner became much more relaxed and enjoyable. Garrett and I even indulged in our favorite chocolate dessert when we had finished our dinner and wine. Our drive home after dinner was more enjoyable and comfortable as well. We even listened to *Jingle Bell Rock* all the way home. Sure enough when we got home, Holly was sound asleep on the floor in her bean bag and Nicholas was sound asleep on the couch.

Garrett and I looked at the kids and in unison said, "Thank you Sara."

I couldn't help but say, "Okay that was a little weird."

Garrett looked at me and smiled as he asked, "Well I guess that's what you get after 16 years, right?" Then he kissed me on my ear.

I really didn't want to make our great babysitter Sara uncomfortable. I opened my purse to get some money out to pay her as I walked her to the door. "Thanks again Sara, we really appreciate you watching the kids on such short notice."

Sara cheerfully replied, "No problem. The kids are always great. Plus, I really needed some extra spending money for next week so this worked out perfect for me too."

After Sara left I carried my little Nicholas up and put him to bed while Garrett carried Holly up to her bed. We each kissed our extraordinary children goodnight, a perfect end to a not so perfect day.

CHAPTER 11

Garrett had already left for work when it was time to wake the kids up for school. I always try to wake up Holly first because she takes the longest to actually get out of bed.

I went into Holly's room and loudly said, "Wake up....wake up....it's time to get ready for school. You don't want your brother to beat you in getting dressed do you?" Usually if I throw the competition comment in for Holly, it tends to make her get out of her bed as soon as she hears her brother get out of his bed. Holly loves to win and so she does get dressed quite quickly to try and beat her brother. But without the competition comment, it takes Holly two to three times longer to get dressed.

Next, I went to wake up my little Nicholas. I was about to tell him to wake up when I saw his Santa suit sitting on the bed. I smiled to myself and I thought his dad must have decided to give him back the Santa suit already. I stood next to my sleeping Nicholas so I could wake him up and show him his daddy had left the Santa suit on the bed for him.

I bent down and whispered in his ear, "Nicholas....Nicholas sweetheart....wake up....you need to see what your daddy left for you on your bed."

The thought of a present made Nicholas sit right up in his bed. He looked around before asking, "What Mimi....what did daddy leave for me?"

At first I thought Nicholas must have something wrong with his eyes. Was he all of a sudden color blind? Did he not see his bright red Santa suit setting on his bed?

I looked at Nicholas intensely as I asked, "Nicholas, are you okay? Can you see okay? Is there anything blurry in here?"

From the way Nicholas was staring at me, I could obviously tell, I was the one who appeared to have the problem this morning. Nicholas continued staring at me until he finally asked, "Mimi what are you talking about? I feel just fine Mimi and I can see just fine too. Are you okay Mimi?"

I was so excited Garrett had given Nicholas back his Santa suit so I quickly replied, "Yes of course I am fine Nicholas. I am just really excited to see daddy gave you back your Santa suit. Daddy must have put your Santa suit on your bed this morning before he left for work. Aren't you happy about your Santa suit Nicholas?

Once again Nicholas looked at me a bit strangely before replying, "Mimi, daddy didn't give me back my Santa suit."

Okay I'm not stupid. I knew I was holding my son's Santa suit Garrett had taken away and hidden. I didn't understand what Nicholas was talking about. I had to ask, "Nicholas this is your Santa suit daddy took away from you and hid, right? How else would it be lying on your bed if daddy didn't put it there?"

Much to my surprise Nicholas quickly responded, "Mimi daddy didn't put it there. The elves saw where daddy hid my Santa suit. So when Jack came to get me last night, he found my Santa suit and gave it back to me."

Nicholas told me about elves watching us and Jack the elf sneaking around our house to get the hidden Santa suit like it was something, which happened every day. I was pretty sure my mouth fell open as Nicholas was telling me all of this. I simply didn't know quite how to respond about an elf walking around our house as we slept peacefully through the night. I decided to leave the wandering elf issue alone. All of a sudden it dawned on me that my son was at the North Pole last night. Why had he been at the North Pole? It was only spring time. It's not even anywhere near Christmas time yet.

I calmly asked, "Nicholas sweetheart, were you at the North Pole last night?"

Nicholas quickly replied, "Yes Mimi, I was at the North Pole last night. I am not there all of the time and there are a lot of important duties I have at the North Pole since I am the new real Santa Claus."

I was suddenly very curious so I asked, "Nicholas what did you get to do at the North Pole last night?"

Once again Nicholas quickly replied, "Well first of all Jack had me put my Santa suit on. I do have to say Jack was very proud of himself when he found out where daddy had hid my Santa suit. The elves were all very upset with daddy because he hid my Santa suit from me, especially Jack. The elves didn't want me to come back to my house here. They all wanted me to stay at the North Pole with them. But I convinced the elves I needed to come back to my own home. I also told the elves my daddy was going to be trying very, very hard to be a believer."

I was shocked. Not because Nicholas had gone to the North Pole last night but that the elves had wanted him to stay at the North Pole. I had to tell Nicholas, "No Nicholas, you have to tell the elves you live here. I am your Mimi so you have to live with me. Nicholas I need you to please….please promise me you will always come home from the North Pole to your Mimi. I just….we just couldn't live without you. We need you here. So please promise….I need you to promise me right now. And I need you to really mean your promise to me that you will always come home from the North Pole to me, your Mimi."

Nicholas looked at me square in the eyes as he replied, "Mimi I will always come home from the North Pole to you. I love you too Mimi and I couldn't live without you either. So please don't worry about me not coming home because I promise….I super duper promise….and I pinky swear, I will always come home to you Mimi. Okay?"

Well I did feel a little better after Nicholas promised he would always come home to me so I replied, "Okay." And he gave me a great big hug, which made me feel a whole lot better.

I calmly told Nicholas, "Come on get out of bed. I think I already hear your sissy getting dressed. You don't want your sissy to beat you, do you?"

Luckily the whole competition thing worked for Nicholas as well. So he jumped out of bed and started getting dressed right away. Holly came running into the room as Nicholas finished putting his last shoe on.

So I had to call it, "Tie, it's a tie. You both finished at the same time. I guess you will have to each try a little harder next time if you want to win."

Out of the corner of my eye, I saw Nicholas grab his Santa suit and go running down the stairs. I wasn't sure what his plans were for his Santa suit. At first I thought maybe Nicholas was taking his Santa suit to put it somewhere secret for safe keeping. But as I got downstairs, I caught him stuffing his Santa suit into his back pack.

I quickly screamed, "No," to get his attention.

Nicholas about jumped out of his skin. I didn't mean to scare him so bad. I only wanted to get his attention so he knew I was watching him stick his Santa suit into his back pack.

Nicholas quickly began to defend his actions, "Mimi, I am just going to share my Santa suit....that's it....just share my Santa suit."

I knew it was only Monday so I had to clarify, "Nicholas you do realize it's only Monday, right? Isn't share day on Friday?"

Nicholas was obviously all prepared for questions from me because he quickly replied, "Well Mimi....okay....yes, share day is on Friday but I won't play with it. Besides Mimi, the rule at preschool is that we aren't supposed to bring any toys to school except for on share days on Friday's. But really Mimi is a Santa suit really a toy? I think not. So I know taking my Santa suit to preschool would be just fine."

I was amazed by my little Nicholas's excellent reasoning skills and I did have to agree with him. The rule at preschool is to not bring toys to school but Nicholas was right, there was no mention of a Santa suit. Plus a Santa suit did not qualify as a toy. So I decided I would make a deal with my little Nicholas. "Okay Nicholas I will let you take your Santa suit to school today but you can't put it on. You need to leave it in your bag. Okay?"

Hesitantly Nicholas replied, "Okay fine Mimi, I will leave it in my back pack at school."

The kids finished eating breakfast before we loaded up into the car so I could drop them off at school. I had remembered to grab the paper with the information on it to schedule the admission testing and interview for Nicholas at Holly's private school. Nicholas is very intelligent so I knew he would have no problem with the admission test. My only concern was the interview portion. But I was pretty confident if I told Nicholas to not mention the fact that he is the new real Santa Claus then he wouldn't mention it.

I dropped Holly off at school first and of course Nicholas had to tell her, "Don't trip and fall sissy."

Even though my little Nicholas and Holly were getting along so well lately, I could tell it bugged Holly a bit when her brother says it every day.

Holly graciously smiled though and told Nicholas and I, "Goodbye."

On the way to drop Nicholas off at preschool, I reminded Nicholas of our agreement to keep his Santa suit inside his back pack on the way to school as well as when I walked him into school and signed him in. After dropping off Nicholas, I went to work to start my fabulous day.

I had been busy at work so I was lucky to have made time at my lunch to call and schedule the appointment for the admission test as well as for the admission interview. I really had been expecting to have Nicholas scheduled for those sometime during the summer. But I guess I failed to realize all admissions to Valley View Academy, the school where Holly attends, were to be completed prior to the end of the existing school year.

They scheduled Nicholas for both his admission test and his admission interview on the same day, which I guess was fine. At least he would be done with both on the same day. The only part I was nervous about was the fact they were scheduled for the upcoming Friday. I was a bit nervous because Friday was only four days away. I wanted to be relaxed by the time I discussed the test and interview with Nicholas. Therefore, I was still debating when I should tell him about the testing.

He already knew he was going to have an admission interview and an admission test so he could attend school at the same school as his sissy. However, he didn't know it was going to be so soon. But of course I hadn't known either until today. I had every bit of confidence in my son though. I knew he would do a fabulous job in the interview and the school staff would absolutely adore him.

Later that afternoon, I was running a bit late to pick up Nicholas because the traffic had been so bad and just plain out of control at Holly's school when I went to pick her up. As soon as I parked, Holly and I jumped out of the car and rushed into the preschool to get little Nicholas. He is usually very conscious about the time and he knows exactly what time I usually pick him up by. I went and signed him out before we went to look for him. Obviously today was not one of those days he was watching the time or else he would have already been out of his Santa suit by the time we arrived. It had been so hot outside today and there sat Nicholas dressed in his Santa suit, playing in the sand box.

I went right over to Nicholas and asked, "Sir, what do you think you are doing?"

Nicholas quickly replied, "Oh Mimi I....I....well I thought it would be okay to wear my Santa suit in the sandbox."

By the look on my face, my little Nicholas knew it wasn't okay. Of course Ms. Carrie had to come over and talk to me about the Santa suit. "Oh, I wanted to let you know Nicholas put his Santa costume on…."

Okay I had already previously corrected Ms. Carrie so I felt the need to once again correct her. I exclaimed, "Oh you mean his Santa suit."

Ms. Carrie finished what she was saying, "Well yes his um….his Santa suit. Nicholas put his Santa suit on right after you left this morning."

I really didn't want Ms. Carrie to think or even have an inkling that Nicholas was actually in big trouble with me so I replied, "Oh that's okay. I let him bring it to school today so he could wear it if he needed to." Then I smiled, grabbed Nicholas's hand and we walked away.

I think at this point as we were walking out to the car, Nicholas was assuming he had gotten out of trouble because of what I had said to Ms. Carrie. Little did my Nicholas know being the new real Santa Claus absolutely does not get him out of trouble. He is still required to obey his parents no matter what. And I had explicitly told him, he was to leave his Santa suit in his back pack. So yes, he was going to get into at least a little trouble for wearing the Santa suit all day at school.

But as soon as we got into the car, Nicholas spoke first. "Mimi, I am so sorry but I just had to wear my Santa suit. I couldn't help it. I am so sorry I didn't obey you Mimi."

I sternly responded, "Thank you for acknowledging the fact you disobeyed your Mimi. Also thank you for apologizing to Mimi for disobeying as well. But your Santa suit is now taken away for one week. I am not going to tell daddy Jack found where he had hid your Santa suit. In fact, I am not even going to tell your daddy you disobeyed your Mimi today by wearing your Santa suit at preschool. In one week, when you get your Santa suit back from Mimi we aren't going to tell daddy you even have your Santa suit. And you are only allowed to wear your Santa suit when daddy is NOT around. Understood?"

Nicholas quickly replied, "Understood Mimi. Thank you Mimi."

Obviously Nicholas realized he was in trouble for disobeying me. But I knew he also realized he was being rewarded for Jack finding his Santa suit where daddy had hid it. I really hadn't agreed with Garrett not giving Nicholas back his Santa suit. When I saw the Santa suit on Nicholas's bed this morning I had truly hoped it was Garrett who had given it back. But it wasn't.

CHAPTER 12

Jack the head elf had once again come through the porthole in Nicholas's room to take Nicholas back to the North Pole so Nicholas could complete a few more of his Santa duties. Jack had decided not to wake up Nicholas this time. So he picked up Nicholas in his arms and carried him through the porthole and back to the North Pole. Nicholas must have been very tired because the next time he woke up, he was in his Santa Claus house and in his Santa Claus bed at the North Pole. Nicholas woke up to the smell of bacon cooking and hot chocolate being made. He was a bit startled to find out he was at the North Pole again. He was especially surprised to see his Santa suit hanging on the coat rack in his Santa Claus room at the North Pole.

Nicholas wiped his eyes as he quickly jumped out of bed to go and find Jack. "Jack, Jack….are you here Jack?" As Nicholas made his way to the kitchen he saw it was Jack who was making him breakfast.

As soon as Jack saw Nicholas, he greeted him. "Good Morning Santa. Did you sleep well? I sure hope you did because we have a very busy day today."

Nicholas quickly asked, "Wait Jack, won't my parents wonder where I am at today?"

Jack looked at Nicholas for a moment before replying, "Well Santa we have you for one full day only. We did a little bit of magic like we do on Christmas Eve. But the magic only lengthens the night where you live by one full day. So it is very….and I mean very important for you to complete the entire list of chores I have for you today."

Nicholas eagerly asked, "Do I get to see and play with the reindeers today? Will I get to see all of the other elves? Will I get to play with the other elves too?"

Jack was a bit taken a back as to how eager Nicholas was. "Okay, okay Santa we will try to make time for all of that. I do think you will find our list of chores that we will be doing together quite fun. At least I hope you will find them fun."

Nicholas still a bit too eager replied, "Of course they will be fun Jack. We always have fun together Jack, right? You do have fun with me too don't you?"

Jack calmly replied, "Yes of course we always have fun together Santa. I do have to say I find it nice that you are so young and like to have fun. So let's hurry up and eat so we can start our day together."

Jack and Nicholas enjoyed good conversation during their breakfast together and as soon as they were done eating breakfast, Nicholas went into his Santa Claus room to put his Santa suit on. Then they were off to visit the reindeers first.

As soon as they arrived at the reindeer stables Jack took the list of chores out of his pocket. "Okay Santa your first chore is to play with the reindeers."

Nicholas smiled. "That's it? Just play with the reindeers? How is playing a chore? I love playing with the reindeers!"

Jack smiled as he answered, "Well Santa I am really happy you like playing with the reindeers so much. But besides playing with the reindeers you need to watch them do their workout and their practice. You need to make sure they are all trying their best and doing a good, no exceptional job."

Nicholas replied, "That sounds fun."

Nicholas ran to the reindeers and let each of them out of their own stable in the barn. Nicholas truly loved all of the reindeers. He went and got their food out to feed all of them. Then he took all the reindeers to the practice area. He ran and played with all of them and he made sure they were all doing an exceptional job. Nicholas did notice all of the reindeers were doing quite well. Well, all of the reindeers except for Vixen, were doing quite well with their take offs and their landings. Vixen however wasn't even able to take off at all. Finally, Nicholas decided he needed to find out what was wrong with him.

Nicholas called out, "Vixen, come over here Vixen."

Vixen came right over to Nicholas. Nicholas looked Vixen over twice through but he still couldn't figure out what was wrong with him. Nicholas said, "Vixen what's wrong? Are you hurt?"

Vixen held up his left leg. So Nicholas went over to examine it. Sure enough there was a nail stuck in the bottom of Vixen's foot. Nicholas was a little bit annoyed at first that nobody had noticed Vixen was hurt. But he was happy he was the one who had figured it out. Nicholas had Vixen lay down on a bed of straw as he grabbed the reindeer medical kit. Nicholas put a little bit of topical anesthetic around the nail in Vixen's foot and then he removed the nail. Nicholas wrapped up Vixen's hoof and helped him back to his stall to rest. Nicholas told Vixen there would be no practicing for the rest of the week so his hoof would be able to heal properly.

Just then Jack reappeared and asked, "Santa, are you all done with the reindeers?"

Nicholas replied, "Yes Jack, I am all done with the reindeers for now. But I do want you to know Vixen had a nail in his hoof. But don't worry, I removed it and I told Vixen he needed to stay off of his hoof for about a week. So Jack, I will need to either be back here in a week to check on Vixen or else I need you or another elf to check on Vixen in a week. Otherwise, all of the reindeers are doing very well."

Jack looked at Nicholas, thinking for a moment before he replied, "Okay Santa I am still going to have to think about that because I am a bit unsure right now if I can bring you back to the North Pole in a week or not. But don't worry about it, I will figure it out later. Right now I need you to complete your chore list."

Nicholas excitedly asked, "Okay Jack what's next on the list that I get to do?"

Jack took the list out of his pocket and took his time reviewing before replying, "Well Santa it looks as if the elves are next on the list. So let's...."

Nicholas abruptly interrupted Jack and asked, "The elves? What chore do I have with the elves? Is it already time to review the naughty and nice list this year?"

Jack patiently waited until Nicholas had finished before he replied, "Santa we have a lot of very important items to complete on this chore list. So you need to listen carefully to my instructions and not interrupt me. Okay?"

Nicholas quickly answered, "Sorry Jack, it's just I am so excited. But Jack, I promise I will listen and try my very best to complete everything on my chore list."

Jack cracked a smile as he replied, "So Sorry Santa, I am not trying to be strict with you. But it's my job to help you finish this list. So thank you Santa for understanding. Enough of that though, let's get on with our list. Like I said Santa you will be with the elves next. So come on let's go and I will tell you on the way what you will be doing with the elves today."

Nicholas told each and every one of the reindeer's goodbye and asked Donner to keep a close eye on Vixen while he was gone. After all of the goodbyes were done Jack and Nicholas left the reindeers and headed off to see the elves. Nicholas was a bit sad to leave his reindeer friends because he loved each and every reindeer so very much. Nicholas continued to look back and wave goodbye to the reindeers until he could no longer see them anymore. Jack knew little Nicholas never liked leaving the reindeers. So he was very patient with Nicholas and his long goodbye to the reindeers.

As soon as Nicholas was done with his reindeer goodbye Jack began to brief Nicholas on his next chore with the elves. "Okay Santa now we are going to see the elves at the toy factory first. You need to check the quality of the toys the elves have been making. You get to check the quality of the toys at the factory by playing with them. If any of the toys break then you need to go to Feldman the head elf at the toy factory. You take him the broken toy and he takes care of fixing the reason why the toy broke. Do you have any questions Santa?"

Nicholas smiled that huge smile of his before replying, "Nope, I don't have any questions. It sounds like it will be super cool to go play with toys. I never get a fun chore like that at home. My chores at home are actual work not fun stuff like playing with reindeer and playing with toys."

Jack sternly replied, "Santa your chores on my list are very serious too. I am very happy you have so much fun doing the chores I give you. But you need to understand they are very serious chores. We must make sure all of the toys you take to the children all over the world are safe enough for them. We don't want any child getting hurt from one of our toys made here at our toy factory."

Nicholas stood up straight quickly replying, "Oh I know Jack....I know the chores....well all of the chores you are giving me are very serious. I promise I will be very serious about each chore. I....well I guess I am just happy your chores for me are so much fun."

Jack cracked a smile on his little elf face before responding, "Okay Santa, I guess I am pretty happy you have been having so much fun with all of the chores I am giving you. We just have to make sure we concentrate on each of the chores as we go down the list. I have a limited amount of time with you and I want to make sure we use our time together efficiently, deal?"

Of course Nicholas was excited he had made Jack happy but even more excited he had actually cracked a smile on Jack's sometimes, way too business like face. Looking at Jack, Nicholas couldn't help but smile before responding, "Deal!"

Nicholas was enjoying the walk to the toy factory but he began to wonder how much further away the toy factory was. Nicholas was about to ask Jack how much longer they were going to have to walk when all of a sudden Jack said, "Here we are Santa."

Nicholas looked up and gazed at the enormous entrance at the front of the toy factory. He thought for a moment to himself as he looked at the huge candy canes and gum drops at the entrance of the toy factory and he wondered why he couldn't remember this entrance to the toy factory. Nicholas knew he had been to the toy factory before but for some reason he couldn't remember this entrance.

Jack must have noticed the confusion and wonderment on the face of little Nicholas because he quickly attempted to clear up any of the confusion. "Don't worry Santa you have never seen this entrance to the toy factory before. Usually I take you to the toy factory through your secret entrance from your house. This entrance though is the main entrance the elves usually use."

Nicholas breathed a sigh a relief as he replied, "Whew! I thought I was losin' it there for a minute Jack. I know I have been in the toy factory a lot of times before but I didn't remember this entrance. These candy canes are amazing!!!!!! I wish they were real though."

Jack looked at Nicholas as he smiled again, "Santa they are real, go ahead take a lick."

Nicholas looked at Jack a bit strangely. Nicholas knew his sissy was always teasing him and he had been trying really hard to not be so gullible lately. He thought for a moment and then he leaned forward and smelled the huge candy cane. Nicholas thought the huge candy cane smelled like the sweetest peppermint candy cane ever. So he thought maybe, just maybe it really was a real candy cane. Then all of a sudden before he could even stop himself Nicholas leaned over and licked the candy cane.

Nicholas straightened up as he loudly exclaimed, "Oh my goodness this is like the bestest candy cane ever! I thought you were just teasing me but you weren't. Can I have another lick Jack? Oh wait does everyone lick this candy cane?"

Jack looked at Nicholas and wondered to himself why Santa is always so quirky before replying, "Santa this is the North Pole and this is all yours, you are Santa Claus! Let's see....how can I put this? Ummmm, ok I know. Santa you are the king of the North Pole. Everything here is yours and all of the elves and I are just here to help you. So no, nobody else licks these candy canes. They are for you and you alone. If one of the elves wants a candy cane then they go and get their own."

Nicholas was in thought the entire time Jack was talking to him. But Nicholas does worry about germs and he wanted to be perfectly clear about the candy cane thing so Nicholas asked, "Okay well what if one of the elves were to say; sneak a lick of one of my candy canes?"

Jack quickly responded, "Santa you know there are elves watching children all of the time, right?"

Nicholas quickly answered, "Yes but who watches the elves?"

Jack shook his head as he responded back to little Nicholas, "Santa, Santa, Santa. Seriously! You deliver presents to the elves too. There are elves that are watching the elves too. I know I have showed you the elf surveillance department before."

Nicholas eagerly responded, "Yes Jack you have a few times but I didn't know they watch the other elves too! I thought they just watched....um....you know....regular people."

Jack couldn't help but laugh before he responded back to little Nicholas. "What Santa, did you think elves didn't have to behave to stay on the nice list? But Santa I do have to say you have the best elves. All of us think you are....umm....lets see how do I put this? Okay Santa all of us elves think you are the coolest! You are the best Santa ever! All of us elves here love that you are so much fun. So thanks Santa."

Nicholas smiled, threw his arms up into the air, loudly exclaiming, "Thank you Jack! Thank you for making it so fun to be here at the North Pole. I think....no I know I am the luckiest person in the world because I am Santa. I love coming to the North Pole, I love all of the elves, I love all of the reindeers and I do have to say I really love the hot chocolate here at the North Pole! I have never, ever, ever had better hot chocolate than here at the North Pole."

Jack smiled and responded, "Ok Santa we have a lot of work to do today so let's go on inside."

Nicholas smiled and followed closely behind Jack. Even though Nicholas had already been to the North Pole numerous times, he was still in awe of everything here at the North Pole especially the toy factory. Nicholas had never ever seen so many toys in his entire life and he loved all of the toys the elves make. In fact he remembered how hard it had been last Christmas when he was forced to make the critical decision of what to ask the elves to make for his Christmas presents. Nicholas remembered the elves finally had to give him a deadline to put in his present requests and Jack had visited Nicholas the night of the 'present deadline' so he could be sure to deliver the list on time to the elves at the toy factory. Little Nicholas was so deep in thought about Jack and the toy factory until all of a sudden his thoughts were abruptly interrupted.

"It's Santa! It's Santa! Look everyone its Santa!" Isabella the elf had spotted little Nicholas from all the way across the toy factory and was screaming his name as she ran towards him.

Nicholas had met Isabella on his very first trip to the North Pole and for some reason she had almost immediately became Nicholas's favorite elf. To Nicholas she seems as if she is the smallest but most inspirational elf at the North Pole. There was something different about Isabella that Nicholas couldn't seem to put his finger on.

Isabella was running towards Santa as fast as she could but she felt like it was taking her for ever to reach him. As she approached Santa, she stretched her arms out all the way and gave him a nice big hug as soon as she reached him. She squeezed him so tightly, Nicholas felt as if he wasn't going to be able to breathe again.

When Isabella finally released Nicholas from her tight squeeze, he took a deep breath in and exclaimed,

"Isabella I've missed you! Do you think you can come around the North Pole with me today and do my chores with me?"

Both Nicholas and Isabella turned to look at Jack, asking in unison, "Please Jack, please can we do the chores together today?"

Jack paused for a few moments and Nicholas and Isabella were unsure as to what jack would say in response. A few moments seemed like an eternity as they waited for Jack to answer their very important question.

Jack looked at both of them with the usual serious look upon his face as he finally answered their question. "First of all, you both must understand there are a lot of important and I mean very important chores on my list for Santa to complete today. Therefore, you both must be able to focus on the chores at hand in order to complete all of them. I want you both to have fun with the chores but you have to be serious about actually completing them."

In unison, they loudly exclaimed, "Yes, yes, yes we will finish all of the chores we promise!"

Jack smiled as he responded, "Okay then, you may do the chores together today."

Once again in unison Nicholas and Isabella exclaimed, "Whew!"

Jack serious once again, stated, "Okay then, both of you come along we need to go to the room of completed toys."

Jack was quiet and walking so fast that Nicholas and Isabella were practically running so they could keep up with him. Nicholas knew Jack was in a hurry because he was a bit stressed Nicholas wouldn't finish all of the chores he had to complete today. But Nicholas truly loved Jack and wanted to make Jack happy. Nicholas also wanted so badly for Jack to know he was very serious about his job as the new real Santa Claus. Inside though, Nicholas had no doubts whatsoever he had would complete the chore list because he had already made the commitment to himself to finish every single chore on Jack's list.

Nicholas got tired of the quietness during the walk so he decided to break the silence by exclaiming, "Ok Jack, Isabella and I are so ready to go and play with all of the toys! Are we almost there?"

Jack sternly looked at Nicholas and replied, "Yes Santa, we are almost there. It is just up ahead and to the left."

Nicholas smiled and responded, "Thanks Jack," as he grabbed Isabella's arm and they skipped down the hallway after Jack.

The three of them had taken a left turn down the hallway but they quickly reached the end. Nicholas looked to his right and then to his left but he didn't see a door to any room. So he asked Jack, "Did you bring us the wrong way? There isn't a room this way Jack! Where are we going?"

Jack looked at Nicholas and exclaimed, "Slow down Santa! Haven't you realized yet there is magic here at the North Pole? Watch and see my little Santa Claus!"

Nicholas was a bit confused but he did know one thing, he did fully trust Jack so he waited and he watched. Then all of a sudden the hallway right in front of them opened up. Nicholas stood there in awe of what was now happening. What had seemed like a plain end of a hallway was now opening up to expose a huge toy room. Not just any toy room or even what one could call an ordinary room. No, it was a huge room with red walls, gold trim and a red and white checkered tile floor. There were so many toys that Nicholas began to feel a bit overwhelmed at first. But then before he could stop himself, he found himself running into the room with his hands up in the air.

Nicholas stopped running as he reached the center of the toy room, he spun in a circle in order to take in everything around him. But he quickly stopped as soon as he saw little Isabella just standing in the doorway.

Nicholas put his little hands up to his mouth as he screamed, "Isabella get your little elf self over here right now! For goodness sake this is a toy room and we gotta play with all of these toys! What are you waiting for?"

Little Isabella stood there for a moment before taking off in a mad dash towards little Nicholas. Jack watched Santa and little Isabella the elf as they began to play with all of the toys. Jack found himself really truly happy that

Nicholas was taking to the current chore so quickly and so well.

At quite some distance on the other side of the room, Jack saw Feldman wave to him so he decided to leave so Feldman could help Santa with the toy chore.

Feldman spotted Nicholas as soon as he had walked in but he had decided to watch him for a bit before introducing himself. But after about five minutes or so, Feldman finally decided it was time to approach the new little Santa Claus. He was a bit nervous because he hadn't actually officially met the new little Santa Claus yet. He had seen him from a far but he suddenly found himself very excited to actually be meeting him face to face.

Feldman walked right up to Nicholas to introduce himself. "So you must be the new Santa Claus I presume? Well, I am Feldman the elf and I am in charge of making sure all of the toys you deliver to all of the children all over the world are safe and age appropriate for them. So did Jack let you know what you would be doing here today?"

Nicholas found himself staring at Feldman the elf as Feldman was speaking. Nicholas was taken a back when he saw Feldman for the first time. Nicholas remembered his Mimi had told him not to stare at others just because they may look a little different. But Nicholas couldn't take his eyes off of Feldman no matter how hard he tried. Feldman was an average height for an elf so it wasn't his height one would stare at. It was Feldman's big ears and big hair, which one could not avoid staring at. Nicholas could not believe how big Feldman's ears were. They stuck out from his head a bit too much for an average elf. Nicholas thought briefly to himself 'they looked like the elephant's ears at the zoo'. But once Nicholas was able to accept those big ears, he couldn't keep his eyes off of the hair. Feldman had dark curly brown hair which stuck out everywhere. Nicholas was unsure whether or not Feldman couldn't brush his hair or if his hair stuck out like that even after being brushed.

Luckily, due to the fact Nicholas hadn't spoken up yet, Isabella answered, "Of course we know what we are doing here Feldman! We are here to play with the toys! All of the toys!"

Feldman began to laugh as he looked at both Isabella and Nicholas before replying, "Yes you are both here to play with the toys but please….please….understand this is a very, very important chore! You see Santa, if you deliver a toy to a child and the child gets hurt from your toy it could jeopardize the entire North Pole operation here. You Santa would be held responsible for the incident. So you two need to play with all of these toys and I mean really play with them. Then after you finish playing with each toy at a station, all you do is press the red button at the station and I will come over to the station to see how the toy testing went. After you report about all of the toys tested at a station then I will take you to the next station. Now do either of you have any questions?"

Both Nicholas and Isabella looked at each other and shook their heads 'no' in unison.

Feldman watched the two of them shake their heads 'no' in response. Feldman took them to the first toy station. When they saw it, Isabella and little Nicholas ran in and immediately started playing with the toys. There ended up being ten toy stations in all and Nicholas and Isabella had fun and loved every toy at each station. But like all the other chores, there was always an end. They were a bit sad when they had completed the last station. They really truly wished they could keep playing with the toys.

Nicholas noticed Isabella wasn't smiling anymore so he tried to make her feel better. "It's okay my littlest elf, I am sure there will be another play day in here soon. I will ask Jack if you can help me next time like you did today. I know he will say 'yes' especially since we completed this chore in like half the time because we did it together!"

Isabella looked over at Nicholas with a smile as she replied, "Thanks Santa, I had a lot of fun with you today playing with the toys. I am happy I got to help you."

Just then Jack walked over and stated, "Well Feldman told me the two of you did a really good job here today. Thank you Isabella for helping Santa but you are needed back at your toy station and Santa has more chores on his list to complete. So let's take you back to your toy station right now."

Isabella was truly happy Jack had let her help Santa today so she gave Jack a great big hug and told him,

"Thank you Jack, I had a super fun day today! But can I please come back next time? And can you please bring Santa to visit me the next time he is here at the North Pole visiting...or...at least tell me when he....when Santa is here next time....please....please? You see Jack....Santa....well um....Santa you see is my only real friend and I miss him super bad when he is not at the North Pole."

Jack looked at little Isabella the elf and his heart went out to her. He knew she had a hard time making friends here at the North Pole and she really did feel left out a lot of the time. So he happily replied, "Yes my little Isabella, I will try my best to always let you know when Santa is here or when he will be here."

Isabella smiled and simply replied, "Thanks", before she skipped off down the hall with little Nicholas and back to her job at the toy factory.

Next Nicholas needed to review the naughty and nice lists, which did take quite a bit of time. He was getting use to the naughty and nice lists and he was also learning who the habitually naughty people were around the world. This review of the naughty and the nice lists would not be the last review before the end of the year. There would be one more review sometime around the summer and then one last review right before Christmas. Nicholas knew everyone who was currently on the naughty list would still have two more opportunities to be placed on the nice list so he didn't feel as if today's review was very important. He did value the naughty list and the nice list. It just was not his favorite chore even though he knew it was an important chore and it had to be done.

Nicholas was both happy and relieved when he finally decided he had completed the chore. Actually though, Nicholas had not fully completed the naughty and nice list chore. He had decided to say he was done with the chore so he could move onto a more fun chore. Nicholas knew he shouldn't lie but he thought it would be okay because it was only a small lie and no one would ever find out he really hadn't finished the lists. He had simply rolled up the lists he had not finished yet and he put them into the secret inside pocket of his Santa suit jacket.

As soon as Nicholas hid his lists, he jumped up out of his seat and announced, "Okay I am finally done with the naughty and nice list chore so what's next?"

Jack looked at Nicholas and replied, "Wow you sure are finishing all of the chores on my list quite quickly today Santa. In fact you are finishing them a lot faster than I thought you would. Your next chore, I think you will like a lot. You are going to go and play with the elves."

Nicholas quickly asked, "What? I am going to play with the elves? Which elves do I get to play with?"

Jack was both surprised and happy Santa had finished all of the chores today with such efficiency. So he answered, "Well Santa this is kind of a fun chore. You see Santa there are still some elves you haven't met because they were either busy or working on the days you have been here before. And it is a policy here at the North Pole that Santa has to get to know all of the elves and all of the elves get an opportunity to meet you Santa. So this is your chore, you get to go and play in the snow with the elves you haven't met. Then there is only one more chore on your list. Your last chore will be to check your sleigh for needed repairs and to say goodbye to the reindeers."

Nicholas jumped up and exclaimed, "Ok Jack, well lets get going then!"

Nicholas loved to exercise and he knew exercise was important but he was tired of all of the walking he had been doing today. Whenever he was tired of walking he would always tell his Mimi his legs were broken but Nicholas knew telling Jack his legs were broken probably, no definitely wouldn't be an appropriate thing to say at the North Pole. So Nicholas continued to walk with Jack to meet the elves. Nicholas finally began to enjoy the walk because they were walking through an area of the North Pole he had never seen before.

"Wow Jack, it is beautiful over here but where are we going?" Nicholas asked.

Jack looked at Nicholas and replied, "We are going to the big Snowball Park. That is--"

Before Jack could finish his statement Nicholas loudly exclaimed, "A Snowball Park! Oh my goodness, I have never ever even seen a snow ball park! Are there really snow balls? Are there toys to play and climb on? Is there...."

Jack had to interrupt little Nicholas because he could see in his eyes, he still had a hundred more questions to ask about Snowball Park. "Ok, ok slow down Santa! We are almost there and then you will get to see it all for yourself. I do guarantee you will have more fun at the snow ball park than you have ever had at any other park before! Here we are Santa."

Nicholas had been so curious about Snowball Park he hadn't even noticed they had arrived. He stood at the edge of the park in awe of what he saw before him. Jack had been so right, was all he could think. This truly was the best park ever. Nicholas had never seen so many snow balls in his entire life. It seemed as if there was no end to the big white Snowball Park. Nicholas had never seen a park this big before. The fresh white snow glistened like diamonds as the sun shined upon it. He continued to stand there looking around at the beautiful park.

Then like a flash of light, Nicholas looked across the park and could see what looked to be a hundred elves running towards him. Nicholas knew the elves were running way too fast to stop in time before they reached him. He thought for sure they were going to knock him right off his feet.

Nicholas was in utter shock to say the least as to the number of elves running towards him and he tried his best to get the elves to slow down. He screamed as loud as he could, "Slow down! Slow dow......"

Boom! Nicholas flew into a huge pile of snow along with all of the elves who were running towards him.

"Santa? Santa? Seriously guys did you have to run Santa over? Can you please help me pick Santa up?" asked Jack angrily.

The elves all tried to lend a hand as quickly as they could to help Nicholas out of the snow pile. Nicholas had only sunk a few inches into the snow so it only took about ten seconds to retrieve him up and out of the snow pile. Jack felt as if it had taken hours. Jack made it very obvious to all of the elves how protective he is of Santa.

"Santa! Santa! Are you hurt Santa?" Jack uttered in a scared voice.

"Awesome!" exclaimed Nicholas.

And in a flash Nicholas jumped up shaking all of the snow off of himself with a huge smile on his face with his face glowing with excitement. Jack had obviously scared the elves by his overly protective reaction. The elves were standing there, a bit unsure of what to do next.

Nicholas could sense the elves insecurity so he said, "Come on over friends! I want to meet each and every one of you and then we get to play in this cool park. After all of you introduce yourselves to me, the first thing I want to play is snow ball fight. There is a huge pile of snow balls over there and they have all of our names written all over them." Nicholas now saw there were only twenty five elves but their speed was so amazingly fast no one could have counted the true amount.

One by one each of the twenty-five elves introduced themselves to Nicholas. He was trying his best to remember all of their names and faces. There was Sally, Cooper, Carson, Bella, Trio and Geegon and...the list went on and on. Nicholas was happy when they had finally all introduced themselves to him.

When the introductions were all done Nicholas screamed, "Snow ball fight!"

As soon as Nicholas shouted 'snow ball fight' everyone took off in a mad dash to grab and throw as many snow balls as possible. Nicholas hadn't even noticed Jack had left him by himself with the elves at Snowball Park.

All the elves were getting tired during the snow ball fight. One by one the elves gave up until Nicholas was the only one left. He diligently looked around the park as best as possible in search of Jack but he still couldn't find him.

Nicholas shouted, "Jack....Jack....Jack....Jack?" getting louder each time he spoke.

Still there was no answer. Nicholas began running around the park in every which way. His heart began to pound and Nicholas became very worried about where Jack could be. Just then Nicholas felt a tap on his left shoulder, which made him quickly turn his head to the left.

Nicholas let out a big sigh as he exclaimed, "Oh my goodness Jack, I thought you were gone! Why didn't you tell me you were going leave?"

Jack took in a deep breath and tried to hide a smile before answering, "Santa we are at the North Pole and so I left you with the elves at Snowball Park! It's not like I left you all alone in a dark abandoned alley or something like that. Weren't you having fun playing here at the park with the elves?"

Nicholas quickly replied, "Well of course I was having fun with the elves. But Jack I guess….well….I guess I like to always know where you are at."

Just then Nicholas reached over to Jack and whispered into his ear, "Jack I thought you were the boss of me?"

Jack began to laugh out loud before reaching over and whispering back to Nicholas, "No Santa actually you are the boss of me. I am only your assistant."

Nicholas stared at Jack for a moment, a bit confused. Nicholas knew he was the new real Santa Claus but until this moment he hadn't actually realized he was technically the boss of the North Pole. This was definitely a very new and big revelation for little Nicholas to think about. Nicholas told himself he would think about it later and talk to Mimi about it later too.

Unsure of how to respond back to Jack after what he had been told, Nicholas simply said, "Okay Jack so now we are off to check the sleigh and tell the reindeer's goodbye, right? But I want to tell everyone here goodbye really quick first. Okay?"

"That sounds perfect Santa," answered Jack.

Nicholas told each and every one of his new elf friend's goodbye for now and thanked all of them for such a fun time at Snowball Park.

Then he was off to check on the sleigh with Jack. Nicholas was extremely happy it was such a short walk to the sleigh holding area by the reindeers. It had seemed as if it had taken no time at all to get there.

As soon as they arrived, Jack opened the big holding area doors to the sleigh and said, "Okay Santa here it is! Now you need to make sure the sleigh is all ready for you for Christmas Eve. Now I know we still have some time before Christmas Eve and we both know you will be back before Christmas Eve but the sleigh is so extremely important in the delivery of all of the presents for Christmas. Basically, if the sleigh is not working then there is no delivery of presents and we do not want that to ever happen. Therefore, we need to always keep the sleigh in perfect working order. If you ever notice anything on the sleigh which is not working perfectly then you need to let me know and I will make the arrangements for the necessary repairs."

Nicholas quickly replied, "Yes sir Jack! I never want the sleigh to crash or anything and I would really be sad if I was unable to deliver all of my presents to everyone."

Jack knew Nicholas had been worried when he had left Snowball Park so he told Nicholas, "All right then Santa, I am going to leave you alone for a little bit so you can check the sleigh and I am going right next door to see the reindeers. Okay?"

"Okay!" replied Nicholas as he was already beginning to check the sleigh.

Nicholas was all by himself in the sleigh holding area, which he thought was nice because now he was able to concentrate on every part of the sleigh. He checked the computer system, the rails, the present storage area, the seats, the handles and even the hookups on the sleigh for the reindeer's. Then he went next door to find Jack when he was all through. Nicholas knew his visit to the North Pole this time would be coming to an end very shortly and he knew he wanted to make sure to get back to his house before his Mimi, daddy or sissy woke up. He didn't want to worry anyone about where he was at.

When Nicholas arrived at the reindeer area he began calling, "Jack, Jack, I am all done Jack."

Jack appeared and answered, "Wow Santa sleigh inspection didn't take too long at all. So how did the sleigh look?"

Nicholas replied, "Well both the driver seat and the passenger seats are a bit wobbly so I would like them tightened up, the right bottom rail is a little bit bent inward so it needs to be straightened out. Also the computer should have a system check ran on it because it is almost due for that. But everything else on the sleigh looks to be in perfect working order."

"Wow Santa, thank you for being so thorough with the sleigh inspection, it is greatly appreciated. Now all you have left to do is tell the reindeer's goodbye and don't forget to check on Vixen. But please hurry because I do have to have you back home and in bed in one hour," said Jack.

Nicholas looked at Jack as he replied, "I know, I know, I would not forget about Vixen. He has been in my thoughts since I left here earlier today. I will try my best to hurry Jack. I would hate to be back late because everyone at home would be very worried about me."

Nicholas first went to check on Vixen but he was asleep so Nicholas was trying to be quite not to disturb him. Nicholas went in and quietly sat on the blanket right next to Vixen, carefully picking up his hoof to inspect the injury. The redness and swelling seemed to have already gone down a bit and it looked as if it was healing nicely. All seemed to be well with the reindeers as Nicholas told them all goodbye. Nicholas then started on the walk back to his house at the North Pole with Jack.

On the walk back Nicholas turned to Jack and said, "Thanks Jack, I had a fun day here at the North Pole again today. I already can't wait until the next time I get to come back....,"

Nicholas stopped midstream in his sentence as soon as he noticed he no longer had the lists in his pocket. He didn't say anything to Jack he simply turned around and started running back towards the sleigh holding area as fast as he could. On the way back to the sleigh holding area all Nicholas could think was maybe, just maybe the lists had fallen out while he was doing the sleigh inspection. He thought he could run back to the sleigh and pick it up. Nicholas was also diligently looking around while he was running back to the sleigh holding area in case the lists had some how fallen out of his pocket after they had left the reindeers. There were no signs of the lists on the ground, so as soon as he arrived at the sleigh holding area Nicholas frantically began to look around everywhere for the lists. It really wasn't a big area so it didn't take long for Nicholas to realize the lists were not there.

Next he ran over to the reindeer area trying to run the same path he had taken earlier when he had gone to say goodbye. Just after Nicholas had entered the reindeer stables, Jack arrived as well.

"Santa you do not have time to play with the reindeer's anymore today. I have already told you, I need to get you back home with your parents," Jack said.

Nicholas wasn't trying to ignore Jack. But he didn't answer Jack because he was concentrating so hard on finding where the lists were. Just then Nicholas spotted Lester, one of the youngest reindeers eating something in the corner of the barn. Nicholas ran over to him and saw the remnants of the lists lying on the ground beneath Lester. Nicholas did not know what to do with the damaged lists. He knew the damage was already done so he sat down on the floor and began to cry.

Jack had absolutely no idea what was going on with little Nicholas but he became even more worried as soon he saw Nicholas begin to cry. Jack ran over to him and asked, "Santa what's wrong? Are you okay? Was I rushing you to leave the North Pole? Was someone not nice to you today?"

Nicholas softly answered, "No Jack everyone was great today. I messed up. I did something really, really awful. I am so sorry Jack. I hope I still get to be Santa Claus even though now I really don't deserve to be Santa Claus anymore."

Jack completely puzzled as to what was going on said, "Santa you are a great Santa. In fact you are actually the best and most fun Santa we have ever had. How did you mess up?"

Nicholas really didn't want to tell anyone but he knew he had to so he told Jack the whole story about hiding the last part of the naughty list and the last part of the nice list in his pocket. He told Jack he thought he could finish reviewing both lists later. He also promised Jack he would never do anything like this again.

When Nicholas was all finished telling him the story, Jack replied, "Well Santa what's done is done. So now we have to figure out how we can fix this."

Jack stood there for a few moments thinking about what he should do first and which elf he should contact in the Naughty and Nice List Department. He finally decided it would be best to go straight to Carl the head elf of the Naughty and Nice List Department. Jack really didn't want to contact Carl because he knew Carl would hang this situation over his little elf head for a very long time.

Carl was a very smart elf like Jack. He was a bit taller than Jack with a very round face, his light brown hair was always combed perfectly, which Nicholas always thought made him look a bit funny. Carl always obeyed all of the rules and some of the elves didn't like him because he was stricter than Jack about all of the elves following the rules. Even though Nicholas didn't know how old Jack was, he knew Jack and Carl were the same age because Jack had told Nicholas they had grown up together. Jack and Carl use to be best friends.

Five years ago it had come down to Jack and Carl for the North Pole head elf position, which was ultimately given to Jack. Carl has let everyone know the North Pole head elf position should have been his and he deserved the position more. However, it was based on an election by all of the elves at the North Pole and Jack had won fair and square by an overwhelming amount of votes.

Jack slowly took his two-way radio out of his pocket and called out on the radio, "Carl, Carl are you there? It's Jack....please pick up Carl....there is a....um....Carl there is a situation."

Obviously Carl was ignoring Jack when he first heard the radio transmission but he finally responded, "Situation?

What kind of a situation? You're the head elf here at the North Pole so you take care of it."

This needed to be taken care of as soon as possible and Jack knew what he had to do. So Jack responded back with a very serious and authoritative tone in his voice, "Carl a situation has arisen, which directly involves your department. This is a sensitive situation and I am ordering you to report to the reindeer area immediately!"

Carl really wasn't in the mood to see Jack today but since he was ordered to the reindeer area he knew he was required to go and report to Jack. It was about a ten minute walk to the reindeer area from the Naughty and Nice List Department and at first he was going to take his time in walking to the reindeer area. But then his sensible side overtook his prideful side and he had a feeling he should get to the reindeer area immediately. Carl jumped into his little elf cart and quickly drove over to see Jack.

When he arrived, he saw Santa and Jack standing outside the barn at the reindeer area. He quickly parked the cart and jumped out to greet them. "Hi Santa, how are you?" He reached down and gave Santa a big hug and then he turned to Jack and shook his hand as he sarcastically asked, "Ok Mr. head elf, what situation do you need help with?"

Jack certainly didn't appreciate the sarcasm by Carl but he chose to rise above the sarcasm and ignored it. Jack needed to quickly deal with the situation at hand so there was no time to show authority to Carl. Jack politely replied, "Thanks you so much Carl for responding to the situation at hand so quickly. You see Carl, Santa had actually not finished reviewing the naughty and nice list today. He thought he could take the last part of the naughty list and the last part of the nice list to review at his other home."

Carl abruptly interrupted Jack, "What….wait….where is the list? Give it to me Santa…..I want the naughty list and the nice list back now….and….well I know that you are Santa and all…..but I want those lists back now! Well….where are the lists?"

Jack calmly replied, "Well Carl you need to let me finish explaining the full situation and then you can ask me your questions. Santa doesn't exactly have the lists anymore. You see Carl while Santa was tending to the reindeer's the lists must have fallen out of his pocket and Lester ate both of the lists. So we need to calmly, rationally and intelligently figure out how we are going to fix this problem together. So can we please agree to put our differences aside right now and try to work together Carl?"

Even though Jack was not Carl's favorite person he still loved the North Pole and everything it stood for. Carl knew he had to reply, "Yes, I will Jack. Let's all brainstorm and try to figure out what we are going to do. We do need to try and keep this just between us for now in order to prevent widespread panic among all of the elves across the North Pole."

And that is exactly what the three of them began to do. However Jack, Carl and Nicholas were so concerned about fixing the situation they completely forgot about returning Nicholas back home.

CHAPTER 13

Meanwhile, back at Nicholas's parent's house everyone was beginning to stir in their beds and wake up.

Holly was the first one to wake up. She got up and went over to see Nicholas. His bedroom door was still shut so she knocked on his door but there was no reply. She figured oddly enough he must be sleeping in this morning.

Holly quietly opened Nicholas's bedroom door and called out, "Nicholas....Nicholas....wake up bro bro."

But as Holly reached his bed she saw he was no longer there. She ran into my room asking me where Nicholas was at. I was still sound asleep so she took it upon herself to wake me up. "Mom....mom....mom....where is Nicholas mom? He isn't in his bed. Did he already go downstairs?"

Since I was in a sound sleep, I was finding it very hard to even open my eyes. I am definitely not a good morning person and I was a bit disoriented at first. I had absolutely no idea what Holly was talking about. As I sat up in bed trying to force myself awake, I looked down at my clock on the bedside table. I couldn't help but ask Holly, "Why are you up sweetheart? You still have about fifteen minutes until you have to get up for school. Nicholas is probably sleeping in and please let him sleep in. He has his admission testing for Valley View Academy tomorrow and I want him to be well rested."

Holly replied, "Mom....seriously....Nicholas is not in his bed or in his room!"

Realizing she was getting absolutely nowhere with me, she ran out of my room, down the stairs and all throughout the house calling out, "Nicholas....Nicholas....Nicholas....Nicholas this isn't funny anymore! Where are you Nicholas? You are going to be in big and I mean big trouble if you don't come out from where you are hiding!"

Holly was getting extremely worried about her little brother and I could tell by the tone of her voice she had a bad feeling way down deep in the pit of her stomach. She was trying to remember everything that had happened the day before trying to remember if she had hurt his feelings at all. Everything had been fine the day before though and she even read him a bedtime story last night. So where was he? Did he run away? Oh my goodness was he kidnapped? So many bad thoughts were running through her head but all she wanted was to have her brother right there again.

I knew Holly was getting very upset so I checked Nicholas's room before I came down the stairs. I saw for myself he wasn't in his room. When I saw a very worried Holly standing in the kitchen, I knew something was wrong, no very wrong. I ran over to Holly and asked, "Holly sweetheart what is wrong? Did you find out where your brother was hiding down here?"

Holly was so upset, frustrated and worried she screamed back at me, "He is gone mom! Nicholas is gone!" Holly couldn't hold back the tears anymore and she began to cry uncontrollably.

I was still calm at this point in time. I knew my little Nicholas must be hiding. He loved to hide from his sister and he was probably tricking her. But now the joke had gone too far and Holly was very upset.

So I began to call out to Nicholas, "Okay Santa you won. We can't find you so we give up and we make you the grand prize winner."

Still there was no response from Nicholas not even a winning giggle could be heard. I began to get extremely worried at this point. There had never been a time Nicholas hadn't come out from his spot once he was announced as the winner, especially the grand prize winner.

I was trying to remain calm for Holly's sake but I found I couldn't even remain a little calm anymore. Frantically, I ran over to my purse to grab my cell phone. I knew Garrett can always fix everything. There had never been a situation Garrett couldn't fix. He has always been my rock so I knew he would be able to calm my fear.

I used the speed dial on my cell phone to call Garrett and immediately I felt a sigh of relief when he answered on the first ring. His sweet voice asking, "Good morning, gorgeous how are you doing this--"

I couldn't help it. I had to interrupt him because I felt I had a lot to tell him with so little time. "Garrett honey, its Nicholas, I can't find our baby boy he's gone, he's gone, you just have to fix it so find him please. Please, find our baby boy, I need him, I need my Santa! Where is he, where is he?" I suddenly felt an overwhelming amount of tears welling up in my eyes and I couldn't hold back the tears any longer.

Garrett had no idea what was going on but he knew I needed him. He told me, "I will be right there, don't worry everything will be fine. I am here. We will find our baby boy I promise."

Garrett stayed on the phone even though I couldn't say anything anymore and through my tears he did this so we could feel close to each other. I listened as he quickly told his boss there was an emergency at home and told him he would call when he had things under control. He worked quite close to home but for some reason it felt as if it was taking ten times longer for Garrett to drive home today.

I was watching out the front window for him so I dropped the phone, ran out the front door and threw myself into his arms as soon as I saw him. As he held me for a moment he felt my pain and tears began to stream down his face.

As soon as he felt the tears stream down his face he quickly wiped them away and asked, "Can you please calm down for a minute so you can tell me exactly what is going on?"

I tried my best to compose myself as we walked up the walkway towards the house. We went in and sat down on the couch where Holly was sitting.

I told Garrett, "Well it's pretty simple honey Nicholas is gone. Holly got out of bed first this morning and she came and woke me up when she couldn't find him. We have searched the entire house and there is no sign of him anywhere."

Garrett calmly responded, "Okay first we need to call and report him missing. Then we can go from there. But I do need you to think of the answers to a few questions the officers will ask us when they get here. Were any doors or windows unlocked? Did he take anything with him?"

Garrett was always so calm in situations like this and I knew it was due to his training in law enforcement but all I wanted him to do was to fix everything and to find Nicholas.

I was still not calm but I said, "Fine go call we need to find him now. I need him, I can't....I can't....I just need you to find him now."

Garrett left the room to call the police and reported Nicholas missing. Since Nicholas was only five and wasn't a trouble child they knew he hadn't just ran away. The police arrived in a matter of minutes. Garrett took care of everything and I held Holly in the other room. We didn't say a word to each other we just held each other for support.

I knew we would find him, I didn't know where or when but I needed him now. I wanted to help....I needed to help so I got up and went to my computer to start designing missing person posters to hang up. I found I couldn't help but cry as I searched through the photos of Nicholas on my computer. I had to find the best one to put on the missing posters. I felt a little better when Holy came over to the computer to sit with me, I needed her next to me. We chose the photo of Nicholas together. It was one of my favorite photographs I have of Nicholas. The photo had been taken on his first day of pre-K and he was so excited to be going to school.

The police were still at our home but Holly and I had printed up a hundred missing posters and we were ready to go out to hang them up all over town. I didn't care what I looked like or even that we still had our pajamas on. All I cared about was finding my baby boy.

Garrett saw me grabbing my car keys and asked, "Where are you two going?"

I quickly responded, "Out....Holly and I printed up missing posters so we are going to go around town and hang them up. I will have my phone so please call me if you know anything....anything at all. I need you to stay here though in case he comes back here."

Garrett kissed me and Holly goodbye and we were off. We drove all over town hanging up posters and we actually hung up the hundred posters quicker than I thought we could. We agreed to go back home to print more.

On the drive back home Holly asked, "Can we please play *Jingle Bell Rock*? I need to hear it right now; I think it will make us feel closer to Nicholas."

I was already turning *Jingle Bell Rock* on as I replied, "Of course we can!"

We sang it the rest of the way home crying through most of the song. It wasn't the same without Nicholas being in the car singing it with us. But Holly had been right. It did make me feel closer to Nicholas.

We pulled into the garage and as I shut the car off. Holly asked, "Mom....wait mom....I need to ask you something. Do you....okay don't think I am crazy mom....um....do think that....well that....okay fine I will just say it. Do you think that Nicholas is at the North Pole?"

I sat there thinking about what Holly had asked. I had been praying for a thread of hope the entire time we were putting up the posters. So I replied, "Holly, maybe he is. It's just he is always back by the morning. But maybe something happened and he couldn't come home. I have an idea, come on."

When we got home the police were still there talking to Garrett. I didn't want to share my idea with my husband yet. I knew he wouldn't understand and I didn't want him to say anything to the police. Holly and I walked into the house and I tried to be inconspicuous as I took Holly up into my room.

I closed my bedroom door and I told Holly, "Sit on the bed while I look for something."

Holly was definitely unsure what in the world I was doing. She asked, "What mom? What are you looking for?"

I searched all over the closet but I couldn't find it any where. It wasn't here, it was gone too. Finally I told Holly, "You are so smart! He must be at the North Pole. We just don't know why he didn't come home last night. There is nothing we can do. We just have to wait for him to come home."

Holly even more confused definitely thinking her mom had gone crazy asked, "Mom what are you talking about? Please tell me mom, what are you talking about?"

I excitedly said, "It's not here. His Santa suit is gone so he must be at the North Pole. I hadn't even thought he could be at the North Pole. But we need to keep this between the two of us. Everyone including your father will think we are crazy if we tell them Nicholas is at the North Pole."

Holly and I agreed to keep this new information just between the two of us. Neither of us had any idea when he would come home but we believed he would come home eventually. We went through the motions and continued to hang up the posters and search for Nicholas in case we were wrong about him being at the North Pole. Later that afternoon, I wasn't in the mood for any visitors but I answered the door only because I had looked and saw it was Holly's friend Mary at the front door.

As soon as I answered the door Mary quietly said, "Hi Mrs. Johnson, I heard about Nicholas and I wanted to come by to check on Holly to see how she was doing."

"Come on in, I will let her know you are here," I replied.

I was a bit shocked to see Mary there because I wasn't sure if Holly and her were back to being best friends or not. I knew Mary had apologized to Holly after teasing her about Nicholas being Santa Claus, but I didn't know how everything was going between them lately.

I walked upstairs to Holly's room and told her, "Honey you have a visitor. Mary is here to see you."

Obviously the two of them were the best of friends again because Holly jumped up and ran down the stairs. As soon as Holly got downstairs they gave each other a big hug. Holly led Mary upstairs to her room.

I hadn't let any other visitors stay but Mary is such a sweet girl and I knew it would be good for Holly to have her friend with her so I had her spend the rest of the day at the house to play with Holly.

CHAPTER 14

    I was quite embarrassed when I had to call and cancel Nicholas's admission testing at Valley View but luckily they were okay about canceling the appointment. A day had passed and we were still waiting for Nicholas to come home. I couldn't go to work and I didn't make Holly go to school either. Upon my insisting Garrett go back to work, he finally agreed and went back. Holly and I just waited.

    I hadn't been able to sleep the first night he had been gone. It was now the second night he had missing and I still couldn't sleep. All I could do was lie down on the couch and watch television. Sometime during one of the many movies I had been watching, I somehow fell asleep. I was startled awake by a loud noise outside. I jumped up off of the couch and looked out the window. I didn't see anything out of the ordinary so I went and sat back on the couch. I found I couldn't sit still. I was really missing Nicholas so I decided to sit up in his room to feel close to him.

    I opened his door and as I walked over to his bed I stopped. I couldn't move nor could I speak. I could see the red sleeve of his Santa suit sticking out of the blanket of his bed. I said a quiet prayer then I began screaming,

"He is back….our Santa is home….Nicholas is here….our baby is back!"

I reached down and I scooped him up into my arms holding him tightly. I never wanted to let go of my little Nicholas ever again. Holly and Garrett came running in as fast as they could. We all started to cry as we hugged our little Santa. I didn't want to let go of Nicholas, in fact I know none of us ever wanted to let go of each other ever again.

The law enforcement side of Garrett took over all of a sudden and he began to interrogate Nicholas, "Where have you been? Did someone take you? How did you get back in your bed? Wait….wait….I need to know why you have your Santa suit on! Where did you find it?"

The interrogation was getting to be too much very fast so I interrupted, "Stop it! We all need to appreciate Nicholas is home."

Nicholas was obviously tired but he chose to answer some of his interrogation questions. "I have been at the North Pole. Vixen hurt his leg. I had chores to do and then a situation happened. I was very busy and…."

Garrett obviously very annoyed interrupted Nicholas mid stream in his story and said, "Stop….seriously Nicholas, this needs to stop. There have been a lot of people out there looking for you and I don't know where you have been hiding but this better never happen again. Do you understand?"

Nicholas quickly replied, "But dad it's the truth, I promise. I was at the North Pole and the elves they--"

Once again Garrett felt the need to interrupt Nicholas, "You were not at the North Pole and I don't want to hear that again. You are in serious trouble mister!"

I felt the need to comment, "No fighting! Garrett you just go and call the police to let them know that by some great miracle our little Nicholas is home."

Thankfully Garrett did as I asked. All I wanted to do was to hold on tightly to my little Nicholas and to never let him go again.

"Can Nicholas and I get the sleeping bags and sleep in the tent?" asked Holly.

I knew she had missed him almost as much as I had and I really wanted to keep Nicholas right by my side so at first I said, "No."

"Mom can I talk to you for a minute?" asked Holly.

"Okay come here, what do you want to talk about?" I asked.

Holly looked at me very seriously and began her story, "Well Mom, Mary and I are best friends again and I need to talk to Nicholas about getting Mary back onto the nice list. Plus I really missed brother and I need to talk to him. So please mom, please can we sleep in the tent tonight?"

I knew Holly obviously really needed to talk to her brother so I finally agreed to the sleeping bag tent night for the two of them. It also seemed very important to Holly to make sure Mary was placed back on the nice list. Mary had helped Holly so much while Nicholas was missing so I wanted to make sure she was back on the nice list as well.

The next day was a long day but a good day. We had a lot of friends and family stop in to see little Nicholas. It was great to see how many people were worried about our baby boy. From that point on, I decided any time someone went missing from the area I would try my best to help all I could. I truly did realize we are the lucky ones. Unfortunately, most of the time, those missing are not found safe and sound

After Holly and Nicholas had been put to bed, I felt I needed to discuss a few issues with Garrett. I told Garrett, "You know you really shouldn't have interrogated Nicholas so much when he got home last night. We need to get past this and maybe this happened so we would appreciate each other more."

Garrett obviously had things on his mind as well because he started right in with what he had to say. "Let's get one thing straight, I do not want our son going out in public anymore in the Santa suit. We can let him wear it around the house but that is it. Maybe this whole thing happened because I took the Santa suit completely away."

I could see Garrett was blaming himself for Nicholas's disappearance. I felt I had to tell him, "No, it's not your fault. He was at the North Pole. Being the new real Santa is a big responsibility for our little Nicholas. He has a lot of things he has to do at the North Pole."

I definitely had more to say in the defense of Nicholas but I stopped because Garrett started uncontrollably laughing at me. He finally did stop laughing enough to say, "Our son is not the new real Santa Claus. He is a five year old little boy with a big imagination, which is fine but this time his imagination went too far. Everyone wants to know where he was and I can't tell them because I don't know either. And a lot of people spent a lot of time and energy searching for Nicholas. We need to move him onto something else so he will forget about the whole Santa thing. I did as you asked me to and I tried to start believing in Nicholas but all believing did was make us loose our son for a little while."

As you might imagine, I was steaming mad at Garrett by this point so I couldn't help but say, "Look, I will honor your request that he can only wear the Santa suit in our house but sooner or later you will realize our little Nicholas is the new real Santa Claus. One more thing, I will not let you mess with his imagination. It is his imagination and I don't feel we have the right to mess with it. Agreed?"

Garrett, a bit reluctantly said, "Agreed." And we left it at that.

CHAPTER 15

I couldn't believe it was already the day of Kindergarten admission testing. Luckily Nicholas had no problem with putting on the nice slacks and collared shirt I had picked out for him to wear during the testing. I had taken the day off work so I could take Nicholas to his tests. Everyone at home was in a happy mood, which was perfect for me. I needed Nicholas to feel he was in a really positive environment. I wanted to make sure he would have no stress leading up to the testing. We had our pancake and bacon breakfast before Holly, Nicholas and I loaded up into the car.

Before Holly or Nicholas could call their song for the morning, I told them, "Nobody gets a song choice this morning. We need to discuss testing on the way to school today."

Holly quickly interjected, "And bro, bro you better do well on your testing today because I really want you to come to my school next year."

I had a lot to discuss with Nicholas and I didn't want to waste any of the time we had on our short drive to school. So I said, "Okay let's just relax Holly. We want your brother to be relaxed and not stressed out about his testing. Nicholas you need to go in there and be yourself.

With one important and I mean very important exception. You can't mention anything about Santa Claus. I mean you being the new real Santa Claus, the North Pole, the elves and absolutely nothing about Christmas. This is very important..."

Nicholas interrupted me with a bit of irritation in his voice, "But Mimi, Santa is who I am! How can I go into somewhere and be myself if I can't really be myself?"

I somehow knew when it came right down to it Nicholas would have a bit of a problem not mentioning he is the new real Santa Claus. I didn't want to hurt his feelings at all so I was trying very hard to deal with this very gently, "Nicholas sweetheart, I completely understand it is very important to you being the new real Santa....but....well....other people don't understand. Remember we have had discussions before about non believers and sometimes you can't change their minds no matter what. Well, I don't want there to be any Santa non believers on the admission board today."

Nicholas smiled as he said, "Well Mimi, its okay if there are Santa non-believers on the missions board today. I will just switch them over to Santa believers."

It never ceases to amaze me as to the amount of positive energy my son has. He always tries his best to look on the bright side, which seems to create even more positive energy. I needed to get my point across to him though. But I couldn't help but smile as I gently told him, "Look Nicholas, Mimi is very serious. Sometimes Santa non believers aren't so easy to switch over to Santa believers. Sometimes, it.... well it takes a bit of time. That is why I want you to concentrate on getting in and then you can try your best later on to make them Santa believers if they aren't already."

Nicholas looked at me and with a very serious tone told me, "Mimi I promised Jack I wouldn't tell lies anymore but I think this will be okay because it is a little different than lying. I will make them see I am smart and I will follow all of their rules at school."

I was happy to say the least but I was kind of concerned about what lie Nicholas had told to Jack that would make him have to promise not to lie anymore. I tried as hard as I could to put it out of my mind though. I made a little mental note to myself to volunteer to put the kids to bed tonight and I would ask Nicholas then. Before I knew it, we were already at the school.

As soon as I had parked the car, Holly said, "Bye mom, bye bro, bro and yes bro, bro, I won't trip and fall. Oh and good luck bro, bro you will do great. You really are awesome!" She quickly kissed both of us before she jumped out of the car and she was gone, merging into her group of friends in a flash.

I had Nicholas unbuckle his seatbelt and come up to the front seat for one more pep talk before he went into testing. I asked, "You okay? You do know sissy was right. You will do great because you are really awesome? And you do know we are all proud of you no matter what, right?"

Nicholas reached over and gave me a big squeeze and proudly told me, "Thanks Mimi! I will try my best and I will try my best not to mention anything about Santa to them today."

I whispered, "Thanks." And we got out of the car walking hand in hand over to room A8 where we were told to report for the testing.

A bright a chipper older lady greeted us as soon as we walked in, "Hi and you must be Nicholas."

Nicholas immediately smiled one of those big smiles of his and answered, "Yes of course I am Nicholas and I am here for my missions testing."

The chipper older lady introduced herself as Ms. Wicket and told me, "Testing for Nicholas will be about two hours. First he will do the one on one testing of his current knowledge next he will meet with the admission board and they will interview him to see if he would be a good fit for Valley View Academy. You have the choice to come back in two hours or you are more than welcome to stay over in the office during the testing."

I really didn't want to leave him there by himself because I didn't want him to feel like he was alone. I had brought a few magazines with me so I politely stated, "Okay, I will just go and wait in the office until he is done." I gave Nicholas a kiss on the cheek and I whispered, "Good luck," into his ear.

"Very well, I will bring Nicholas to the office as soon as he is done with his testing," replied a still chipper Ms. Wicket.

I walked to the office and I knew I was the nervous one. Why was I nervous? I wasn't the one taking the test, Nicholas was the one taking the stressful test right now. But maybe I was taking on all of his nervousness so he could go in there and be himself without being nervous. Or maybe that was what I was wishing for. I tried my best to concentrate on the magazines I was reading but I found it a bit difficult to think about anything except Nicholas and his test.

It had been what seemed to be an eternity but the two hour mark had come and I was relieved he would be done any minute with the testing. I heard the door handle of the office door move and Nicholas ran over to me giving me a great big hug. Nicholas proclaimed with quite a bit of confidence, "I did perfect Mimi, they loved me!"

I smiled as Ms. Wicket nicely commented, "Yes, Nicholas did do a very good job. Next week we'll begin making our final selections of the children we would like to join us at Valley View Academy for kindergarten next year. You should receive a letter within a month as to whether or not Nicholas was accepted."

"Well thank you for your time and it was nice meeting you Ms. Wicket," I politely replied.

Nicholas and I silently walked out to the car. I really didn't want to say anything until we were in the car to make sure nobody at Valley View Academy heard any of our comments. I knew it was only kindergarten and the school had been rated as one of the top in the state but for heavens sake why did they have to test them and interview them simply to get in? I did appreciate the quality of education there. I guess it seemed too serious though and I wished it would be a bit more fun to go to school there.

As soon as we had pulled out of the parking lot, I began my interrogation, "So Nicholas how did it really go? What did they ask you? Were they nice?"

Nicholas smiled and said, "Gosh Mimi you sure have a lot of questions! But okay I will tell you everything. Oh and before I tell you about the testing, I wanted to let you know I didn't say anything about being the new real Santa Claus. I kept my promise and I also didn't say anything about the elves, Christmas or even the North Pole. Well let's see they took me in and they showed me numbers, letters, colors and shapes and I had to say what they were. Then I had to count as high as I could but they stopped me when I got to two-hundred so I guess I had counted high enough. I also had to say my ABC's but I didn't want to just say them so I sang the ABC song. They let me have a snack after that and then they asked me some math questions about adding numbers. It was a little boring but it was more fun when they interviewed me."

All I could think was great, at least he didn't let them in on the Santa secret so maybe he will get in. I wanted him to tell me about the interview though. So I asked,

"Okay that sounds great but what did they say in the interview part?"

Nicholas was a bit annoyed I had interrupted him but he looked at me in the rear view mirror with a smirk as he continued on with his story, "There were five people sitting behind a big table and they all took turns asking me questions. They even asked me what my name was, which I didn't know why because everyone had already said 'Hi Nicholas' to me. But I thought maybe they forgot my name or something. I told them about you and sissy and daddy. They also asked about what animals we have at home. But you know what my favorite question was?"

Oh no, was all I was thinking. I knew he had probably showed them his quirky side too. I remained calm and asked, "What....what was your favorite question?"

Nicholas laughed as he said, "They asked me what my favorite toy was and you know what I said?"

By the laugh and the sarcasm in Nicholas's voice I knew he had provided a very off the wall answer to their question. Once again I remained calm and asked, "Um....did you say, The Hulk?"

Nicholas laughed and shook his head 'no'.

Great my guess again. I waited a minute trying to think of what toy he could have possibly picked as his favorite toy. I finally answered, "I know, your big green dinosaur that walks and roars with the little remote." Nicholas again shook his head. I gave a few more guesses but I ran out of what I thought it could be. I really didn't have anymore possible guesses. He could have chosen anything in the world to be his favorite toy. So eventually I gave up.

"Nicolas just tell me, I have no idea what you picked," I said.

Nicholas took a bit of a serious tone and said, "I think I should keep making you guess Mimi....but....I really want to tell you what I said. So here it is....a bucket....yes Mimi I said a bucket!"

Okay yes, I was a bit shocked to say the least and yes, I know my child is generally very low maintenance and doesn't require a lot of toys to make him happy but he said his favorite toy is a bucket. A bucket? Seriously why would he say a bucket? What does he do with a bucket? Five minutes ago I was thinking he had a good shot of getting into Valley View and now I think his chances are probably slim to none.

My first instinct was to scream but instead I chose to take a deep breath in and relax before I replied.

As calmly as I could I asked, "Oh a bucket? Did you say anything about the bucket?"

Nicholas laughed and said, "Of course I did Mimi. It was weird though they all looked at me funny after I said bucket but then a really funny lady behind the table smiled at me....um....I....I think her name was Ms. Lulu. Yes, her name was Ms. Lulu."

Nicholas then repeated what Ms. Lulu said, "Boy I love that answer. Now tell me what do you do with a bucket?"

"The other people behind the table just looked at Ms. Lulu and told her they didn't need to know what I did with the bucket but Ms. Lulu told me to go ahead and say what I do with a bucket so I did," said Nicholas.

Okay this was getting worse. Obviously the other people on the board didn't like the bucket answer Nicholas had given but suddenly I was very curious about why he had chosen a bucket. So I asked, "Well Nicholas what did you say about the bucket?"

Nicholas laughed again before he answered me, "Mimi I just told them what I do with a bucket. I told them I dig a big huge hole in the sandbox, I fill the bucket up with water, I take the bucket back to the sandbox and I pour the water in my big huge hole."

"That's it?" I asked.

"No Mimi the best part is what I do next. I get in the hole and I get really, really dirty!"

Okay so the bucket answer was quite imaginative. Nicholas really is an out of the box thinker. It never ceases to amaze me how he can turn something one may think is plain and simple into something fun and creative. After Nicholas had finished his story, I did get a level of confidence back that he still had a good chance to get into Valley View. I was also glad to hear Ms. Lulu was on the admission board. Sometimes she seems as if she is the only fun part of Valley View.

Ms. Lulu had been Holly's first grade teacher at Valley View. In my mind Ms. Lulu is the most fabulous teacher I have ever met. She always has a smile on her face and her clothes are phenomenal. It doesn't matter what she is wearing, she always looks great. She is not quiet at all. In fact, I don't think there is a quiet bone in her body. Ms. Lulu is never afraid to tell it like it is. The first time we met Ms. Lulu was on Holly's second day of kindergarten. I was walking Holly to her classroom when we heard Ms. Lulu behind us say, 'Girl, you look like you could be a *Breck* girl.' We had absolutely no idea she was talking to Holly so we had continued walking. Ms. Lulu had tapped Holly on the shoulder so we stopped and looked at her as she continued, 'Girl, your hair is gorgeous. Don't you remember those *Breck* shampoo commercials with the girls with long perfect and shiny hair? You look like you could be one of those *Breck* girls.' From that point on we have been a huge fan of Ms. Lulu.

Holly and I had both loved her first grade school year very much. Ms. Lulu always let me help in the classroom as much as I had wanted to. She made the classroom fun and you could always tell she really cared greatly about each and every child. The children seemed to enjoy learning in her classroom as much as she enjoyed teaching them. It was obvious though some people didn't like or agree with the teaching style of Ms Lulu. But I liked her and I was happy Holly had her for a teacher in first grade.

Nicholas and I agreed to go home and spend the rest of the day playing since I had the day off of work. We went home and played board games, played outside on the swing set, we even made a picnic lunch for each other eating it in the backyard. During our picnic, Nicholas finally told me the whole story about why he had gotten stuck at the North Pole and why he had promised Jack he wouldn't lie anymore. Nicholas informed me the naughty list and the nice list situation did finally get taken care of.

"Mimi I was super lucky because I thought I had taken the current list to review later but I actually hadn't. Carl had gone back over to the Naughty and Nice List Department and found out I had actually grabbed the old list. It did take quite a bit of time to figure that out though. Carl was so thorough looking over the list to make sure he had the right lists." Nicholas said happily.

I was happy Nicholas had finally told me the reason why he had been late getting home from the North Pole and before long it was already time for us to pick up Holly.

"How was it bro, bro? Did you do great in the testing today?" asked Holly as soon as she got into the car.

"Thanks sissy, I think I did great. I hope I get in so we can be at the same school together," replied a happy Nicholas.

Now all we had to do was wait for a month to see if he got in. I have always strongly believed in fate so I felt completely at peace with the entire kindergarten situation. If Nicholas was meant to get in then he would. If he was meant to go somewhere else then he wouldn't get in. Everything happens for a reason and we would have to wait and see. I put kindergarten in the very back of my mind.

CHAPTER 16

'Twas the night before the first day of kindergarten for the new real Santa however neither of the children in our house was snug in their beds yet. The new school year was starting tomorrow! Nicholas would be starting kindergarten and Holly would be starting fifth grade. They had their new back packs, their new lunch pails and their new clothes, laid out for their first day but I wasn't sure if I was ready for them to go back to school.

We had such a fabulous summer! All of us were so excited when we received the acceptance letter for Nicholas. He had gotten into Valley View Academy. We went to Hawaii in July for our summer vacation and the summer seemed to have flown right by. I know people say time goes by even faster the older you get but I didn't think I was old yet!

Nicholas had agreed to not wear his Santa suit to school. There was a dress code at school but Nicholas did try to convince us his Santa suit jacket could be his 'regular' jacket. We told him we would discuss that issue later on when it started to get cold out, which he had reluctantly agreed to.

I finally had gotten Holly and Nicholas to bed while Garrett was downstairs making their lunches for the next day. Nicholas had woke me up super early this morning because he had his days confused and he thought today was the first day of kindergarten. I had sent him back to bed but I had been unable to fall back asleep. I had reluctantly gotten out of bed and of all things, I cleaned the house. I was very tired and I was ready to go to bed myself.

Garrett and I ended the night with a kiss and telling each other to have pleasant dreams.

I was sound asleep when all of a sudden I heard Nicholas saying, "Mimi, Mimi wake up it's the first day of kindergarten and I have to show you something."

I was so not ready to get up out of bed but Nicholas kept shaking me and trying to open my eyes until I finally said, "Okay Nicholas what do you want to show me? It is still very early and you still have about two hours until you have to wake up for school."

Nicholas softly replied, "I know Mimi....just come here....please Mimi."

Obviously it was important because of the way he tried to pull me from the bed. I somehow found enough energy and with his assistance, I rolled out of bed. Nicholas took me by the hand and led me into his room. I guess I was able to find the energy to get out of bed because I was a bit curious as to what my little Nicholas wanted to show me.

Nicholas pulled me all the way into his room and quietly shut the door behind us. He quickly flipped his light switch on as he exclaimed as quietly as he could, "Look Mimi....look what the elves gave me for my first day of school!"

There it was lying on the bed and I had no idea at first as to how I should even respond to what Nicholas was showing me. I took a long deep breath in before I was able to respond appropriately.

After a moment I excitedly asked, "Oh my goodness Nicholas when did you get this? This is so awesome! Is it new pajamas?"

"Um....no....Mimi the elves gave me this last night! It was a present for my first day of school. And....no Mimi of course it is not pajamas! It is to wear under my clothes at school since I can't wear my Santa suit. Isn't it great? They gave me one shirt without sleeves for when it's hot and then another shirt with long sleeves for when it is cold."

I was looking at a Santa suit but it was thin, like it was made out of t-shirt material. There were pants, which were red except for the print at the bottom of each pant cuff that resembled white fur. The shirts resembled Nicholas's red Santa suit jacket with the white fur print down the front of the shirt at the cuffs and collar.

Then it dawned on me, he must have went to the North Pole. 'What?' I thought to myself. Why had he been at the North Pole the day before his first day of kindergarten? Nicholas knew his first day of kindergarten was very important and he knew I would not approve of him going to the North Pole on a school night, so I started to get a little upset.

But he was so excited the elves had remembered him on the night before his first day of kindergarten. I changed my feelings and was happy he had chosen to wake me up and share it with me. I really couldn't get upset, I wanted only to be happy and positive so I chose to embrace the fact he had gone to the North Pole on that night.

I smiled and quietly exclaimed, "Whew, I love it! I bet it was so exciting seeing all of your elves on the night before your first day of kindergarten. This will go perfectly under your school clothes. Just remember we don't talk about Santa stuff at school yet. Okay?"

Nicholas smiled and replied, "I know Mimi. Thanks for coming in, to see my present from the elves."

I gave my little Nicholas a great big hug then I put him back into his bed. I was still tired and went back to my bed as well. I wanted a little more sleep before we all had to get up and get ready for the day. But before I knew it my alarm was going off quite loudly.

I was shocked I had actually been able to fall back asleep after Nicholas had gotten me up. I knew this was not one of those days I could press the snooze button a million times as usual. I forced myself to get up and out of bed with no snoozes.

I walked into Nicholas's room to wake Nicholas up but there was no need to. He was already dressed and ready to go to school. He even had on his new shoes. I was also almost positive he had on his new 'under Santa suit' he had been given by the elves. I figured I would ask later.

I said to Nicholas, "Thanks for getting up and getting dressed by yourself. Come downstairs and I will make you some breakfast."

Holly's light was on so I was assuming she was already up and getting ready as well. But I knew it would be best if I checked to make sure she was actually getting ready for school. I walked into her room and sure enough she was already dressed and ready to go to school as well. I knew I should thoroughly enjoy the fact my children were able to get up and ready without having to be told. I knew this would not last long.

I told Holly, "You look beautiful! Come downstairs in a minute and I will make you something for breakfast."

I was happy Holly and Nicholas were in such great moods this morning and so excited to be going to school together. As I walked downstairs, I was so surprised to see Garrett making breakfast in the kitchen. Obviously I was unaware he didn't have to go to work today. I was happy, it's just he hadn't told me he had taken the day off.

As soon as he saw me walking down the stairs he walked towards the stairs and greeted me with a kiss. "Good morning and surprise! I wanted to go with you today to take the kids to their first day of school. I knew you had taken the day off so I took the day off too," he said.

I kissed him back and told him, "I am very happy you took the day off! Thank you, the kids are going to be so excited to have you home and they are going to have pancakes for breakfast this morning."

Nicholas and Holly heard us talking. They came running down the stairs screaming, "I want pancakes daddy."

I simply looked at Garrett and said, "See I told you!"

What a great start to the day. Garrett fed the kids breakfast and I went and got ready to take the kids to school. I was still a little nervous because there were older kids at Valley View Academy. Kids that had over the years for some reason or another had become non believers and I wanted those kids to stay away from my little Nicholas. I wanted him to have fun at school and I wanted to just keep the Santa thing quiet for now.

On the way to school Holly asked, "Can we please take Nicholas to his classroom first so I can help?"

Nicholas was happy Holly wanted to help take him to his classroom on his first day of kindergarten. After he heard that he asked us, "Please Mimi....please daddy can sissy come with us to my classroom first."

After hearing that of course we weren't going to say 'no'. We happily agreed to let Holly come with us to take him to his classroom.

We had received a classroom assignment of B6 from Valley View for Nicholas. But when we arrived, we learned it was a different teacher than what we had been told. I checked the number on the outside of the door, even though I knew we were in B6. I looked around the classroom and I eventually went up to what looked like a teacher at the front of the classroom. I thought well maybe Ms. Leah was out sick or something but when I approached the woman at the front of the classroom, she told me Ms Leah had been replaced. I was a bit taken back but I was trying my best not to show it.

    I asked, "Oh....well if....if Ms. Leah isn't the teacher then who is going to be my little Nicholas's teacher?"

    The woman proudly announced, "Well of course I am. I am Ms. Broomer and I am the new kindergarten teacher."

    "Oh, well nice to meet you then," I politely stated before I turned and walked back to Garrett.

    We told Nicholas 'goodbye' from across the room and waved because he was already talking with some new friends he was making. We were very happy to see this and so we left. We walked Holly to her classroom next. We said our 'goodbye' at the door because I guess in fifth grade it must not be cool to have your parents walk you into the classroom. Garrett and I walked slowly back to our car.

    I was trying my best to keep my mouth shut until we were safely in the car. But as soon as Garrett's car door shut, I couldn't stay quiet any longer. I asked, "Okay so Nicholas was suppose to have a nice sweet teacher and now he has someone who looks like a wicked witch? I wanted him to have Ms. Leah not Ms. Broomer."

Garrett quickly responded, "What? Aren't you always the positive thinking queen? Let's wait and see how it goes for Nicholas in her classroom first."

He was right, I really was being a bit negative about Ms. Broomer and I didn't even really know her yet. So I agreed to give her the benefit of the doubt and be positive about her.

The day together with Garrett went by so quickly. We went to a movie, we had lunch together and before we knew it was already time to pick up the kids from school. We drove up to the front of the school to pick up the kids but we only saw Holly. At first I thought maybe Holly had forgotten to go and pick up her brother at his classroom. This was understandable because it was the first day of school and her routine was a little different now.

As soon as we reached where Holly was standing, she climbed into the car and before I could even ask where Nicholas was at, she quickly said, "Um you need to park the car and you both need to go to the office now."

I knew it obviously involved Nicholas and so a million questions began to fill my head and I began to panic about my little Nicholas. I had to ask Holly some essential questions as we were parking the car. "Is

Nicholas okay? Did he get hurt? Was someone not nice to him? Did they not want you to pick him up from his classroom? Come on Holly what's going on with your brother?" I asked impatiently.

Holly answered, "Slow down mom Nicholas is fine he didn't get hurt or anything. It's just that....well....he is in the principal's office. Mom, please don't get upset but he brought his Santa suit to school."

I abruptly interrupted Holly's story and asked, "What? Nicholas brought his Santa suit to school?"

Holly hesitantly replied, "Well....yes mom....but....well....he needed it today. I knew he was going to bring it and I didn't stop him. He told me about it this morning but he promised me he would leave it in his backpack the whole day. I'm so sorry mom, I should have stopped him and I should have told you."

Garrett was trying to park the car as fast as he could but the parking lot is always crazy in the afternoons. It always seems as if parents forget how to drive when they come to pick their child up from school. Finally though, the car was parked and we were on our way to the office.

I could see the tension building up in Garrett's face and neck. I told Garrett, "Just relax sweetheart and remember we need to completely support our little Nicholas in this situation no matter what."

"Um....okay but just know that we will have a huge talk with him about this at home," he replied a bit agitated.

When we arrived in the office, the receptionist had us sit down while she let the principal know we were there. It seemed as if the principal was making us wait forever before he finally came out to see us.

The principal approached us and said, "Hi....and you must be the parents of Nicholas. I am Principal Riley and I am sorry we couldn't be meeting under better terms but there was a bit of a disturbance today involving your son."

We followed him back to his office and we saw Nicholas sitting in a big black leather chair. Mr. Riley pushed his big black thick rimmed square glasses back up onto his nose as he continued, "It appears to us that Nicholas brought a costume to school today. Another child in his class opened his backpack and found the costume."

I had to ask myself why everyone keeps insisting on calling his Santa suit a costume. It's a suit and not a costume. For some unknown reason I was suddenly overcome with the need to clarify the issue with the principal.

"Principal Riley before you go any further you need to understand something. Nicholas has a Santa suit not a costume," I confidently stated.

Garrett looked at me a bit odd to say the least but I felt such a deep need to defend my sons Santa suit. I had made the commitment to always stand up for him as the new real Santa Claus and that is exactly what I was going to do. So out of respect for Nicholas as the new real Santa Claus, I had no other choice but to clarify the fact about the Santa suit.

Principal Riley continued this time though with quite a bit more sarcasm in his squeaky little voice, "Okay, well I am so sorry about that but the fact is he brought the costume….um the suit to school. Then he told all of his classmates he is the new real Santa Claus. We depend highly on honesty in this school and so we would appreciate you discussing this honesty issue more in depth with Nicholas at home. But I also wanted to let you know it caused quite a bit of disruption in the classroom as well and so eventually Ms. Broomer had no other choice but to send Nicholas to the office."

I didn't think it was appropriate at this time to argue the fact that Nicholas is the new real Santa. I decided to choose my words very carefully before saying, "Well his backpack is his personal possession and the other child had no business getting into my sons backpack. We will make sure Nicholas no longer brings his Santa suit to school but I would also like the guarantee that my sons stuff is going to be safe here at Valley View Academy. I do not want his belongings messed with by anyone anymore."

"Oh of course all of us always try our best to protect the possessions of each of the children here at Valley View Academy. I will try my best to insure nobody touches your son's possessions again," Mr. Riley quickly answered.

I was more than a bit annoyed at the events which had transpired today. I wanted to take all of my family home so I nicely asked Mr. Riley, "And is there anything else or can we take Nicholas home now?"

"Nicholas is all set to go home. As you can see he was given back his backpack and inside is his cost.... I mean Santa suit. I want to strongly encourage you to take care of this situation as soon as possible, hopefully today so there will no longer be any type of problems here at the school," stated Principal Riley. Then he shook our hands and showed the three of us to the door.

I grabbed Nicholas's hand and Garrett grabbed Holly's who was waiting in the waiting area of the office as we all quietly walked out to the car. It was almost dead silent in the car the entire ride home. I was pretty sure we were each trying to figure out what we were going to say to each other during the imminent family meeting when we got home. However, when we got home, Garrett went over to Nicholas's backpack and took his Santa suit out of the bag and went upstairs by himself.

About five minutes later Garrett came back down the stairs and announced to all of us, "Nicholas the Santa suit is gone. It is not gone for good but it is gone for now. You may have it back the day after Thanksgiving to wear for the Christmas season but then we put the suit back away the day after Christmas. Okay kids, anyone up for video games?"

We were all shocked by the fact we were obviously not having a family meeting as well as the fact, Garrett had taken the Santa suit away without even any type of discussion. Nicholas however was a bit relieved he wasn't getting into anymore trouble even though he had taken his Santa suit to school. I on the other hand, I didn't know exactly how or even what to think at that moment in time. I had such a range of mixed emotions in my head and I was trying to comprehend all of the emotions I was feeling.

That night Garrett volunteered to put Nicholas to bed first while I put Holly to bed. He was definitely taking his time putting Nicholas to bed but I could hear from the hallway they were having a discussion and so I didn't want to disturb them. I was definitely curious as to the content of their discussion but I knew it was none of my business and I wanted the two of them to get along so they could have a good father son relationship. I ended up staying in with Holly longer, which was nice because it had given me the opportunity to thank Holly for being supportive of her brother as the new real Santa.

Garrett finally came in to Holly's room and announced, "Time to switch," with a smile on his face. I took that as a good sign things had gone well during his big discussion with Nicholas.

I kissed Holly and told her, "Goodnight," and I went in to see my little Santa Claus.

As I entered his bedroom, I saw him lying in bed with a smile on his face. But I could also see a thinking expression on his face, which definitely let me know whatever Garrett must have told him, was making him think.

"Did you pick out a bedtime book?" I asked him softly trying to break his intense thought mode.

He looked up and muttered, "Um….a….what?"

I smiled and asked a bit louder this time thinking maybe he hadn't heard me the first time, "A book silly….did you pick out a book yet for Mimi to read to you?"

He was still a bit out of it but eventually replied, "Um….no….a book….I don't know what book to pick."

I went over to my little Nicholas and I kissed him on the cheek. I whispered into his ear, "I love you Santa and I will always believe in you Santa."

That was just what he needed to hear because he reached up and gave me a great big hug and said, "I love you too Mimi….thanks Mimi."

Nicholas jumped up out of bed and went to his book shelf to grab a book. "How about this book Mimi?"

I looked at which book he had chosen and I was delighted to see he had picked *I Love You Forever* by Robert Musch. "That is perfect Nicholas," I replied with a smile on my face.

"Come on up then Mimi, I saved you a spot right next to me," said Nicholas gleefully as he patted the spot right next to him up on his bed.

Little Nicholas and I both know this book by heart so we found ourselves saying the memorized words together and not really reading the book. When we finished the book, I crawled down off of his bed and I kissed him goodnight. I still was unsure as to whether or not I should ask what he and his father had talked about. So I kissed my little Santa goodnight and I headed for the door but I couldn't resist asking him about the conversation.

I turned the light switch back on, I walked over to him in his bed and I quietly asked, "Are you okay? Are you and daddy okay?"

I was unsure as to what his response was going to be and all I wanted was a positive response. I needed to know everything was going to be okay between him and his dad.

Nicholas looked up at me with his big beautiful eyes and whispered softly, "Mimi don't worry, I know daddy loves me. I think it may just take a little more time for daddy to really believe I am the new real Santa Claus. But its okay Mimi because I know daddy loves me no matter what. He even told me a secret!"

I couldn't help but interrupt Nicholas and ask, "Secret? What do you mean daddy told you a secret?"

He giggled quietly and answered, "Mimi I wasn't supposed to tell you but daddy said that if you got really curious then I could tell you."

"Okay Nicholas, I am really, really curious so tell me," I said eagerly.

Still giggling he replied, "Daddy is going to be my soccer coach! He already signed up and everything. I am super excited Mimi."

I quietly let out a "Whew!"

I kissed my Santa goodnight one more time and I happily left his room. Wow, I was excited Garrett was actually going to coach his son's soccer team. I knew Garrett had played soccer as a kid and he was really good athletically in sports but I thought it was absolutely amazing he was actually going to coach Nicholas's team.

Obviously the big smile on my face gave it away to Garrett that I knew the secret because as soon as he saw me, he smiled too and asked, "So I am guessing he told you, right?"

I went over and gave him a big hug, a kiss and excitedly exclaimed, "Uh….yes….of course he told me! It is going to be so awesome having you as the coach of his soccer team! But wait did you call and volunteer or did they call you?"

"Actually someone from the soccer league called me yesterday to see if I was interested in coaching because they were short on coaches. They told me I would be able to be Nicholas's team coach. So I said, 'yes'. I thought it would be fun and maybe it would take his mind off of Santa Claus and give him something else to think about," Garrett said proudly.

"Well thanks….thanks for thinking of Nicholas and for being such a great dad," I said thankfully.

I wasn't so keen on the idea he had decided to coach so Nicholas would get his mind off of Santa but I was happy as well as thankful he wanted to spend time with Nicholas and to be the soccer coach for his team.

CHAPTER 17

I was excited to help Garrett run the soccer team in any way I could.

"No Nicholas you have to wear the soccer uniform they gave you. You can't wear whatever you want to," I sternly told him.

It was the morning of his first soccer game and Nicholas was insisting he could wear his Santa hat during the game. I had been telling him all week he couldn't wear it but he wouldn't stop asking. At the moment I was really wishing Garrett wasn't the soccer coach because then we could have told Nicholas he couldn't go to the game. But since Garrett is the coach, Nicholas and I both needed to be there.

I guess I am a push over because I finally agreed to let Nicholas take his Santa hat to the game. The agreement though was the hat would stay in the bag while he was playing and he could only wear it when he sat on the sidelines and wasn't playing.

Nicholas had agreed to the terms I had set forth and I was really hoping he would keep to those terms at the soccer game. Nicholas played the first quarter very well. I was so proud of how well he focused and how energetic he was playing. It was his turn to sit out of the game during the second quarter. Of course the first thing he did was run over to his soccer bag to grab his Santa hat out of the bag. Nicholas proudly put his Santa hat on his head and went to sit on the sidelines by his teammates.

At first people young and old stared at Nicholas probably wondering why he was wearing a Santa hat in the early fall. I really didn't mind the stares and neither did Nicholas. I never minded the stares, in fact I guess I kind of like the attention Nicholas gets from them. On the other hand though, I absolutely hate it when people young or old decide to take it upon themselves to say something completely negative or just plain inappropriate.

Across the field I saw a strange looking man who seemed out of place staring at Nicholas. The strange man was a bit overweight with glasses and shoulder length brown scraggly hair, which I guess really is none of my business. At first, I thought maybe he was staring at Nicholas because then he wasn't the only one to seem so out of place. I was hoping the man across the field was not one to voice his negative opinions and I was hopeful he would keep all comments running through his head to himself.

The team was playing so well I had forgotten all about the strange man. We actually won the first soccer game. Our soccer team had been so great. The kids played without any fear. All of us were on a winning high so I never even noticed the strange looking man cross the field. Nor had I noticed him standing right next to us. As I saw the strange man up close, all that was going through my mind was it should be illegal for anyone to wear shorts so short and tight, out in public. I was nice though and I kept my mouth shut about his weird looking shorts so why couldn't he keep his mouth shut about my son?

The strange man walked right up to Nicholas and sarcastically said, "Hey kid it's not Christmas yet. Who do you think you are Santa or something?"

I was so extremely proud of my little Nicholas because he didn't get mad or anything. He looked up at the strange man and politely said, "Well actually….actually I am the new real Santa Claus so you better watch what you say to people or else your name will stay on the naughty list."

It was pretty funny because Nicholas had really thrown this guy off with his wonderful response. So much so the strange man had turned and walked away, unable to respond.

Garrett and Holly walked up to us. Garrett asked, "Hey is everything okay? Was the weird tight short guy talking to you two?"

I laughed and said, "Tell you later."

Garrett and I ended up having a good long laugh about the tight short guy later in the evening during our wine time. Garrett had actually been fine about Nicholas wearing his Santa hat on the sidelines today at the soccer game which made me happy. Hopefully this meant he was coming around and maybe he would become a Santa believer soon.

My personal target goal was for Garrett to become a Santa believer by this Christmas day. I thought maybe seeing Nicholas experience another Christmas as the new real Santa Claus would put him over the edge to the Santa believer side.

Nicholas is a smart child and he was getting really good grades in Kindergarten but he was still spending a good portion of school time in the principals office. He got along with most all of the kids in his class. There were only a few kids who seemed to tease him quite a bit. Nicholas was nice to the kids who were teasing him but he always seemed to take their bait.

One of the biggest bullies would tease Nicholas and say, "There is no such thing as Santa," or "Hey Santa where are your reindeers?" or "Where's your beard Santa?" to name a few.

Nicholas always responded back nicely saying, "I am the new real Santa," and "All of my reindeer are at the North Pole."

Mrs. Broomer would always send him to the principal claiming Nicholas was being disruptive in the classroom to the other children. Mrs. Broomer claimed Nicholas needed to control his imagination and wanted us to tell him he was not the new real Santa Claus. I of course adamantly refused to do any such thing.

Nicholas and Holly both had the day off from school and I had totally forgotten it wasn't a school day for them. However, it was obvious to me they both needed a break from school. But I had so many errands to run and so much to do during the day, I had the feeling everything was going to take me twice as long with two kids along for the day. I decided to make the best of it though and I promised Holly and Nicholas we would go to the zoo at the end of the day if I finished everything I needed to do. I was sure the promise of the zoo at the end of the day would definitely insure a smooth day for all three of us and I do have to say I was right.

Holly and Nicholas were dressed and ready to go quite quickly. Nicholas of course was in his Santa suit for the day. I had absolutely no idea how or where he had found his Santa suit but I was happy he had found it. I have to admit, I had really missed those bright red Santa pants with the soft white fur at the bottom as well as the Santa jacket with the bright and shinny brass buttons. Not to mention how the Santa hat fits my little Nicholas so perfectly. I suddenly felt extremely excited and fortunate to be able to spend the day with my fabulous daughter Holly as well as my very own Santa Claus.

The three of us loaded up into the car and we were off to complete my 'To do List'. My goal was set for all three us to get the chance to spend the last part of the day in the zoo and to get there as soon as possible. We didn't finish everything on the list until about three o'clock. Finally arriving at the zoo at about thirty minutes later, which was later than I had hoped. This actually worked out great because it gave us about an hour and a half before the zoo closed. Since it was near closing time, I was hoping there wouldn't be many people left crowding the displays.

As we entered the gates of the zoo parking lot, I knew I was batting a thousand today. My day was working out perfectly, was all I could think to myself. I was right, there were hardly any people left at the zoo. I was able to get a front row parking spot just a few feet from the entrance. It was Nicholas's turn to show my identification and the zoo pass to the man at the gate. As soon as we were through, Holly and Nicholas were off to see the seals. After the seals, we made our way to the alligator, which was really neat because the alligator was right near the fence so we could all see him really well. As we left the alligator and made our way to see the flamingos and the Meerkats, we began to see all of the Christmas decorations the zoo had begun to put up. All I could think to myself was it wasn't even Thanksgiving yet so how could there already be so many Christmas decorations out. Nicholas on the other hand was a bit excited to say the least, by the site of all of the Christmas decorations already displayed.

Nicholas threw out his arms and asked, "It's beautiful Mimi don't you love all of the decorations?"

We continued to walk deeper into the zoo interior coming around the corner before our destination. Nicholas got even more excited. "Oh my goodness Mimi they are already setting up a spot for me. Look at the presents at the entrance and I think maybe some of my reindeer will come here too. Oh Mimi, this is the best I have ever seen. Can I go in and see where I am going to be sitting?"

I quickly responded before Nicholas crossed into the construction area, which had large yellow tape across the entrance warning no admittance to non authorized personnel. "No sweetheart they are still working on it, preparing it for you. It's not quite ready. You should probably wait until they finish it all the way."

Nicholas turned and looked at me for a moment then happily responded, "You're right Mimi. I don't want to mess up anything they are working on for me. I will wait until they are all finished. Come on lets go, the Meerkats are waiting to see me. Oh and I know Mr. Komodo Dragon has definitely missed me."

Nicholas went running off to see the Meerkats first as if he owned the zoo. I think he would seriously consider living part time or even full time at the zoo if he could. Even though there were not a lot of people left at the zoo, the ones still here were fascinated by little Nicholas dressed as Santa Claus. Most of the little kids were waving to Nicholas and he was waving back at them with a huge smile. Some of the adults waved and said 'Hi Santa' but about a third of the adults just stared at Nicholas unsure of what exactly to think or say. It was as if some were a bit afraid to actually believe.

We made our way around the zoo and we saw Mr. Komodo Dragon, the Koala bears, the Kangaroos and even the Zebra's. But as we were walking towards the Gorilla's, I caught a little boy staring at my Nicholas. It was a different kind of stare, one I can't even begin to explain. All I knew about the stare of the little boy was it was a stare of amazement. Nothing like I had ever seen before.

We watched all of the Gorilla's play but I felt someone was not too far behind us and that we were being followed. I couldn't help myself so I had to look behind the three of us. Much to my surprise there was the little boy again. The same little boy who had been staring at Nicholas a few minutes prior and now he was with whom I believed was his dad. I kind of wanted them to pass by us because I wasn't quite sure why the little boy was so fascinated with my little Nicholas. I decided I would have Holly, Nicholas and I stop at the Tortoises.

I was trying not to be too obvious to the little boy and his dad so I quietly told the kids, "Hey, let's stop and look at the Tortoises. We haven't spent time with the Tortoises in quite awhile."

Holly and Nicholas kind of looked at me a bit funny as they stopped to look at the Tortoises with me.

I thought the little boy and his dad had walked by but then I heard a little voice say, "Daddy lets stop here next to Santa and look at the turtles with Santa."

I turned my head so quickly towards the little voice, I felt as if my head was going to spin right off. There stood the little boy with his dad. I could tell the dad was a bit embarrassed by his son's infatuation with my little Nicholas as Santa Claus. I guess I should have realized earlier the little boy was following us because he wanted to be near to Nicholas, the new real Santa Claus. Suddenly I began to understand the little boy's stare as he stared at my Nicholas once again. It was the stare of believing. I don't mean any believing, no the true believing in Santa Claus with absolutely no inhibitions or doubts whatsoever. Up to this point, I had seen believers in my son as the new real Santa Claus but never to this extent.

I could feel a strong sense of pride welling up inside of me after seeing the little boy's stare, an overcoming pride that I was lucky enough to be the Mimi of Santa Claus. I was proud because I get to see Santa Claus every single day and proud other people can see the big, jolly and selfless heart little Nicholas has too.

We continued our walk through the zoo seeing the Chimpanzee's, the Hippo and the Lions. I felt proud. I was seeing the zoo with Santa Claus right by my side. I no longer minded the little boy following us through the zoo.

I was lost in thought as we walked around the zoo until all of a sudden I heard a loud squeal from my little Nicholas. "Yeaaaaaaaaa! I can't believe it! It's out! It's out! Look Mimi, look sissy the Snow Leopard is out from behind its rock!"

Holly and Nicholas took off across the path to the Snow Leopard's home. Sure enough the Snow Leopard was actually out and walking around. The three of us stood there in awe at the extreme beauty of the Snow Leopard. Our moment of 'awe' was quickly interrupted by the little boy who had been following us through the zoo. He came up to where the three of us were standing in front of the bars and stood to the left side of Nicholas. I looked over and saw him staring at my Nicholas and I could tell he wanted to say something to him.

When the little boy couldn't keep his thought in anymore, he turned to Nicholas and asked him, "Are you the real Santa Claus?"

After the little boy asked this oh so important question to my little Nicholas, I couldn't help but wonder how Nicholas would answer this question. Is he just going to say 'yes' and expect the little boy to leave it at that? Would the little boy leave it at 'yes'? Would he keep asking my Nicholas questions? What if Nicholas didn't know what to say? What if…..? As a million questions of obvious negativity were going through my head, I noticed Nicholas was ready to answer this oh so important question the little boy had asked him.

As I glanced over at my Nicholas I saw him tilting his head down toward the little boy, I saw a huge smile flash upon his face and then I heard him answer, "Yes, I am the new real Santa Claus."

The little boy got very excited. He jumped up and screamed, "I knew it, I knew it! See daddy I told you he's the real Santa!"

Nicholas continued to have a huge smile on his face as he decided to assume his new jolly and friendly duties as the new real Santa Claus. He began to talk to the little boy. "Now have you seen all of the decorations my elves and I have been putting up around the zoo? I hope you like all of the Christmas trees and wreaths we have put up too. Oh and have you seen the lights we have been putting up? We have been working very hard but we aren't done decorating yet. So come back after Thanksgiving and you can see all of the finished decorations."

The little boys eyes were very big as he intently listened to Nicholas. When Nicholas was done asking the little boy about the decorations, the little boy exclaimed loudly, "Yes, yes, I love all of the decorations. You and the elves have done a great job!"

By this time, I really had the distinct feeling the little boy's dad was very ready to go. I soon found out, I was right. But as I stood there watching my Nicholas, the new real Santa Claus, I relished in the fact I am his Mimi. I couldn't help but continue to be so proud of how great of a job he was doing as the new real Santa Claus. I truly noticed how articulate and mature my Nicholas had now become. My thoughts though were once again interrupted, this time though by the little boy's dad.

"Come on son, it is time to go. We need to get home soon", said the little boy's dad.

The little boy really didn't want to leave his new famous friend but his dad grabbed his hand and led him away. The entire time the little boy was looking back at the new real Santa Claus waving and saying, "Bye Santa Claus, thank you Santa Claus. I know you know I have been really good this year Santa. Bye Santa…..bye Santa….."

Nicholas stood there and waved to the little boy until he could no longer see nor hear the little boy anymore. He stood there for a moment longer before he turned back around to see Holly and I standing there watching him. Holly and I were still in a bit of shock and amazement at what had transpired at the zoo. I was quite thankful I was not the new real Santa Claus. I don't think I could have pulled off what Nicholas had so eloquently pulled off. My Nicholas had helped the little boy's excitement in Christmas by being himself.

We made our way through the rest of the zoo before heading to the exit. Of course we could not exit the zoo without Nicholas telling the alligator goodbye one last time and Holly telling the seal goodbye one last time. It's always funny to watch the kids telling the animal's at the zoo goodbye before we leave for the day. They tend to say goodbye to the animal's as if they are never going to see them again. I think they must forget we maintain a yearly pass to the zoo. I never mind bringing them to the zoo because we always learn new things about at least one of the animals every time we come.

We were walking out to the car holding hands when all of a sudden Nicholas stopped right in his tracks. "Mimi, please don't tell daddy I wore my Santa suit to the zoo. Remember, he said I couldn't wear my suit out in public anymore except on Christmas because it causes too much of a strick?"

"Too much of a what Nicholas?" I asked quickly but then I remembered exactly what Nicholas was talking about. "Oh you mean too much of a stir. Well sweetheart all three of us had a fabulous day today and we should all be proud of our day. I know daddy wouldn't be happy I let you wear your Santa suit out of the house before Christmas. So mum's the word. None of us will talk about today except between the three of us."

The three of us quietly continued our walk to the car. I never keep anything from Garrett but he was out of town for training and truthfully, I didn't agree with his decision to not let Nicholas wear his Santa suit year round. I am so past the point of caring what other people think about my children. I don't care anymore if someone has a problem with what Holly or Nicholas wears or imagines. In defense of Garrett though, I do understand it is hard at first to accept your child as they are. But I do accept Holly and Nicholas for who they are. I have learned to appreciate everything about them and to let them be who they really are. I do know Garrett will one day come to understand the importance of accepting our children no matter what. My only hope is it will be sooner rather than later for the sake of Holly and Nicholas but also for his sake.

After Nicholas had taken his Santa suit off to put his pajamas on, I neatly folded up his Santa suit and I put it on the high shelf in Garrett's closet. I was hopeful Garrett wouldn't notice the suit had been moved. In fact, I still wasn't sure where Garrett had originally hid the Santa suit. But Nicholas had found it and I didn't feel the need to put the Santa suit back in Garrett's exact original hiding location. Besides Nicholas had once told me it didn't really matter where his Santa suit was hidden because the elves would always either get the Santa suit for him or tell him where the Santa suit was hidden.

"Mimi I want....well actually....Mimi I need to tell you that I will be going to the North Pole soon. I think it should only be for the night but I do have a whole lot of stuff to check on before Christmas Eve," said Nicholas in a very serious tone.

I knew Christmas was fast approaching so I already knew Jack would be coming to get him soon. I knowingly replied, "Sweetheart I understand you have a lot to work on. So it's okay if you are gone all night, you just concentrate on what needs to be done to get ready for Christmas."

I had fully accepted my son as the new real Santa Claus and I was so proud of how many responsibilities he was taking on at the North Pole. He loved being Santa and he took his job quite seriously. I was so excited for Christmas morning. I had been so surprised and amazed with last year, I found myself getting extremely anxious for this year. Santa had brought all of us the best and most meaningful presents last year so I was curious what Santa would do this year.

CHAPTER 18

As soon as Nicholas arrived at the North Pole he turned to Jack and confidently said, "Thanks Jack for coming and getting me one last time before Christmas Eve. I have made a list of stuff I need to do and when I am done with my list you can let me know if there is anything else I need to complete before Christmas Eve."

"Wow Santa, you sure are prepared this year. I am really proud you thought ahead and made a list of chores for yourself. I have been working on a lot of stuff at the North Pole too so I have arranged for a different elf to take you around as you are completing your chores tonight," responded Jack trying not to smile.

Nicholas responded in utter shock, "What? But Jack....you....you are the head elf....you're my head elf. You are the one who is suppose to take me around because--"

Just then a little voice came from behind the chair interrupting Nicholas, "What Santa? Am I not good enough to take you around?"

Nicholas looked around and smiled as he saw his very best elf friend Isabella standing there. He ran up to Isabella, gave her a great big hug and told her, "Of course you can be my tour guide elf today at the North Pole," then

Nicholas turned and smiled at Jack and said, "Thanks Jack!"

Jack knew Santa and Isabella were such good friends so he knew Santa would love to spend the time with Isabella while he did his chores around the North Pole.

Before the two of them started with their chores, Isabella told Nicholas, "Okay Santa let's go outside, I have one more surprise for you!"

Nicholas saw it as soon as he walked out the front door and he let out a loud, "Awesome!"

Isabella had arranged to have a bright red golf cart to drive Santa around the North Pole that night. She knew Santa didn't like to walk from place to place very much and he had loved being driven around in a golf cart at the North Pole earlier in the year.

She already knew the answer but she had to ask, "Do you like it Santa?"

Nicholas looked at her and said, "No I don't like it....I love it! It is perfect. Can I drive it later tonight? I will drive really well, I promise!"

Isabella smiled and said, "Get in Santa....what are you waiting for?"

Nicholas jumped into the golf cart and they were off to the reindeer area first. Tonight Nicholas would be announcing the names of the eight reindeers he had chosen to be his team for Christmas this year. He was a little nervous because he didn't want to hurt any of the reindeer's feelings. He knew all of the reindeer had been working extremely hard this year to be a part of his team. But he was confident in his decision.

As they approached the reindeer area Nicholas was amazed at how many of the elves had shown up to hear the reindeer team announcement. The elves and the reindeer were already outside waiting for Santa to arrive so Isabella drove the golf cart right up to where they were all waiting.

Nicholas was so excited he leaped out of the golf cart before Isabella came to a complete stop. As soon as he had jumped out, he walked right up in front of the waiting elves and reindeers and announced, "Okay everyone, I know all of you are very eager and excited for my announcement tonight and so am I. But first, before I announce the eight reindeers I have chosen to be my sleigh team this year, I want to make it clear to everyone this was not an easy decision. All of the reindeer did work very hard this year and I am proud of all of my reindeer."

"Go ahead then....tell all of us which reindeer you chose," said an obviously over eager elf in the crowd.

So Nicholas began, "Okay, okay I will tell you in no specific order. I have chosen Donner, Prancer, Comet, Cupid, Rudolph, Dasher, Blitzen and last but certainly not least, I have chosen Dancer."

One by one, each of the chosen reindeer made their way up to the front to stand by Santa as they heard their name called. The crowd cheered after they had heard Santa name all of the reindeer for the sleigh team. All of the reindeers chosen were so proud to have been picked by Santa. It was truly a great honor to be a part of Santa's sleigh team.

After Nicholas had congratulated all of the reindeers he had chosen for his sleigh team, he turned to Isabella and told her, "I will be right back. You just wait here. There is something I need to do."

Isabella had no idea what Santa needed to do. She knew he had a big job with a lot of responsibilities so she happily replied, "Perfect. I will be waiting right here for you so come back here as soon as you are done."

Nicholas had known Vixen would be upset because he had not been chosen to be a part of the sleigh team this year. But Nicholas knew Vixen had still been having a little bit of trouble with his foot since he had injured it earlier in the year. Nicholas did not want to put Vixen at risk of hurting the foot again.

Vixen was lying down in the corner of the barn facing towards the wall with his head hanging down when Nicholas finally spotted him. He was obviously upset and hurt but Nicholas knew he had done what he had to do. Nicholas wanted to make Vixen feel better. Nicholas was unsure of what to even say to Vixen to make him feel better so he sat down on the floor of the barn right next to him.

After a few quiet moments of sitting there next to Vixen, Nicholas turned and gently said, "I am so sorry Vixen.....I wanted.....I really did want to pick you. It's just that....well....it's just that I was worried about you. I was worried you could possibly hurt your foot more if you were on my sleigh team this year."

Vixen murmured softly, "My foot is fine Santa."

Nicholas replied very honestly, "No Vixen your foot is not fine. Your foot still has some healing to do and I understand you are strong Vixen but you need to take it easy so your foot has time to heal correctly."

Vixen shook his head and replied, "Santa I just wanted to be a part of your sleigh team. That is what all of us reindeers work so hard for all year long. I am tough and I am strong so I know I would be fine on your sleigh team."

The niceness angle wasn't working and Nicholas knew it so he firmly responded back to Vixen saying, "Look Vixen, you are one of my reindeers and I care about you very much so I make the rules. You are not to work out until the first day of next year. I want you better and on my sleigh team next year."

Vixen knew Santa was serious by the tone of his voice so he replied, "Fine Santa, I will do everything you say only because you are Santa and you watch, I will be on the sleigh team next year and I will be bigger and better than ever before."

"I know you will be Vixen and I can't wait," replied Nicholas.

Santa knew Vixen was extremely competitive so he knew Vixen would be a part of his sleigh team the next year. He gave Vixen a great big hug and left to meet Isabella outside.

When Nicholas got outside, Isabella was already waiting for him in the golf cart. As he was getting in she asked, "Everything okay Santa?"

Nicholas smiled as best he could and replied, "Yes its okay let's just get on to our next chore, the toy factory toy check."

"Then we're off to the infamous toy factory Santa!" Isabella exclaimed as they sped away.

It was a bit of a drive to the toy factory and Isabella knew Santa very badly wanted to drive the golf cart. When they were about half way to the toy factory, Isabella pulled the golf cart over and jumped out.

Nicholas quickly asked, "Ms. Isabella....what....what are you doing?"

She giggled and told him, "Get out Santa it's your turn to drive!"

"What? Are you serious? I get to drive?" Nicholas asked in utter amazement and shock.

Before Isabella could even answer any of the questions he was already jumping into the driver's seat. It was a bit rough at first but they had tons of fun and couldn't stop laughing the rest of the way to the toy factory.

Nicholas was so happy to see how organized and efficient the elves were at the toy factory this year. The elves were already finished making all of the toys for this Christmas. All Nicholas had to do was to inspect the quality and workmanship of the toys. This chore really didn't take him long to complete because he had been inspecting the toys all throughout the year already.

When Nicholas finished his inspection, he grabbed a megaphone and climbed up on top of a ladder in the toy factory, announcing, "Elves, come on over here….all of you….I have an announcement to make."

The elves loved Santa and they were eager to hear what he had to say so they quickly gathered around the base of the ladder.

"I want to say thank you, to all of you. All of you have done an extraordinary job this year with the toys. I have never seen such quality toys before. Your attention to detail really shows through all of the toys each and every one of you chose to make. All of your work raised you above being just ordinary elf toy makers. These toys show me and people all over the world who will be receiving them, the elves here in my workshop are extraordinary elf toy makers. You elves truly rock!" Nicholas announced proudly.

Every elf had a smile on their face as Nicholas thanked them. They were all so pleased to hear Santa was so proud of them. Some of the toys the elves had been designing last year had been boring and Nicholas hadn't found those toys to be much fun. He had encouraged the elves to have fun making and designing the toys and not to be so serious all the time. Nicholas even had Jack install a stereo system in the toy factory so the elves could listen to fun music as they worked.

Nicholas told all of the elves, "Goodbye my elf friends and I will see all of you very soon when I come back on Christmas Eve," he waved and was off to his last chore.

Nicholas had made sure to really concentrate on the nice list and the naughty list. There were a few kids he was unsure whether or not they deserved to be on the naughty list. They were the bullies at school who had been teasing him. Nicholas was trying very hard to be impartial when it came to them. He was finding it so very hard to do, he knew he needed to speak with Carl.

Carl was still a bit overprotective of both the nice list and the naughty list since the 'situation' earlier in the year but luckily he wasn't mad anymore about what had happened. Nicholas had been very positive about the 'situation' because it ended up being for the best. Jack and Carl were once again the best of friends and they helped each other in their duties at the North Pole now.

Nicholas felt perfectly comfortable with Carl so he had no problem going right up to him and asking, "Um....Carl....I have something important about the lists I need to talk to you about. But wait....don't worry both of the lists are fine....I didn't lose anything."

Carl smiled and said, "Go on....you can ask me whatever you want."

"Well Carl....it's just that....well there are those bullies in my class who tease me about being Santa

Claus....and....well I don't know whether I should put them on the naughty or the nice list. I want to be fair like I am with all of the children," explained a confused little Nicholas.

Carl thought for a moment before answering, "Well Santa, I want you to know I have watched some of the video footage of how those bullies treat you and it isn't nice at all. I don't like how they treat you and it does make me more upset because you are Santa. They're behavior towards you, well it's not acceptable. It is always your final decision Santa but you don't need to feel bad at all if you put the bullies on the naughty list."

Nicholas always enjoyed the insightfulness of Carl and he was happy he had asked Carl. He told Carl, "Thanks," and went back over to his desk to think about his big decision a little more.

Both the nice list and the naughty list are very important and Nicholas valued both of them very much. On this day, Nicholas had spent a lot of quality time on the lists. He hoped as the years go by, reviewing the lists would begin to get easier and easier.

When Nicholas was all finished with the lists, he got up from his desk to get Isabella so they could report back to Jack. Nicholas was really trying his best to get back home before anyone got up that morning and he was trying to get home in enough time so he could get a little bit of sleep too.

He found Isabella still sitting in the corner watching the monitors with some of the other elves "Come on Isabella, I think you have had enough video watching for the day."

Isabella was having a fun time but she was happy he was finally finished with the lists. Usually she only worked in the toy factory so she hadn't ever been allowed to come to the behavior room to watch how kids were behaving all over the world. It was actually very entertaining. She was amazed by the number of temper tantrums some kids throw. Isabella also was extremely amazed at how naughty some kids were when no one was looking and how they would lie about it. She was happy she lived at the North Pole and not with all of the naughty children.

It was a quiet ride in the golf cart on the way back to meet up with Jack. Nicholas was happy he had come to the North Pole tonight, it was so beautiful. He found himself looking in every which way all around the North Pole. The elves always worked so hard to keep everything looking really nice there. The brass doors and poles were always so bright and polished. The windows were always clean with no smudges and it seemed as if there was never anything out of place at the North Pole.

On the other hand Isabella found herself being quiet because she always hated when it was time for Santa to leave the North Pole. She had felt very lucky this time though. She was grateful Jack had chosen her to be Santa's tour guide at the North Pole tonight. Every year a team of elves were chosen as the elf sleigh team. The elves chosen to be a part of the sleigh team would get everything in Santa's sleigh ready for Christmas Eve and then they would be in charge of all radio contact with Santa during present deliveries. It did make Isabella feel a bit better about Santa leaving because he had chosen her to be a part of the elf sleigh team this year. So Isabella knew she would get to see Santa on Christmas Eve.

Before long they were already back at the house and there was Jack waiting out front to greet them. "So how did every thing go you two?" He asked.

Nicholas and Isabella turned and looked at each other as they said in unison, "Fabulous!"

He chuckled a little bit and replied, "Well thank you Isabella for taking Santa around the North Pole today and we will both be seeing you again on Christmas Eve."

Isabella quickly replied, "No Jack, I thank you for choosing me to take Santa around the North Pole. It truly was an honor to be able to do that. But it is getting late and I know Santa needs to be leaving soon so goodbye Santa and goodbye Jack thanks for all the fun tonight!" And in a flash she was gone speeding off in the little red golf cart.

As soon as she was gone Jack turned to Nicholas taking on a bit of a serious tone he said, "Santa, I will be taking you back home very soon but we need to go inside and go over what you did today."

Nicholas always enjoyed spending time with Jack. He had been looking forward to sitting down, having a nice cup of hot chocolate with Jack and discussing the night at the North Pole. He quickly walked into the sitting area of the house, checking to see if there was a cup of hot chocolate setting by his chair.

As soon as he reached the sitting area he smiled when he saw his Santa mug setting by his chair. He turned around and told Jack, "Thank you Jack for making me my hot chocolate. I thought you might have forgotten all about my hot chocolate today."

Jack smiled and replied, "You're welcome. I hope you enjoy it. But Santa you know I make you your hot chocolate every time you come to the North Pole. Did you seriously think I would forget something as important as your hot chocolate?"

Nicholas smiled and said, "Okay I knew you wouldn't forget....well I was hopeful you hadn't forgotten my hot chocolate."

"Okay Santa enough of that now, we need to get down to business," replied Jack.

Nicholas told Jack everything he had accomplished and even which reindeers he had chosen as his sleigh team for this Christmas. Jack was amazed Santa had completed all of those chores so perfectly that day. In fact, Jack had nothing left on his list for Santa to do during this trip. It looked as if everything was ready for Christmas Eve and now all they had to do was wait for the wonderful day, which was fast approaching.

"Ok Santa it is time for you to go back to your house now. I don't want you to be late again like last time. That was horrible, although all of us here at the North Pole did enjoy having you here for those few extra days. This time though Santa I won't be accompanying you back to your mom and dads house," announced Jack.

Nicholas paused for a moment unsure exactly what to think. Jack had always taken him through the port hole he had never gone by himself before. What if he got stuck in the port hole or what if the porthole took him to the wrong house? It seemed as if a million questions were buzzing through his head and he didn't know how to make them stop.

Jack saw the confused and scared look on his face so he reassuringly told him, "Santa you will be fine! I have always gone with you home to supervise you but I am so proud of you because you don't need supervision anymore. You are running things here at the North Pole very efficiently and you are very, very smart so I know you will be fine. Plus, I will be watching you from the video room the entire time. Okay?"

"Okay Jack. I know I will be fine, it's just I always enjoyed it when you take me home after each visit to the North Pole," said Nicholas as he tried his best to keep a smile on his face.

Jack walked Nicholas to the port hole and gave him a great big hug and then he was gone. Jack had raced over to the video room as he had promised so he could watch Santa arrive back at his house with his parents. He knew Santa would be okay but he was still a little nervous to say the least about Santa's first trip in the port hole by himself. It seemed as if it took forever but finally Santa arrived back at his house with his parents and luckily everyone was still asleep when he arrived. Jack breathed a huge sigh of relief before returning to his daily duties.

Nicholas was very tired when he arrived home from the North Pole. He climbed out of the port hole and went straight off to bed. It seemed as if he had only been asleep for a moment when he heard his sissy running into his room to wake him up. He slowly peeled open his eyes and saw his sissy was staring directly at him.

"I know where you were last night bro, bro," whispered Holly.

"What do you mean you know where I was last night?" asked Nicholas.

"I know you went to the North Pole Nicholas 'cause I came in your room to check on you last night and you weren't here," replied Holly.

Nicholas knew Holly was happy he had gone to the North Pole because she knew how much he loved it there. There was no reason to not be honest with Holly thought Nicholas. Plus he knew exactly where she was going with this conversation so he decided to ask her before she could ask him.

"So sissy, are you helping me out this Christmas Eve again?" asked Nicholas.

Holly couldn't help but smile as she replied with excitement, "Um….only if you want me to bro, bro."

"Of course I want you to help me with the present delivery on Christmas Eve. You are an expert now and I don't want to deliver presents without you. It would not be the same without you!" announced a proud Nicholas.

Holly gave her brother a great big hug and said, "Come on let's go wake up mom and dad so they can make us breakfast!"

They ran and jumped up on their parent's bed as if it was a trampoline. They were happy their daddy was back from is trip and everyone was craving daddy's pancakes. So it was a pancake breakfast morning for the entire family.

CHAPTER 19

I could hardily believe it was already Thanksgiving Day again. It seemed as if this year had flown by. On the way to Thanksgiving dinner at grandma's house, Garrett had asked if it would be okay if we left a bit early from grandma's house. He wanted some family time of our own on Thanksgiving this year, just the four of us. I was happy because I always enjoy spending time with Garrett and the kids. Sometimes life seems to pass right by and we forget to make enough time for each other.

Thanksgiving dinner was so delicious and there was probably enough food there to feed at least another twenty people. My grandma loves to cook and I know she always wants to make sure there is enough food for everyone.

We each ate a piece of my mom's mouth watering pumpkin pie before we said our goodbyes and headed back home. On the drive home Garrett called his song first so he turned on *Jingle Bell Rock* and we all found ourselves singing along.

As we drove into the driveway, Garrett stopped when we were about halfway into the garage and announced, "Okay everyone we left grandma's house early because we are going to have family fun night tonight. When we get inside I want everyone to get their pajamas on and report back down to the family room for some fun."

'Wow', was the only word running through my head. I was so proud Garrett had planned a family night for all of us tonight. Actually all of us were extremely excited but taken a bit off guard by the surprise. Nicholas and Holly raced upstairs to quickly put their pajamas on with Garrett and I not far behind them.

Within three minutes Holly and Nicholas were already back downstairs in the family room waiting impatiently. I heard Holly announce, "Come on everyone, what's taking everybody so long?"

I was dressed in my pajamas and ready to go back downstairs. I wanted to wait for Garrett to finish getting into his pajamas before I went back downstairs. He looked over at me and saw how impatient I was becoming so he said, "You can go ahead downstairs and be with the kids. I will be there in a few minutes."

"What? Don't you want me to wait for you?" I asked quite curiously.

Garrett turned and smiled at me, "Nope. Go ahead down and sit on the couch and wait for me. I will be down in a few minutes."

I agreed to go downstairs, however I was more than a bit curious as to what Garrett was planning.

"Mimi....Mimi....where is daddy? What's taking so long?" Nicholas asked as soon as he saw me walking down the stairs.

"I don't know sweetheart. But we are all going to sit down on the couch and wait for daddy. He has a fun night planned for all of us," I answered.

Garrett finally came walking down the stairs with a bag in his hands, which made all of us even more curious to say the least. We watched him so intently with our eyes as he finally walked to the front of the couch to face all three of us.

Garrett held his bag in his arms and began, "First of all I want to say what I am thankful for and then each of you will get your own turn to say what you are thankful for right now."

All three of us clapped in excitement and Nicholas asked, "Then what do we get to do daddy?"

"You are going to have to wait and see my little man," Garrett continued, "First of all, I want to say I am thankful for all three of you and you each need to be acknowledged for what is extra special about you in my eyes."

Garrett reached into the bag and pulled out little Nicholas's Santa suit. As soon as he saw his daddy holding his Santa suit he jumped up onto his feet and jumped up and down on the couch. He was so excited. I seriously thought he was going to fall right off of the couch.

"Thank you daddy, thank you daddy!" Nicholas exclaimed unable to control his excitement.

Garrett laughed and said, "Okay, okay I know you are excited but I need to have my turn to tell everyone what I am thankful for."

Nicholas quietly sat back down on the couch with a huge smile remaining on his face.

Garrett continued, "Nicholas here is your Santa suit back. I know it is a day early but that's okay. I am thankful you are my son, the new real Santa Claus. I am thankful you are you and I could never have asked for a better son. I want you to know I am proud of you and proud you are the new real Santa Claus."

Nicholas was handed his Santa suit and his daddy gave him a great big hug. I was still unsure exactly what made Garrett have a sudden change of heart. I guess it didn't matter, I was happy with his change of heart and it really didn't matter where his change of heart had come from, only that it was there.

Garrett turned to Holly, "And next we come to you Holly, my perfect Holly. I am thankful you are you as well. I am thankful you have such a huge heart, you always try your best and you play the game of life full out. Thank you Holly!"

He reached down and gave Holly a great big hug and now I knew it was going to be my turn. I had absolutely no idea what he was going to say about me.

Sure enough Garrett looked at me and continued, "And last but certainly not least, I am thankful for you Mimi. I am so thankful you are so supportive of our children and that you encourage them to always believe....to believe in themselves and you always let them know they are truly exceptional children. I am also thankful for your strength....your strength to believe in our son and your strength to allow him to be the new real Santa Claus. I am truly blessed to have such a wonderful family."

Garrett walked over to the couch and we all gave each other a big family hug. Garrett had other surprises in his bag as well. He had bought a new family picture search game we all played for a few hours but to top it all off, he also bought a new Santa movie for all of us to watch together. Every one of us had a blast and everything in our world felt so perfect.

As I closed my eyes that night, I dreamed of the North Pole and my little Nicholas walking around playing with the elves there in his bright red Santa suit. Usually I tend to dream of the North Pole on the nights after Nicholas tells me a new story about the North Pole. So, I wasn't sure why I was dreaming about my little Nicholas at the North Pole tonight. I guess it was how excited I was about Christmas and way too eager for it to be here especially after the phenomenal Thanksgiving we had this year.

I knew Nicholas had his own list at the North Pole but I had to write out my own list here for family. I think I hate working on my Christmas list about as much as Nicholas hates working on the naughty and nice lists. What do I get my sister for Christmas? What do I get my mom and dad for Christmas? What do I get my aunt for Christmas? And I can't forget about my cousins and my nephew. One always wants to get a nice but genuine gift for the people on their list, at least I do. I know everyone will like whatever I get them it's just I like to give gifts with a meaning.

One by one I was able to check everyone off of my list. All of the presents were wrapped and under the tree. The house was decorated outside with an array of decorations and bright colorful twinkle lights. Inside the house was decorated probably a bit too decorative but oh well Nicholas loved it and he was the one who kept adding decorations. Every time we went to a store he would convince Garrett or me to buy another Christmas decoration. But over decorating was okay, I was happy with how festive our house looked, although I did feel like it was probably starting to look a bit too much like the North Pole. Except for the fact we didn't have the huge edible candy canes everywhere like Nicholas told me there was.

I had wanted to buy an artificial tree this year but Nicholas had pretty much prohibited us from putting up an artificial tree. Nicholas had claimed he needed the smell of a real Christmas tree or the tree didn't count as a Christmas tree. The four of us went to the Christmas tree lot of his choice to buy our tree. He was very picky about the tree he picked for us this year. It wasn't that the tree had to be a certain height or look a certain way. No, it had to smell a certain way. I had never heard about the different smells of Christmas trees but I trusted him and so we let him smell as many trees as he wanted to until he found a perfectly scented tree.

"This one....this tree....it's the one. Come on daddy come get this tree," Nicholas had exclaimed quite loudly at the tree lot.

Garrett set up the tree as soon as we got home and we had all helped decorate it. Nicholas had Holly help him place the new silver star from last Christmas on top of the tree and it looked perfect. And yes it smelled perfect too.

Suddenly it was Christmas Eve and it seemed as if we were eating Thanksgiving dinner yesterday. I was absolutely ready though and so very excited for Christmas morning to come. It was as if I was beginning to feel like a kid again. Nicholas had asked me what I wanted him to deliver for me on Christmas morning and I had told him anything would be perfect and that I wanted him to surprise me again.

Once again this year we left my aunt's house early so Nicholas and Holly could go to bed early. As soon as we arrived home they both went running up to Nicholas's room. I tucked Nicholas in bed and I tucked Holly in her sleeping bag on the floor right next to his bed.

"Goodnight Mimi, we don't need a book tonight. We will wake you up in the morning. Goodnight," they both said almost in unison.

Had they practiced that or what I thought to myself?

As I was closing the door, Nicholas said, "Mimi....Mimi....don't worry we will both be safe. I will watch Holly and keep her safe. I love you Mimi."

Before I could even respond, Holly quickly stated, "Mom I will take care of Nicholas, since I am the oldest."

"You may be the oldest sissy but remember I am Santa Claus!" Nicholas reminded Holly.

I knew this would keep going back and forth so I went back into his room to give them each one more kiss.

Before leaving I whispered loud enough for them both to hear me, "I love you both and both of you need to take care of each other."

How does one make them self go to sleep when they are filled with an overwhelming amount of excitement? As I walked back to my bedroom, I had absolutely no idea how I was going to make myself go to sleep tonight. I could not wait to see what my little Nicholas had brought for all of us this Christmas.

Garrett could see I was having a difficult time going to sleep so he said, "Close your eyes and think happy thoughts about the North Pole. Think about our son and daughter flying across the entire world to deliver presents to people young and old. Imagine the reindeer team Nicholas chose for this year flying through the sky and…."

"Mimi….Mimi….Mimi! Wake up Mimi you gotta come downstairs to see what I brought for everyone," Nicholas said as he was shaking me the best he could to wake me up.

What? Was it already Christmas morning? The last thing I remembered was falling asleep as Garrett told me happy thoughts about the North Pole. I looked at my watch and saw yes....yes it is Christmas morning.

I practically flew out of bed as I was screaming at Garrett, "Wake up honey....wake up....it's Christmas....it's Christmas morning!"

Garrett knew I was so overly eager for Christmas morning he jumped right out of bed and the four of us ran downstairs together. Of course Garrett and I did grab the camera and the camcorder but this year I let us all run down together.

Nicholas had an extreme amount of energy this morning and he was the first one to get downstairs. He flipped on the lights to the family room and all of us stopped right in our footsteps. It was even more perfect and beautiful than last year. I had been unsure as to how Nicholas would top last year but he did.

"It's perfect Nicholas! I love it!" I exclaimed as soon as I could speak.

Nicholas simply smiled a huge smile of his and ran over to the fireplace with Holly, Garrett and I close behind him so we could see all of the wonderful gifts. This year though, there wasn't a big present setting out for Holly. I saw her look around a bit and I was proud she managed to stay excited even though she didn't see a big present for herself.

Nicholas quickly grabbed a small package lying underneath her stocking, which hung from the fireplace. Nicholas handed Holly the small package as he was trying his very best to contain his excitement. I had absolutely no idea what he had gotten Holly in the small package but I was very eager to find out.

"Sissy you need to open this one first....go ahead open it....now!" Nicholas loudly exclaimed.

I could definitely tell Holly was a bit unsure of what exactly was in the small package. But she followed her brother's directions, quickly ripping the paper off and opening the box. She stared at the box for a moment and I could tell this is not what she had asked Santa to get her for Christmas.

Nicholas was obviously starting to get a bit impatient with his sissy when he shouted, "Seriously sissy open the paper up and read it out loud!"

So Holly took out the small piece of paper and read out loud, "Go out to the garage and find me."

Obviously it all clicked for Holly as soon as she read those words out loud because she dropped the piece of paper and the box. She ran out to the garage and stopped as she exited. There it sat in the garage right by the back door. As soon as I saw it, I looked over at Nicholas and I continued looking at him until he caught my eyes staring at him.

Nicholas walked over to me and motioned for me to bend down so he could tell me something. "Mimi....it's Christmas....and....well it's what sissy wanted and has been wanting for a really long time," he whispered.

I watched Holly as she reached down and unlatched the lock on the door from the crate. She reached in and gently took out the cutest Yorkshire Terrier from the crate and cuddled him. Holly was so overwhelmed and happy tears began to stream down her face as she snuggled up and softly spoke to her new little puppy. Nicholas knew Holly couldn't speak so he went over to her and she put her empty arm around him until she could speak.

In a soft and quiet tone she said, "Thanks Santa….he….he is perfect. I love him!"

"Okay well bring him inside so we can all open our present's sissy," said an excited little Nicholas.

As soon as we were all back inside Nicholas ran over to the fireplace, grabbed my stocking and brought it over to me. I looked in my stocking and I was so excited to see another box wrapped in silver paper with a bright red ribbon this year. I had no idea what gift Nicholas could have gotten me to even come close to the incredible necklace he had given me last Christmas. I never take the necklace he gave me off. It is my most prized possession and I never have the desire to take it off because I always want it right with me.

I lifted the soft lid off of the box and I couldn't believe what I saw. How could a little boy get the right gift for his Mimi every year? I slowly took it out of the box so I could get a closer look at it. It was absolutely beautiful and like no other bracelet I had ever seen.

Nicholas was looking at me intently and he couldn't keep his words in any longer, "Mimi it's a charm bracelet. Do you like it? It's going to have only charms about me being the new real Santa Claus. Look the first charm is me in my Santa suit. I also had the elves make you a charm that says 'Mimi'."

Nicholas stood up proudly announcing, "Okay everyone I want all of you to pour out your stockings because all of us have a matching present."

All of us did as Nicholas asked and we poured out our stockings. We all found a small silver key inscribed with the word 'Believe.'

I put my arms around him and I gave my Santa a great big hug. He is always so thoughtful. He loves to see others happy and it shows. As I hugged my little Santa, tears of joy began to run down my face. This was truly another great Christmas and I wasn't even upset he had given his sissy a puppy without consulting his Mimi first.

CHAPTER 20

It turned out once again to be the perfect Christmas and perfect New Years. I was so excited to start the New Year with all four of us on the same page in life. All of us had come to appreciate and to accept each other for who we are. But I did know life always likes to throw you those sudden curve balls and little did I know the curve ball we would be receiving in the New Year.

Life is one step at a time and one must live life day by day but we were all having a great year so far and I wasn't at all prepared for a bump in the road of our perfect life. The bump in the road came up quite suddenly one beautiful March afternoon. I knew it wasn't my fault because I got the mail. But I wish I had never even gone to the mailbox that day. I know inevitably I would have received the letter no matter what but I wish I had never received the letter.

I remember unlocking the mailbox and taking the stack of mail out of the mailbox. The letter was the one on top and as soon as I saw it was a letter from the school I froze. I didn't know what to do but a strange feeling came over me and I knew it wasn't a good letter. It wasn't report card time and the letter looked too official. It was an envelope made of expensive paper stock and addressee said, "To the Parents of Nicholas Johnson."

    I didn't want Holly or Nicholas to see me open up the letter so I made them their after school snack and I let them know I would be right back downstairs. Holding tightly on to the envelope I closed my bedroom door locking it behind me and I sat down on my bed. Quickly I opened the envelope and pulled out the neatly folded letter. Tears began to stream down my face as I read the letter.

To the parents of Nicholas Johnson,

    Valley View Academy values its atmosphere of teaching students to be a valuable asset in the world with the best curriculum and teaching staff available. Many feel your son Nicholas would be best suited elsewhere. Therefore, we thank you for enrolling him at Valley View Academy for his kindergarten year but he will not be asked back for his first grade year next year. Once again we thank you for allowing us to educate Nicholas this current school year but you will need to seek an alternative school for next year.

    Best Regards,
    Principal Riley

Okay now what? Why would a school not ask a student back because he is the new real Santa Claus? I was trying to think of something, anything I could do to help my baby boy. How could someone do this to my little Nicholas? Maybe I should take both Holly and Nicholas out of Valley View Academy. Yes, that is exactly what I am going to do I thought to myself. So I wiped my tears off, walked to the bathroom sink, splashed some cold water onto my face and went back down stairs.

As I got back downstairs, Nicholas and Holly were finishing up their snack so I asked, "Okay who wants to go on a bike ride?"

Nicholas raised his hand and excitedly yelled, "Me!"

Holly grabbed their plates as she jumped up and screamed loudly, "Me too!"

I smiled and said, "Perfect then come on let's go and get our bikes out."

Nicholas and Holly rode their bikes in front of me racing each other the entire time. Fortunately, there is a park right close to our house with a bike path so we didn't have to ride our bikes on the street very far. We rode our bikes around the path, enough for me to regain composure then headed back home.

As soon as we were on our street Holly yelled, "First one home is the grand prize bike rider for the day!"

We all took off as fast as we could and Holly is such a fast bike rider. She could have quite easily blown all of us out of the water in the race but I could tell she was letting her brother keep up with her so I decreased my speed a little bit too.

Holly and Nicholas rode their bikes up the driveway at virtually the same time. I rode up right after them then clapped and happily announced, "It's a tie! You are both the grand prize bike riders for the day!"

Holly and Nicholas smiled at the announcement and we all put our bikes back away.

"Come on kids let's go inside and make dinner before daddy gets home," I said as we put the bikes back in their places in the garage.

"Can we have spaghetti night tonight?" Nicholas asked.

"I think spaghetti night sounds perfect Nicholas," I replied.

Nicholas helped cook the noodles and set the table, Holly made the garlic bread and the salad while I made the sauce. Dinner was almost ready by the time Garrett arrived home.

Garrett obviously could smell the spaghetti and garlic bread cooking as he walked in the door because before we even saw him we heard him say, "Mmmm, something smells good in here."

As soon as the kids heard their dad, they ran to greet him. They gave each other great big hugs. I walked over and decided to join in the group hug.

I didn't want dinner to get cold so I told Garrett, "Hurry upstairs and get changed. Dinner is almost ready."

No one needed to know about the letter yet. All I wanted was a normal evening with my family. During dinner I did catch Garrett staring at me and I looked away so I was almost positive he knew something was up. Luckily, he waited until the kids were in bed asleep before he brought anything up.

Once Garrett was sure the kids were asleep he turned to me and asked, "Okay, spill it....what's going on?"

I laughed and replied, "What? Just because I actually make dinner for once you think something is going on?"

Garrett looked at me quite seriously and asked again, "What's going on?"

I didn't want to cry again but I found tears began to stream down my face and I couldn't say anything. Garrett reached over and held me close, which he knew always made me feel better.

Unsure of what exactly to say to Garrett or how to start, I decided he needed to read the letter. As I was running upstairs, I could hear Garrett following right behind me.

I reached into the drawer of my dresser where I had hidden the letter then I handed it to Garrett and told him, "Here honey, you need to read this."

He sat down on the bed and I could see his face drop as he tried to understand the contents. He sat there and stared at the letter for a moment. I wanted to give him the opportunity to think about the letter and I didn't want to interrupt his thoughts.

After a few moments, I quietly said, "Its okay honey. I have decided we will take both Holly and Nicholas out of Valley View Academy next school year. We can throw the letter away and be done with Valley View Academy."

Obviously Garrett didn't agree with my idea because he sat there and shook his head 'no' before responding, "No! We are not going to let them do this! Aren't you always the one who stands up for everyone? This time we need to and we have to stand up for our son."

"But how can we?" I asked

"I don't know. Call your sister she's a teacher she'll know what we can do," he replied.

I called my wonderful sister and she told us the principal couldn't kick Nicholas out of school and we would need to go to the next Valley View Academy school board meeting. I was a bit hesitant but I knew I needed to go to the board meeting to stand up for Nicholas. I knew I couldn't hide everything from Nicholas but I didn't know how I was going to tell him what was going on. So I decided not to tell Nicholas or Holly about the letter.

Fortunately, I found out the next school board meeting would be held the following week. I prepared an eloquent speech about my Nicholas and I was feeling quite prepared and empowered against the school board. The only thing left was to present my side to the Valley View school board.

Garrett was staying home with the kids while I went to the meeting by myself. I didn't want Nicholas or Holly to get suspicious by both of us going.

Nicholas was playing in the play room with his dinosaurs so I walked into the playroom and sat right next to him on the floor.

Obviously he could tell something was on my mind because he turned to me and asked, "What's wrong Mimi?"

I looked at him and took his little hands into my hands as I said, "Nicholas honey I want you to know I love you and I will be home in time to put you to bed."

His eyes got really big as he continued staring at me and said, "Okay Mimi....just tell me Mimi if something is wrong."

I smiled as I kissed Nicholas goodbye. I knew he had a feeling something was wrong but I didn't want to upset him. I went downstairs to tell Holly and Garrett goodbye before I was off to the meeting. On the drive to the meeting, I thought about how tonight was not going to be an easy night for me. Life would be so much easier for everyone if people would let kids be kids and let them be who they are. Unfortunately, I continue to find more and more people expecting children to be a certain way and refusing to let children be who they are.

I arrived at the meeting by myself feeling quite lonely as I entered the large wooden doors which led to the meeting. As I entered the room where the meeting was being held, I felt all eyes fall upon me. I held my head high as I sat down trying to keep a smile on my face. I had requested for the non acceptance of Nicholas for the next school year to be put on the agenda. I knew it would be placed last on the agenda list so I waited.

Finally, Principal Riley announced, "There is one remaining item on the agenda for tonight and that is in regards to kindergartner Nicholas Johnson. He has made numerous interruptions in his class this year and he has had to spend an abundance of time in the office with me. His teacher Ms. Broomer and I had a lengthy discussion recently about his disruptive behavior and therefore, I felt it was best to not accept Nicholas back for the next school year at Valley View Academy. His mother has requested for this issue to be placed on the agenda and so she is here to speak in regards to the non-acceptance issue."

Board member Mr. James then asked, "Is Nicholas Johnson's mother here tonight to speak?"

Finally, it was my turn and I found myself jumping up quickly out of my seat. I took a deep breath in to calm down and then I began, "Thank you members of the board. Life is about the journey. We can not and should not confine our children's imaginations. We must let our children be who they really are. Life is about living and it is not about picking and choosing what a child can imagine or believe. I refuse to put my children's imaginations in a box. I will not confine nor control my children's imaginations. I have chosen to lead a positive life for my children and for myself. My son is the new real Santa Claus and I will fully support him. My little Nicholas embodies every bit of the meaning of Santa Claus. He is always happy, jolly and giving and that is what being Santa Claus is all about. I am proud Nicholas is my son and Valley View Academy should be proud to have Nicholas as a student. Therefore, I ask for the non-acceptance of Nicholas to be rescinded."

Principal Riley sternly answered, "Mrs. Johnson, Valley View Academy stands by the non-acceptance, thank you very much though for coming tonight."

"What? Not everyone at Valley View Academy stands by the non-acceptance," Ms. Lulu interjected.

"Principal Riley I think we should discuss this in our side meeting room before we make a final decision," continued Ms. Lulu.

Hesitantly principal Riley agreed and all of the board members went to discuss Nicholas privately.

Meanwhile back at home...

"Daddy, where did Mimi really go tonight?" asked Nicholas.

Garrett hadn't agreed with me not telling Nicholas where I was going tonight and he thought all of us should be at the meeting together. I had refused for either of us to tell Nicholas because I didn't want to damper his spirit.

Garrett had been watching the kids at home as he continued to become increasingly more upset about the entire situation. Therefore, when Nicholas asked about my whereabouts, he let it all spill out. Garrett told Holly and Nicholas about the letter and the board meeting I was at.

When Garrett had finished Holly loudly exclaimed, "We have to go, we need to all be there to support Nicholas and Mimi!"

Garrett shook his head 'no' as he explained, "We can't go, my truck is in the shop so we don't have any way to get there. We have to trust Mimi can do this on her own."

Holly continued protesting, "What, on her own? I thought were supposed to be a family, a team with everyone on the same page? We need to….no we have to be there."

"I would let all of us go right now but we have no way to get there," Garrett stated once again.

Nicholas knew the elves had to be watching what was going on right now because they were always watching him and he knew they would be there to help. "Let's ride our bikes," suggested Nicholas.

Garrett smiled as he said, "Nicholas riding our bikes would take to long but it was a good idea."

Nicholas looked at Holly and Garrett as he stated in a very serious tone, "Believe, let's all believe!"

The three of them raced to the garage to get their bikes out to ride to the meeting. At first, the ride seemed to be taking forever but Nicholas knew the elves would be there to help soon. Sure enough, suddenly it felt as if their bikes had lifted off of the ground and they were magically speeding quite fast to the meeting. Nicholas knew the elves must have helped out somehow. Then out of the corner of his eye he saw Jack flying away on Vixen.

Meanwhile at the Meeting...

I was sitting quietly in my chair saying a prayer in hopes the school board would have a change of heart when suddenly I saw Garrett, Holly and Nicholas burst through the big wooden doors on their bikes as the school board members were walking out of their side room.

"Excuse me, this is an official meeting. We do not allow bike riding in our meeting," stated Principal Riley.

Nicholas got off of his bike, walked right up the walkway and right up to the school board table. He looked at each and every board member before he proudly stated, "I see that some of you are believers but sadly some of you are non believers. I don't know why you are non believers or should I say what made you non believers. But I do know all of you really are good people deep down inside."

Principal Riley obviously felt the extreme need to interrupt my little Nicholas, "You need to go and sit down. Only your mom or dad can speak at this meeting."

Nicholas was very obedient so he turned around with his head hung down and began walking towards me.

Suddenly Ms. Lulu stood up and loudly voiced her opinion, "Boy you come right back up here and you finish what you have to say. You are important and don't ever let anyone tell you differently!"

Nicholas stopped and turned to look at Ms. Lulu. Nicholas smiled as he practically ran back up front to the school board table where he continued, "Thank you Ms. Lulu. I think some of you forgot how to truly believe in something, especially you Principal Riley. I know you are on the naughty list because you close your office door and smoke in your office even though you aren't suppose to. But what's worse Principal Riley is how you lie about smoking in your office to everyone. I love going to school at Valley View Academy but I can't go to a school where kids aren't allowed to dream, aren't allowed to have big imaginations and aren't even allowed to really believe in things. I want each and every one of you to know that everyone needs to believe in something because your beliefs ultimately become your destiny. I truly believe I am the new real Santa Claus and being Santa Claus is my destiny!"

The moment Nicholas finished, Ms. Lulu quickly stood up clapping and exclaimed, "I believe! I believe in you Santa and if you aren't going to be at Valley View Academy next year then neither will I."

At first everyone just stared at each other unsure of what to do next. Then one by one they each stood up and clapped. Nicholas stood there smiling and his smile kept getting bigger and bigger with every person who stood up clapping.

One year later...

"Okay kids all of you need to believe in something and you also need to believe in yourselves. So today we are going to all talk about what we believe in." explained Ms. Lulu to her little first graders.

Ms. Lulu looked around the room and asked, "Who wants to be the first one to tell the class what they believe in?"

Nicholas raised his hand so quickly it looked as if it was going to go right through the ceiling.

Ms. Lulu saw his hand go up first so she smiled and said, "Nicholas tell all of us what you believe in."

Nicholas stood up and smiled before he announced, "Santa! I believe I am Santa Claus! Who's your Santa Ms. Lulu?"

Ms. Lulu smiled and said, "Nicholas you'll always be my Santa!"

Follow Your Imagination Where Ever It Leads You!

ACKNOWLEDGMENTS

First and foremost I am thankful to my Reece who has never stopped believing in me. I could not have written this book without all of your unending love and support. Thanks for everything you do but most of all thanks for just being you. I will always love you and thanks for always loving me no matter how many yellow poles I hit.

I am also extremely grateful to my son Ty, whose fabulous imagination inspired this book. Thank you so much for including me on all of your exciting adventures to the North Pole. Most of all thank you for picking me as your Mimi.

I would also like to thank my precious daughter Ellalyn for believing and protecting your brother and for always singing, dancing and jumping on the couch with me.

I am also happy to thank the many people in my life who have contributed to making my life fabulous. Thank you Constance for introducing me to fabulousness, you are truly the most fabulous person I know and will ever know. Also, a big thanks to Luenell who is such a bright light in this world and is never afraid to tell it like it is.

I would also like to thank the Los Angeles Zoo for making it possible for children of all ages to imagine, dream and believe they are true friends with all of the animals at the zoo.

Finally I would like to thank Happy Bean Publishing for all of their hard work and support to make this book possible.

Kristy Haile graduated from Northeastern University in Boston, and she lives with her husband and two children in California.

Her website is www.iamsantabook.com.

Her E-mail is rkehaile@yahoo.com